"I agree to your plan. With a few conditions."

Tanner stiffened, guarding his heart against the words he expected. *Stay away from the children. Don't forget you're a half-breed.*

"The children must be treated kindly at all times. And I don't want them getting hurt because of the horses."

Nothing about his heritage? Nothing at all?

"Ma'am, there is no need for such conditions. I would never be unkind to a child. Or an adult. Or an animal. Everyone deserves to be treated with respect. And I would never put anyone in danger. For any reason."

"Then we have a deal." Susanne held her hand out.

He took it before she remembered he was a half-breed, and marveled at her firm grip despite the smallness of her hand.

Inside his heart, buried deep, pressed down hard beneath a world of caution, there bubbled to the surface a desire to protect.

The one thing he meant to protect was his heart. No one, especially a fragile blonde woman, would be allowed near it.

"We have a deal," he said.

Their agreement would certainly solve two problems. But he wondered if it would create a whole lot more to take their place.

Linda Ford lives on a ranch in Alberta, Canada, near enough to the Rocky Mountains that she can enjoy them on a daily basis. She and her husband raised fourteen children—four homemade, ten adopted. She currently shares her home and life with her husband, a grown son, a live-in paraplegic client and a continual (and welcome) stream of kids, kids-in-law, grandkids, and assorted friends and relatives.

Books by Linda Ford

Love Inspired Historical

Montana Cowboys

The Cowboy's Ready-Made Family

Christmas in Eden Valley

A Daddy for Christmas
A Baby for Christmas
A Home for Christmas

Journey West

Wagon Train Reunion

Montana Marriages

Big Sky Cowboy
Big Sky Daddy
Big Sky Homecoming

Cowboys of Eden Valley

The Cowboy's Surprise Bride
The Cowboy's Unexpected Family
The Cowboy's Convenient Proposal
Claiming the Cowboy's Heart
Winning Over the Wrangler
Falling for the Rancher Father

Visit the Author Profile page at Harlequin.com for more titles.

The Lord thy God in the midst of thee is mighty; he will save, he will rejoice over thee with joy; he will rest in his love, he will joy over thee with singing.
—*Zephaniah* 3:17

Dedicated to the memory of my grandson, Julien Yake,
who passed away July 2015 at age 19;
and to his mother, who will forever mourn him.

Chapter One

Spring 1899
Near Granite Creek, Montana

The skin on the back of Tanner Harding's neck tingled. Something—or someone—watched him.

He slowly straightened from leaning against the fence but kept his eyes on the horses corralled behind the barricade of intertwined thick branches. He didn't want to alert whatever rustled behind him that he was aware of its presence. He crossed his arms as if his sole purpose was admiring the wild mares he'd captured, but one hand slipped down to the handle of the knife he carried on his belt. Whether it be man or beast, Tanner didn't intend it to succeed in attacking him.

A slight sound indicated the stalker had moved toward Tanner's right, to the little grove of trees. A bear? It was too quiet and it didn't smell. A cougar? A big cat would be up the tree waiting for a chance to pounce. A man? That seemed most likely.

He tensed his muscles, fixed in his thoughts where to strike, and sprang around in a single movement that most men couldn't imitate. But then most men didn't have Lakota blood mixed with white in their veins.

His right arm came up. The steel blade of his knife flashed as he confronted—

A boy? A little boy, with tousled blond hair and blue eyes as wide as moons, who shrank back as far as the tree trunk allowed.

"You gonna kill me?" he squeaked.

Tanner slid the knife back into its sheath as the tension drained from his body. "You're too little to be any danger to me."

The boy drew himself up to the fullest of his barely three feet. "I ain't too little." He crossed his arms and thumped them to his chest. "I'm five."

"Uh-huh." Tanner perched one foot on the nearby fallen tree and leaned over his leg. "You got a name?"

"Robbie."

"Is there a last name goes with that, Robbie?"

"Robbie Collins."

He knew the family. They lived down the valley a bit, scratching out a living on a farm. The mother had died a year or more ago, the father, a few months past. Who was in charge of this child and the other three children in the family? They weren't doing much of a job for this youngster to be a few miles from home.

"What's *your* name?" Robbie spoke with an amusing mix of bravado and innocence.

"Tanner Harding."

Robbie nodded. "You live on that big ranch over there, don'cha?"

"Yup."

"You gots some brothers."

"Two. Johnny and Levi. They're both younger than

me." Was the boy purposely trying to divert Tanner from finding out what he was doing here? "Won't someone be worried about you?"

Robbie ignored the question and moseyed over to the barricade of tree branches. "Those your horses?"

"They are now." Three of the mares for sure were descendants of his mother's mare, which had been turned out to join the wild herd after her death. No one but his mother had been able to ride her. He meant to gentle them, breed them to a top-notch stud and start a herd that would have made his mother proud. He would be proud, too. Might even gain him a little respect from the white men in the area. At least he hoped so. Though it might be too much to hope they would at some point accept him as their equal.

"They're wild horses, right?"

"I'm going to tame them."

Robbie might only be five, but the look he gave Tanner overflowed with so much doubt that Tanner chuckled.

He dropped his booted foot to the ground. "We better get you home."

Robbie's shoulders sank. "Auntie Susanne is not going to be happy with me."

"Oh?"

He hung his head. "I'm not supposed to go away without telling her."

Tanner studied the boy. So Robbie had wandered off before. "Then why do you?"

Robbie shrugged. "Just 'cause," he mumbled. He lifted his head and fixed Tanner with a desperate look. "'Cause things is different now."

Tanner swung to the back of his horse and reached down to lift Robbie up. "Different how?"

"I's got no mama or papa. Just Auntie Susanne." Sorrow dripped from every word.

Tanner felt sorry for this motherless five-year-old boy. Tanner had been seven when Seena, his own ma, died. But his pa was still alive and strong as an ox. A suitable time after Tanner's mother died, Big Sam Harding had married Maisie and provided the three boys with a loving stepmother.

But it wasn't the same. Maisie was blonde and white and sweet as honey. Tanner's ma was a full-blood Lakota Indian and more tough than sweet, though she loved deeply. She'd been injured escaping the Battle of the Little Bighorn and Big Sam had rescued her, nursed her to health, married her and built the ranch for her. After her death, Tanner had felt lost. A half-breed boy in a white world.

Turning the offspring of Ma's mare into a fine herd was meant to correct the lost feeling that lingered to this day.

He took one more look at the mares. The fence was meant only to capture them. He needed solid corrals in which to train them. There were solid corrals back at the ranch, but Pa said he couldn't bring in a bunch of wild horses.

"First thing we know, the wild stallions will be coming around stealing the mares back and taking our stock, too." Pa was right, of course, but being right didn't solve Tanner's dilemma. He'd build a new set of corrals out here, but that would take time he didn't care to spend when he could be training the horses. Somehow he hoped to find an easier solution.

But first he needed to deal with the boy before him.

"Best get you back home," he told Robbie as they headed toward the little farm.

A short time later a low house with smoke rising from the chimney came into view. A cow wandered through some trees to the south, while a big workhorse grazed placidly in the farthest corner of the farm.

A boy climbed the pasture fence, and in the yard two girls chased chickens. Made him think of a poem Maisie used to recite. *Chasing the chickens 'til they won't lay.*

A man rode from the yard on the trail toward the town of Granite Creek, Montana. Seems if he'd come to help, he might have stayed and done a little helping. The fact that he didn't caused Tanner to think the man came for other reasons, though he wasn't prepared to guess what they might be. But a woman alone except for four children would appear, to some, an easy mark. His hands clenched the reins.

He saw no Auntie Susanne as he rode onward, Robbie's arms tight about his waist.

"Auntie Susanne is going to be awfully angry," the boy mumbled. "Maybe you could say it was your fault."

Tanner stopped the horse and turned to Robbie. "I won't lie for you. You have to face the consequences of your actions." How would this woman react to the boy's wandering? "What do you think your aunt might do?"

"I dunno. But she won't be happy." He drew in a deep breath. "I promised I wouldn't disappear again but I forgot my promise when I heard your horses."

The boy would have already been a distance from the farm in order to hear them, but Tanner didn't point that out.

Robbie perked up. "Not sorry I saw them, either. They're fine-looking animals."

Tanner chuckled. "Thanks. I happen to agree." He prodded the horse onward until he entered the yard.

A woman dashed from the barn, dusty skirts flying, blond hair blowing in the wind. She skidded to a halt as she heard the hoofbeats of Tanner's mount and spun about to face him.

From twenty feet away, he could discern this was not an old aunt but a beautiful young woman with blue eyes fringed by dark lashes.

She stared at him, then blinked as if unable to believe her eyes.

He could almost hear her thoughts. *What's this wild Indian doing in my yard?*

If she'd had a man about, he'd most likely come after Tanner with a weapon like Jenny Rosneau's pa had. The man had taken objection to a half-breed wanting to court his daughter.

"Go join the rest of your kin on the reservation," he'd said. Mr. Rosneau obviously did not think being a Harding mattered at all.

Big Sam might have objected had he heard. But Tanner did not tell him. All that mattered was that Jenny shared her pa's opinion. Nothing his pa said would change how people looked at Tanner or how the young ladies ducked into doorways to avoid him.

At least the woman before him appeared unarmed, so he wouldn't have to defend himself.

He reached back for Robbie, lifted him from the horse and lowered him to the ground. "He belong to you?"

* * *

Susanne's mind whirled. What was a stranger doing in her yard? Even more, what was he doing with Robbie? She grabbed Robbie and pulled him to her side. "Did this man hurt you?"

The man in question studied her with ebony eyes. He wore a black hat with a feather in the band and a fringed leather shirt. Leather trousers and dusty cowboy boots completed his outfit except for a large knife at his waist. She glanced about but saw no weapon she could grab. She was defenseless, but if he meant to attack she would fight tooth and nail.

His appearance was the icing on the cake for an already dreadful morning. First, the milk cow was missing. Frank had gone looking for her. He was a responsible boy but, still, he was only eleven. He shouldn't be doing her job. She needed to get the fences fixed so the cow wouldn't get out. But she simply couldn't keep up with all the things that needed doing.

Then Liz went to get the eggs. She was ten but had gathered eggs for her mother even before Susanne had come out to help. But six-year-old Janie had followed her and left the gate open. Now all the chickens were out racing around. If Susanne didn't get them in before dark, some predator would enjoy a chicken dinner.

She thought that was as bad as the morning could get. Then on top of that Robbie had disappeared again. The boy wandered about at will. She had been searching for him when Alfred Morris had shown up with a renewed offer.

"You can't run the farm on your own," Alfred had said, as he did every time he crossed her path—which he made certain occurred with alarming regularity.

"That's obvious to anyone who cares to look. Sell it or abandon it. Swallow your pride and accept my offer of marriage. You'd have a much better life as my wife."

"Mr. Morris, I'm flattered. Truly I am. But I don't want to sell my brother's farm. Someday it will belong to his sons."

Alfred lived in town where he ran a successful mercantile business. She was sure he'd make someone a very good husband. Just not her. No, marriage was simply not in her plans. Hadn't been even before she became the sole guardian of four children.

Her own parents had died, drowned in a flash flood, when she was twelve. Her brother, Jim, was fifteen years older and had already moved west. He'd come for the funeral and made arrangements for Susanne to live with Aunt Ada. But living with her relative was less than ideal. Aunt Ada treated her like a slave. Never had she let Susanne forget how much she owed her aunt for a roof over her head and a bed. Well, more like a cot in the back of the storeroom but, regardless, according to Aunt Ada Susanne should be grateful for small mercies.

When Jim's wife grew ill, he'd sent for Susanne to help care for her and the children. Weeks after her arrival, Alice died. And now Jim was gone, too, dead from pneumonia right after Christmas.

The farm had gone downhill since then. Now it was time to plant the crop, but Susanne wondered how she'd be able to get it in the ground.

Only one thing mattered—the children. Keeping them together and caring for them. She would never see them taken in by others, parceled out to relatives or neighbors and treated poorly as she'd been. Somehow she'd take care of them herself.

But she hadn't counted on having to face an Indian. Didn't he look familiar? Where had she seen him before?

"Auntie Susanne, he gots some of the wild horses."

At Robbie's words, she tore her gaze from the man before her. "Is that where you were?" Her voice came out higher than normal. "You stay away from wild horses. You could get hurt."

"Mr. Harding brought me back."

She jerked back to the man on horseback. So that's why he looked familiar. He was a Harding. The family owned a big ranch—the Sundown Ranch—to the east of Jim's little farm. She hadn't recognized him right away because he'd always worn jeans and a shirt when she'd seen him in town. Why did he dress like an Indian now? "Thank you for seeing him home safely."

"My pleasure, ma'am." He touched the brim of his hat. "Don't guess we've been properly introduced. I'm your neighbor Tanner Harding."

The girls left off chasing the chickens and stared at Mr. Harding.

Frank trotted up. "Aunt Susanne, I can't find the cow." He turned his attention to their visitor. "You an Indian?"

"Frank," Susanne scolded. "You shouldn't ask such a question."

Mr. Harding chuckled. "It's okay. I'm half Indian, half white."

"He gots wild horses in a pen," Robbie said with some importance.

"I'm Frank." The boy held his hand out for a proper introduction.

Mr. Harding swung out of his saddle with more ease

than most men. Certainly with more ease than Alfred Morris, who struggled to get in and out of the saddle.

Mr. Harding took Frank's hand. "Pleased to meet you, neighbor."

Frank's chest swelled at the greeting. "You, too, Mr. Harding."

"Prefer you call me Tanner. Mr. Harding is my pa." He let his gaze touch each of them.

That left Susanne little option but to introduce herself and the others. "I'm Susanne Collins. You've met my nephews. These are my nieces, Liz and Janie."

He doffed his hat at the girls and they giggled.

"Ma'am." He brought his dark eyes back to Susanne. "I know where your milk cow is. I can bring her in if you like."

She hesitated. She didn't like to be owing to anyone. She'd learned that lesson, all right.

"I looked everywhere and couldn't find her," Frank said, half-apologetic.

"She's way on the other side of the trees." Tanner continued to look at Susanne, awaiting her answer.

She wanted to say no but how long would it take to tramp out and persuade Daisy to return to the pasture next to the barn? She wouldn't be comfortable leaving the children while she went, and it would take all day if she took them with her. Which left her with only one option.

Relying on this man—any man—made her shudder. She remembered when she'd learned that lesson firsthand. Four years ago, when Susanne was sixteen, Mr. Befus had offered to take Susanne off Aunt Ada's hands. Had even offered a nice sum of money. Susanne still got angry thinking her aunt had been prepared to sell her like so much merchandise. When Susanne had protested, Aunt Ada had reminded her she had no right to say no. "You are totally dependent on the good-will of others and if Mr. Befus sees fit to offer you a home, you best accept." Reasoning a home with some-one who wanted her would be better than staying with Aunt Ada who clearly didn't, Susanne had agreed to the arrangement.

Aunt Ada had left him alone with Susanne at his re-quest. "I need to know what I'm getting in this bargain," he'd said. As soon as the door closed behind Aunt Ada, he'd grabbed Susanne and started to paw her. Her skin crawled at the memory.

"I'll not marry you until I know you'll be able to pay me back properly."

She'd fought him.

"You owe me, you little wildcat."

She'd broken free and locked herself in the bed-room, refusing to come out until Aunt Ada promised she wouldn't have to go with the man.

The next day she'd sent Jim a letter. It had taken two more years for him to invite her to join him. He'd said he always meant to get back to her, but he got busy with his family and working on the farm. She would have left Aunt Ada's but without Jim's help and without a penny to her name, she would simply be throwing her-self from one situation to another. Better the one she knew and understood.

Ever since then she'd been leery of men offering any form of help, and vowed she would never marry and owe a man the right to do to her as he wished.

But at this moment she had no other recourse.

"If you don't mind bringing her back." She hoped

his offer was only a neighborly gesture and he wouldn't demand repayment.

"Not at all." He swung back onto the saddle without using the stirrups and reined about to trot from the yard.

She stared after him, at a loss to know what to think. She couldn't owe him for fear he'd demand repayment, but what could she do in return? Still, first things first. She turned to the children. "Let's get the chickens back in." And then she absolutely must figure out how to get the field plowed.

Fifteen minutes later and a generous amount of oats thrown into the pen, the chickens were in and the gate closed.

Two minutes afterward, three were out again, having found a hole in the fence. Susanne closed her eyes and prayed for a healthy dose of patience. "Frank, you stand at the hole and keep any more from getting out. I'll find something to fix it with. You others, see if you can catch those hens."

She was knee-deep in the bits and pieces of Jim's supplies in the corner room of the barn when the gentle moo of the cow jerked her about. "So you decided to come home, did you? You're more bother than you're worth."

Tanner rode in behind the cow, ducking through the open door just in time to catch her talking to the cow.

For a moment, her embarrassment made it impossible to speak.

"She got out through a big hole in the pasture fence," he said, without any sign of amusement or censure, which eased her fractured feelings.

"I know. The fences all need repairing. I'm getting it done as fast as I can." If she wrote down everything that needed doing around here it would require several pieces of paper. She was drowning in repairs. "Thanks for bringing the cow back."

He nodded. "You're welcome. Ma'am, I could fix that fence for you. Wouldn't take but a minute."

Her insides twisted with protest. It wasn't as if she didn't need help. As Alfred Morris pointed out regularly, anyone could see she wasn't keeping up with the workload, but help came with a price. The lesson had been drilled into her day after day by Aunt Ada. "No, thank you. I have no wish to be under obligation to you."

His expression hardened. "Ma'am, you aren't the first, nor will you be the last, to want me off their place because I'm half-Indian." He backed his horse out of the barn.

She climbed over the pieces of wood and wire at her feet as fast as she could and ran after him. "It has nothing to do with your heritage," she called.

But he rode away without a backward glance.

She pressed her hand to her forehead. The last thing she wanted was to offend him.

Tanner only offered to help Miss Collins out of neighborly concern. She had her hands more than full with looking after four children, the house and the chores. How was she going to get the crop in? And if she failed to do so, what would she feed the animals through the winter and how would she buy supplies for herself and the children?

He shouldn't be surprised that she objected to having an Indian on her property. He'd come to expect such a reaction. He should just ride away, but something his ma used to say stopped him. "Son, if we see someone in need and walk away, we are guilty of harming them."

He did not want to be responsible for harming a pretty young gal and four orphaned children, but what could he do when Susanne had chased him off the place?

What would his ma do?

He knew the answer. She'd find a way to help. But she wasn't alive to help *him* find a way.

As he rode past the barn, he eyed the corrals. Susanne's brother had certainly built them strong, though the wire fences around the pasture showed signs of neglect.

He rode past the farm, then stopped to look again at the corrals behind him. They were sturdy enough to hold wild horses…and he desperately needed such a corral… A thought began to form, but he squelched it. He couldn't work here. Not with a woman with so many needs and so much resistance. Not with four white kids. Every man, woman and child in the area would protest about him associating with such fine white folk.

He shifted his gaze past the corrals to the overgrown garden spot and beyond to the field where a crop had been harvested last fall and stood waiting to be reseeded. He thought of the disorderly tack room. His gaze rested on the idle plow.

This family needed help. He needed corrals. Was it really that simple?

Only one way to find out. He rode back to the farm and dismounted to face a startled Miss Susanne. "Ma'am, I know you don't want to accept help…"

Her lips pursed.

"But you have something I need so maybe we can help each other."

Her eyes narrowed. She crossed her arms across her chest. "I don't see how."

He half smiled at the challenging tone of her voice. "Let me explain. I have wild horses to train and no place to train them."

"How can that be? You live on a great big ranch."

"My pa doesn't want me bringing wild horses in." He continued on without giving her a chance to ask any more questions. "But you have a set of corrals that's ideal."

For a moment she offered no comment, no question, then she finally spoke. "I fail to see how that would help me."

"Let me suggest a deal. If you let me bring my horses here to work with them and—"

She opened her mouth to protest, but given that she hadn't yet heard how she'd benefit he didn't give her a chance to voice her objections.

"In return, I will plow your field and plant your crop." The offer humbled him. He'd made no secret of the fact he didn't intend to be a farmer. Ever. He only hoped his brothers never found out or they'd tease him endlessly. Even before he finished the thought, he knew they would. He'd simply have to ignore their comments.

"I have no desire to have a bunch of wild horses here. Someone is likely to get hurt."

"You got another way of getting that crop in?" He gave her a second to contemplate that, then added softly, "How will you feed the livestock and provide for the children if you don't?"

She turned away so he couldn't see her face, but he

didn't need to in order to understand that she fought a war between her stubborn pride and her necessity.

Her shoulders sagged and she bowed her head. Slowly she came about to face him. "This morning I prayed that God would provide a way for me to get the crop in. Seems this must be an answer to my prayer."

He was an answer to someone's prayer? He kind of liked that. Maybe he should pray that God would make Himself plain to him. He'd sure like the answer to that prayer, as well.

"So I agree to your plan." Her eyes flashed a warning. "With a few conditions."

He stiffened, guarding his heart against the words he expected. *Stay away from the children. Don't think you can make yourself at home. Don't forget you're a half-breed.* She might not use those exact words but the message would be the same.

"The children must be treated kindly at all times. And I don't want them getting hurt because of the horses."

His mouth fell slack. He was lost for words. Nothing about his heritage? Nothing at all?

"Ma'am, there is no need for such conditions. I would never be unkind to a child. Or an adult. Or an animal. Everyone deserves to be treated with respect. And I would never put anyone in danger. For any reason."

She studied him for several heartbeats. She seemed to be searching beyond the obvious, but for what?

He met her look.

His mouth grew dry. He blinked and shifted away. He saw depths of need and a breadth of longings that left him both hungry to learn more and wishing he saw less.

"Then we have a deal." She held her hand out.

He took it before she remembered he was a half-breed, and marveled at her firm grip despite the smallness of her hand.

Inside his heart, buried deep, pressed down hard beneath a world of caution, there bubbled to the surface a desire to protect.

The one thing he meant to protect was his heart. No one, especially a fragile blonde woman, would be allowed near it.

"We have a deal," he said.

Their agreement would certainly solve two problems. But he wondered if it would create a whole lot more to take their place.

Chapter Two

A little later, Tanner rode into the yard at Sundown
Ranch. His brothers trotted over to the barn as he led
Scout in. Though they were close in age—Johnny was
twenty, a year younger than Tanner, and Levi two years
younger—his brothers were as different from Tanner
as was possible. Johnny lived to please his father and to
prove he was part of the white world. Levi didn't much
care what anyone except Maisie thought.

"You get them?" Johnny asked.

"I sure did. Ten in all. And all three of Ma's horses.
I have them in that little box canyon over the hill."

Big Sam ambled into the barn. "Howdy, boys."

"Hi, Pa," they replied.

"You capture them horses?" he asked Tanner.

"Ten. Now all I got to do is break them."

"Sure wish I could help you out, but you know my
feelings."

Tanner did. They all did. He could hardly wait to
see their surprise when he announced his good news.

The supper bell rang and the four of them crossed to
the house. It was a one-story structure, nothing fancy,

but, as Big Sam often said with a great deal of pride, it was solid.

Maisie waited at the door to greet them. As part of her many rituals, she got a kiss on the cheek from each man as he passed. Not that Tanner was complaining. She was a good, loving mama to Big Sam's boys and had never let their mixed heritage influence her affections for them.

They washed up, sat at the table and automatically reached for one another's hands as Big Sam asked the blessing. Holding hands was another of Maisie's rituals. He'd found the gesture comforting when he was eight and still found it comforting at twenty-one. There was one place he knew he belonged. Right here in this house.

They passed the food and then began another of Maisie's rituals.

"Sam, did you get the cows moved up to summer pasture?" Over the evening meal, Maisie asked each of them about their day, starting with Pa and then proceeding in descending age.

"Sure did. Grass is looking good already. The cows will get lots to eat. Soon there will be calves on the ground."

Tanner listened as Big Sam described every aspect of the herd. He'd grown up hearing this sort of thing and knew the importance of each detail.

When Pa was done, it was Tanner's turn.

Maisie turned to him. "How did your day go? Did you get those horses you wanted?"

"Sure did." Again, he told of his day, describing the horses in more detail for her than he had for his brothers or Pa.

"And I had a visitor."

"Up there?" She sounded as surprised as his brothers looked.

"A young boy." He enjoyed parceling out the information in a way that increased their curiosity.

Maisie sat back, dumbfounded. "What would a child be doing up there? How old was he?"

"Five."

"That's hardly more than a baby. Levi's age when your mama died." She gave Levi a look of love. It was no secret the two of them shared a special bond. She brought her attention back to Tanner. "Was he lost? Abandoned?"

"Nope. Just wandering a little far from home. It was Robbie Collins. You know, from Jim Collins's farm."

Maisie made a sound half distress, half regret. "Why, it's—" She counted on her fingers. "It's four months since he died. I've been meaning to get over there. I hear his sister is caring for the children. That poor girl. They say she hasn't anyone to help. How are they faring?"

"I'd say she was struggling."

"Sam, someone ought to help them." Maisie shook her head, her look part pity, part scolding.

Tanner felt rather pleased that he'd be able to reassure her that someone was. "I have a set of corrals to work the horses."

Maisie, Big Sam and his two brothers looked at him.

Big Sam found his voice first. "You built some already? How'd you manage that?"

"Didn't build some. Found some ready and waiting." He grinned at the curiosity his words triggered.

"Where?"

"How?"

"Are you joshing us?"

"At the Collins place. Pa, did you know Jim Collins had dreams of capturing some of the horses?"

Pa looked thoughtful. "Come to think of it, I might have heard him mention it a time or two. Took it as just that. Talk."

"Nope. It wasn't. He has a set of corrals over there that are just about perfect."

Levi eyed his brother suspiciously. "How's that going to work? You bought them? Rented them?"

"Traded for them." He explained his work agreement with Susanne Collins. That brought a look of complete astonishment from those around the table.

"You're going to farm?" Johnny shook his head. "Never thought I'd see the day."

Tanner knew what Johnny meant. He'd often scoffed at stooping to join the white man in breaking the land and sowing crops. "It'll be worth it to have the use of the corrals."

As if sensing Tanner's brothers might have a whole lot more to say about the subject, perhaps things Tanner didn't care to hear, Maisie turned the conversation to Johnny, asking about his day.

Tanner listened with half his attention, his thoughts on his recent agreement. What had he done by agreeing to farm? He'd never been interested in hitching a horse to a plow, though he'd had to do it a few times as Pa insisted they grow oats for feed and wheat for flour. How many times had Tanner said his Lakota mother would have hated her sons in such a role? They should be on horseback hunting buffalo. But he hadn't been thinking about that earlier today. In fact, all he'd been thinking when he suggested the agreement was what a shame that those corrals weren't being used and that someone

ought to help Susanne no matter how much she insisted she didn't need it. There would be plenty of people saying he wasn't the right sort of man to do it, but no other man had appeared on the scene in months. He'd be fair to her, though, and stay as far away from Susanne and the children as was humanly possible, considering the corrals were a few hundred feet from the house. Like it or not, they needed each other.

Susanne wanted nothing so much as to chase Tanner Harding down and tell him in no uncertain terms she couldn't accept his plan. But the place was falling into rack and ruin. Jim had neglected it the past year or two as he dealt with Alice's illness and then tried to cope with her death. Susanne would be the first to admit she needed help and she would hire a man in a snap if she had the funds to pay one.

She didn't, so that left her no option but to accept help to get the crop into the ground. The rest of the work she'd manage on her own with the children's help. Starting this morning. She called to them. "Let's go fix the fence." They wasted too much time every day chasing the cow and bringing her home.

The girls came readily enough, but Frank and Robbie stared toward the hill, no doubt curious about Tanner's horses. She hadn't seen them or his pen, but Robbie had provided a detailed description. She knew the place where he held the horses. Before Jim's death, she'd loved wandering across the hills, finding wildflowers, watching hawks soar overhead and enjoying nature. She'd always felt close to God out there. She missed those times alone.

"Come on, boys."

The pair had an animated discussion before they trotted toward her. She was certain the topic of their conversation was the wild horses. Robbie had talked of nothing else since Tanner had brought him back yesterday.

When they joined her, she caught Robbie's chin and turned his face to her. "Robbie, I don't want you going to see those horses. They're dangerous. Besides, you shouldn't be wandering about on your own. Something might happen." Tanner had given no indication as to when he'd bring the horses to the corrals; nor when he'd turn his hand to planting the crop. She certainly had no intention of suggesting he should do it sooner rather than later, if she even saw him again. What was to stop him from riding in and out without acknowledging either her or their agreement?

She was getting suspicious. There was no point in blaming Aunt Ada for making her that way, even though the woman had assured Jim she'd give Susanne a good and loving home and she'd done quite the opposite. The experience had made Susanne cautious and more than a little suspicious of seemingly kind offers.

But that was in the past and she did not intend it to color her whole life.

"Yes, Auntie Susanne," Robbie said.

With a kiss to his forehead, she released him. Each day he promised not to wander, but she knew he'd forget it if the urge hit him. So every day she reminded him again. Despite her frustration, she smiled at him and his siblings.

Each of the children handled the loss of their parents in different ways. Robbie wandered. Frank tried too hard to be a man. Liz looked for ways to make things go smoothly. Janie got lost in her dreams. Susanne often found her up a tree or tucked into a corner almost hidden from view talking to her doll.

And what did Susanne do? she asked herself.

She tried to take care of the work.

As she twisted wire together and tacked it to the wobbly post, she tried not to think too hard of all she'd lost. First her parents, then Alice and Jim. It was enough to make her certain she would never let herself care for another soul apart from these children, for fear of more loss. It was a strange world. Those who loved her died, while those who would use her to their own advantage lived to do so.

Never again, she vowed. She'd see to that.

She sought a more pleasant topic for her thoughts and settled on the diamond brooch Jim had given to her. It used to be their mother's and before that, her mother's. She and Jim had laughed together knowing the little stone in the setting was likely only glass. It didn't matter. It represented their mother.

"You can hand it down to your eldest daughter," he'd said.

She'd laughed. "What makes you think I'll get married?"

He'd squeezed her shoulder. "You're beautiful. You'll have dozens of suitors calling."

At the time, she'd been moved by his praise. Not since her parents died had she felt so blessed. But now it didn't matter if she was beautiful or not. She'd not have suitors calling once they heard she had four children to raise as her own. She certainly didn't count Alfred Morris. He was more of a dictator than a suitor. A man who wanted to own her. She knew he would constantly remind her how much she owed him for giving her a fine home.

She'd had enough of that.

And it wasn't as if she'd have time for courting.

She'd thought a time or two of selling the brooch. But it was the only physical reminder she had of her mother and wasn't worth a lot in the way of money. The diamond—if it was such—was so small she could barely see it. Instead, she'd trusted God to lead her to another way to manage.

She'd certainly not considered trading the corrals for seeding the crop and would still refuse if the good Lord would provide another way. *Please, God, perhaps there's an old married man who would work for a crop share.* Straightening, she squinted toward the trail that led to town in the hopes of seeing a wagon headed her way. The breeze lifted a swirl of dust but nothing more. Seems that prayer was not to be answered at the moment. *Anytime soon would do, Lord.* She turned back to the fence.

A few minutes later, she twisted the last wire and straightened. "That should hold."

"Can we go play now?" Robbie asked.

"Yes, you may." She remained at the fence as they scampered off in various directions. "Don't wander away," she thought to call.

Alone for a few minutes and everything momentarily peaceful, she looked about and breathed deeply. She needed this time to think and pray. *Father God, please help me keep the children. That means a way to do the farm work as well as time to tend to the children's needs.* Of course, God didn't need the constant reminding, but she knew no other way to set her worries aside.

She could not linger, and hurried toward the house and the many tasks at hand.

The milk cow trotted away as she neared the yard and headed straight for the hole Susanne had just fixed. Seeing her way blocked, the cow mooed and shook her head.

"Too bad, old girl, you'll have to stay in your pasture from now on." Susanne entered the house and found Liz and Janie sitting at the table.

"Can we eat now?" Liz asked. "We're hungry."

Susanna didn't need to look at the clock over the doorway to the living room to know the morning was almost gone and she'd accomplished so little. Being every bit as hungry as the children, she pulled out a frying pan, wiped it clean and set it on the stove to heat while she cut the leftover potatoes. Once they were browned, she broke in eggs. What did it matter if it was only eleven o'clock?

"Call your brothers and we'll have dinner."

When the boys clattered through the door, she told them to wash up.

She smiled at the way they bumped into each other. Two boys full of energy and playfulness. Guilt stung her throat. When Jim was alive, he'd romped with them, and she'd played quiet games with them. But it had been weeks since she'd had time to play with any of them.

Susanne put the pan in the middle of the table and looked at Liz and Janie on one side, Frank and Robbie on the other. Her gaze lingered on the vacant spot at the end where Jim used to sit. She swallowed hard, missing him yet feeling blessed by the presence of the children. "Let us pray." Her voice caught on the words.

The children obediently clasped their hands together under their chins and bowed their heads.

"Lord, we are so blessed to have each other and to have food to eat. Thank You. Amen."

"Amen!" Frank added with so much enthusiasm that Susanne chuckled.

"It's not like you've been starving to death." She again felt a sting of guilt. Her meals were simple fare. She lacked time for anything else.

She really should do more cooking. Make bread again. It was weeks since they'd had anything but biscuits and fry cakes. Not that both weren't perfectly adequate. Just as fried potatoes and eggs were perfectly fine for a meal. Perhaps not day after day, an inner voice suggested. Susanne promised herself she'd do better... once she got the work on the farm taken care of.

"Robbie, slow down." The child ate as if it was a race.

Frank spoke slowly. "I'm glad Tanner is going to bring his horses here. Pa would have liked that." Frank's jaw grew firm, reminding her of Jim. Tears caught in the back of her throat. She'd waited so long to be reunited with her brother only to lose him again. At least until she got to heaven.

"He planned to capture some of the wild horses himself," Frank explained.

Susanne knew that. In fact, he might well be alive today if not for that dream. He had been following the whereabouts of the herd when he got caught in a downpour that eventually led to his pneumonia.

Frank continued. "He had the corrals all ready and would have gotten his horses for sure except Ma got sick and then he got sick." His voice quavered but he pushed on. "He told me I could help him when he got the horses. He'd have to gentle them first, but then I could help feed them and could talk to them so they'd learn not to be afraid of children." Frank sucked in a ragged breath, as did his brother and sisters. This talk of their father and mother would soon have them all in tears. "I want to help Tanner with the horses."

Susanne jolted back. "I'm sorry, but I must refuse you permission. It simply wouldn't be safe and I sure don't want anything to happen to any of you."

Frank hung his head but not before she caught a glimpse of rebellion in his eyes.

She'd never considered she'd encounter problems with the children. But she must insist. Being around wild horses simply wasn't safe.

The children were subdued throughout the remainder of the meal. Afterward they helped with the dishes, then scattered outside. She should give them more chores but couldn't seem to get any organized for them and she freely admitted she didn't want them to have to work as hard as she had for Aunt Ada.

She glanced about the kitchen. It needed a good cleaning. Alice would be shocked at the way it looked, and Aunt Ada would have had her whipped for the neglect.

But she no longer answered to Aunt Ada or depended on her for a roof over her head and a meal to warm her insides.

She stepped outside when she heard a horse approach. Goodness, months had gone by without anyone but Alfred Morris visiting, and now she had a steady stream of visitors. Or rather, she corrected herself as she recognized the rider, one recurring visitor. Was this what she'd agreed to? For Tanner Harding to come and go at will? Her insides grew brittle at the idea. Frequent visitors, in her mind, came with demands. Demands she didn't care to fulfill. Thinking of Mr. Befus, she shuddered.

Her eyes narrowed as she saw the milk cow bawling and bucking behind Tanner, protesting at being pulled home at the end of a rope. What was he doing with her cow?

"I brought you something," he said, jerking his thumb in the direction of the cow.

"Was she out? I fixed the fence just a few hours ago."

"I saw her jump over the fence where the wires were slack. She was intent on the wide-open spaces."

"What am I going to do with her?"

"You could try tethering her."

She hadn't meant the question for him but if he knew how to keep the cow home, she would like to know. "How do you do that?"

"I'll show you." He led the cow toward the barn.

"You tell me and I can do it myself." Susanne followed hard on his heels, intent on making it clear she didn't need his help. She did not want him to think he could take advantage of her failures.

"You're back," Robbie called to Tanner.

The four children stood in the doorway of the barn, their faces eager.

"I brought your cow home."

"She won't stay," Frank said.

"That's *our* problem," Susanne pointed out, not wanting Tanner to think she couldn't manage. Never mind that there was plenty of proof she wasn't doing well on her own.

Ignoring her protests, Tanner handed the rope to

Frank and went into the tack room, picking his way over the items on the floor.

Susanne's cheeks burned. She'd been meaning to clean up that mess. Another of the chores that never seemed to get done.

Tanner returned, a halter in his hands, and went to the cow, five people watching him, four with keen interest, one with reluctance. Okay, maybe she'd let him do it this time, while she watched and learned. After that, she'd do it herself.

"Let's see if we can train her to stay home." He slipped the halter over her head, found a length of rope on a nail by the door and hooked it to the halter.

"It's long enough we can secure it to anything solid enough to hold her. Which might have to be a tree with a girth of at least six feet."

The children giggled at his explanation as they followed him from the barn. The cow balked, but he leaned into the rope and persuaded her to walk along.

Could this control the stubborn animal? It must. She had no other choice.

"That tree will do." He led them to the spot where the grass was green and the tree stout, and tied the rope about the tree. "Now she needs water."

"I'll get it." Frank ran back to the barn and dragged out a small trough. He put it beside the tree and then hurried to fill it with water.

Tanner stood by and let the boy do it. Robbie insisted on helping and, even though he could only carry half a bucket of water, Frank let him.

Susanne secretly smiled her approval at how the children worked together. Helping each other was the only way the five of them would manage to run this farm.

"That ought to do," Tanner said with some satisfaction.

"Thank you," she said to him. He might have saved her several hours a day by showing her a simple remedy. "I'm sure I can do it in the future." Hopefully her voice didn't sound as uncertain as she felt.

The cow jerked at the end of her rope and mooed a protest.

Little Janie pressed her fingers to her mouth. "Daisy doesn't want to be tied up." Tears pooled in her eyes.

Tanner squatted in front of the little one and wiped the tears from her face. "She'll get used to it. In a little while she'll even learn to like it. Just like we all learn to adjust and even like changes."

Susanne could well argue otherwise but before she organized what she would say, Janie's eyes cleared and she smiled. The little girl reached out and touched his cheek.

"I like you."

Tanner straightened quickly and gave Susanne a dark look.

She pulled Janie to her side. *He's only here for a short while*, she wanted to warn her niece. *Don't get fond of him.*

Frank spoke, his voice breaking the tension. "My pa planned to capture some wild horses, too. But he died." Instead of lightening the moment, Frank's words descended on them like a dark cloud.

Susanne blinked hard, determined not to give way to tears.

"That's why he built that set of corrals," Frank added.

"They look real sturdy," Tanner said.

"They are. Pa said if you're going to train horses, you need to be set up for it."

"That's a fact. I think he would wonder why I didn't plan ahead before I trapped my horses."

"Why didn't you?"

Tanner chuckled. At the sound, the children relaxed visibly, but tension mounted in Susanne. *Be careful, little ones. Guard your hearts.*

"I should have," Tanner said, "but when the horses were hanging about within easy capturing distance, I couldn't resist grabbing the opportunity, trusting something would work out. And, look, it has. Your pa's corrals are going to be used just as he intended they should." With that, Tanner moved toward his horse.

Susanne followed, torn between her need to exert her independence and gratitude to him for showing her a simple solution to her cow problem. "Thank you for your help with Daisy."

He slowed and faced her. "You're welcome."

"And for being kind to little Janie. She's very easily hurt at the moment."

She wondered at the way his expression grew hard, his eyes cool and distant.

"Ma'am, I assure you that both you and the little girls are perfectly safe from me. I would never take advantage of you." His expression hardened like granite. "However, there are those who would not believe that. Who would criticize you, or worse, simply for your association with me…a half-breed."

She recalled his accusation that she'd asked him to leave yesterday based on that fact, something she had never cleared up. Now was the time. "Mr. Harding, it is not the blood of a man that means anything to me. It is his conduct that reveals if his heart is noble or base."

His eyebrows went up in a way that made her think he didn't believe her, then he touched the brim of his hat. "I need to check the corrals and make sure they're ready for use." He strode away.

She didn't have any more faith in his words than he had in hers. Time alone would prove whether or not she was safe in his presence, but it wasn't fear of him physically that made her shudder. No, it was the way the children looked at him. The way he had shown up to help when she floundered to manage on her own and the fact she'd been desperate enough to accept the agreement between them.

She already regretted her decision. Was she to be forever at the mercy of other people's handouts and thus under obligation to them, wondering what they would demand in return?

Chapter Three

The next morning Johnny and Levi accompanied Tanner to help move the horses. Pa had sent three of the hired cowboys to assist.

They rode directly toward the canyon where the horses were penned.

Tanner reined in at the hill closest to the Collins farm. "I'll go warn the family to stay out of the way so they don't spook the horses."

His brothers waved him away and he turned Scout toward the farm.

Frank and Robbie saw him coming and raced down the trail to greet him, yelling about the horses.

Smiling, he waited for them to reach him. "What's all the noise for?"

Frank caught his breath. "You're bringing the horses here today?"

"That's my plan."

"My pa would be glad."

"Then I am, too." He perceived he and Frank shared something special—a desire to please a dead parent.

The two boys trotted by his side as he rode into the yard.

"Where's your aunt? I need to talk to her." He wished he could avoid it. All her fine talk yesterday of accepting a man based on his conduct sounded pure and sweet, but he'd heard it before—specifically from Miss Jenny Rosneau—and he knew untested words had no substance to them.

"In the house," Frank said.

"Auntie Susanne," Robbie yelled loud enough to make Scout snort in surprise.

Susanne came to the door, a kitchen towel in her hands. She smiled, her eyes catching the early-morning sun. "Yes, Robbie?"

Tanner swung down. "Morning, ma'am." She stood framed in the doorway, apparently happy with whatever she was doing.

As her gaze shifted from Robbie to him, the light faded and her smile flattened. Her smile had not been for him. That was obvious.

He hadn't expected otherwise. "Came to say we're bringing the horses over this morning. Won't take anything to spook them, so maybe you and the children could stay inside until we have them penned."

She nodded. "I understand."

He stood there captured by the moment and a dozen thoughts that didn't make sense, most especially that something about Susanne made him think of his ma. They couldn't be any more different. Ma was bronzed, while Susanne's skin glowed like fine porcelain. He shifted his gaze so he could think more clearly. "I'll see to things."

"Thank you."

Her words jerked his attention back to her. "For what?"

She gave a little shrug. "For letting me know."

"You're welcome." He trotted away while he could still think. The two boys followed as he led the cow out to the far corner of the pasture and tethered her securely. They stayed right with him as he dragged the water trough out to the cow and they helped him carry water to fill it. They talked as he scoured the yard, removing anything that might spook the nervous horses. Or rather, they asked questions that he did his best to answer.

"How many horses you bringing?" Frank asked.

"Ten," Tanner said.

"You got lots of help? My pa said getting them into the corrals would be the tricky part."

"That's a fact." He told the boys how many men were with him.

"We could help," Robbie said.

Tanner stopped cleaning up objects in the yard—some branches, a pitchfork, a scrap of rag—and looked into the younger boy's eyes. "Robbie, the best way you can help is to stay inside until we have them in the corrals. Otherwise, you might frighten them. Think you can do that?" He didn't mention that Robbie might be trampled. Tanner's fists curled at the idea.

Robbie nodded.

Tanner gave the yard a sweeping glance. He could see nothing more that would alarm a wild animal. He turned his attention to the corrals. Jim Collins knew what he was doing when he built them. The valley ran from the box canyon downward to the yard, narrowing and providing a natural crowding passageway. By swinging the set of gates outward Tanner created an alleyway that would funnel the horses into the big pen.

Even if the animals wanted to run, the men would have no trouble keeping them contained.

Satisfied, he spoke to the boys. "It's time. Go on inside."

As the boys went toward the house, he swung to Scout's back and rode up to join the others. Tanner opened the barricade and the men slowly edged the animals out of the enclosure and down the coulee.

The animals snorted and neighed but moved easily along the narrow valley. At the yard they balked for a moment but the men had them surrounded and the only direction for the horses to go was into the big holding pen.

Tanner and Johnny both dismounted and closed the gates.

The men gathered round the corrals and admired the milling horses for a few moments before Big Sam's three cowboys rode away on the heels of Tanner's thank-yous.

"Those three are off Ma's mare, if I don't miss my guess," Johnny said as he eyed the horses.

"I'm thinking those two, as well." Tanner pointed out the two he meant.

"I barely remember Ma's mare," Levi said as he joined them.

Tanner grinned at his younger brother. "You were just a tadpole."

"I was five."

"I'm five, too," said a little voice behind them, and all three jerked about.

Tanner's heart raced up his throat when he saw Robbie. He thought he'd made himself clear about staying indoors. Thought the boy understood. "Does your aunt know you're here?"

"Why? You only said we had to stay in until you had the horses in the corrals." He climbed the fence to look at the herd. "Say. They're even better-looking than I recall."

Johnny and Levi grinned at each other.

"Robbie, you get back here!"

They all turned toward Susanne, silhouetted in the doorway.

Her displeasure blared like a trumpet. Did she not want the boy around the horses…or the three half-breed men? Only one way to test her. "It's okay now," he called. "Why not let the children come and see them?"

She stared at him, her expression so full of denial he knew what she would say even before she opened her mouth. "Very well." Susanne turned to the children.

His brain bucked. He'd expected her to refuse. But, of course, she couldn't deny the children this little treat.

Frank was halfway across the yard before she finished speaking.

The girls followed their brother more slowly, perhaps as uncertain as they were curious.

Susanne remained in the doorway.

"That's the aunt?" Levi said.

"I thought she'd be old," Johnny added. "Now I understand why you're willing to turn your hand to farming."

"For the use of the corrals," Tanner growled.

"You want to see them, too, miss?" Johnny said to Susanne, sparing Tanner a look that said far more than he'd dare speak aloud. *Why are you being rude to her? The horses are in her yard. She'll want to look at them.*

Johnny had forgotten to take into consideration a

simple fact. Susanne was white as white could get—
wheat-colored hair, sky-colored eyes and skin like china.

Tanner was clearly a half-breed with black hair, black
eyes and dark skin.

It wasn't rudeness that kept him from speaking. It
was consideration for her situation. And yes, a desire to
avoid the hurtful comments he expected to hear.

He'd best keep his distance from this woman, as
she'd no doubt do with him.

"I'd like to see them." She pulled the door closed behind her and started toward them.

Tanner was too stunned to even think.

Three pairs of eyes watched Susanne as she crossed
the yard. Her world had been shaken up by the pounding of horse hooves as the herd had raced into the corrals. The animals were majestic and her heart thrilled
to watch them even as her mouth went dry. What had
she done, allowing such wild, powerful animals into
the yard? Bad enough she'd agreed to let Tanner plant
her crop, but these horses threatened the safety of the
children.

As she neared them, her mind filled her with a thousand uncertainties. This was what Jim had planned. Did
allowing Tanner to use the corrals fulfill her brother's
dream or mock it?

Would the children be hurt? If not by the horses,
then by their big-eyed admiration of Tanner, which they
made no attempt to disguise.

Knowing how much the wild horses had meant to
Jim, she couldn't resist letting the children see them
more closely or refuse the invitation to see them herself.

She'd warn the children to stay away from the animals after they'd had their look.

The three men smiled at her approach, setting her nerves into an anxious twitch. What did they want? Worse, why had she agreed to something that seemed to give them the right to ride into her yard without invitation?

Tanner stepped forward. "Miss Collins, might I introduce my brothers, Johnny and Levi."

She stilled her nervousness. *Never show fear. Never show emotion of any sort.*

The men were clearly related though vastly different. Johnny wasn't as dark as Tanner and dressed like a well-heeled cowboy with crisp new-looking jeans and clean shirt. Levi was slighter than his brothers and taller. He had a cocky bearing about him. She couldn't quite say how she came to that conclusion. Maybe it was the way he stood with his legs apart and his fingers jammed into the front pockets of his jeans. Or maybe the way he quirked his eyebrows when he greeted her with a smile.

"What do you think of the horses?" Tanner made space for her beside him at the corral fence.

She hesitated but curiosity overcame her and she stepped up on a plank as far from him as she could get and still see. "They're beautiful."

Beside her, Tanner murmured, "They truly are." His voice rang with awe.

She understood his emotion. The animals held their heads and tails proudly. One kicked up her hind legs. Susanne studied them all and picked out the one she admired the most. "That's the best-looking one." She pointed to a bay with a white blaze.

Tanner jerked about to stare at her. "You picked out

the dominant mare. She's the leader of the pack. Once I can handle her, the others will be easier."

"Good eye," Levi said.

"Thanks." Susanne thought it best to keep to herself the fact she was a town girl and knew nothing about horses except what looked nice.

The children all admired the horses, as well.

"They are real pretty," Janie said. "Especially that one." She pointed. "Her name is Pretty Lady."

No one disputed her announcement.

"My pa would have been proud," Frank said, his voice a little uncertain.

Tanner patted his back, a manly gesture. "Your pa built a fine set of corrals and I'm honored to be able to use them."

Frank nodded.

Robbie, not to be outdone, added, "Pa was a good builder."

The men all agreed.

Levi backed away from the fence first. "Guess we better get back before Pa comes looking for us." He said it with so much regret that Susanne chuckled.

"He'll have work for us," he added.

Johnny sighed. "Only Tanner here is getting the summer off to pursue his own interests."

"I'm the oldest," Tanner said, as if to defend himself. "It's time for me to try my hand at other things."

Johnny draped an arm across Tanner's shoulders. "Yeah, I know."

Johnny and Levi ambled back to their horses. Tanner followed his brothers and mounted his, as well.

The children waved to them as they rode away.

Susanne stared after them, a confusion of ideas, regrets and if-onlys filling her head.

If only Jim hadn't died. If only she didn't need help to run the farm. If only she didn't find it so hard to accept help even on fair terms. Then perhaps she could let herself enjoy having visitors, seeing the horses in the corrals, even letting the children befriend Tanner.

But if-onlys were but vapor in the sun, disappearing into the air.

It was time for dinner and she'd prepared nothing. Good thing they all loved fried eggs and potatoes. Again, she realized how little time she spent on household duties. Again, too, she thought of how displeased Aunt Ada would be.

As she made the simple meal she realized how often she thought of Aunt Ada as she worked. Would there ever come a day when she didn't measure every decision, every activity, against her aunt's reaction?

The children came at her call and gathered round the table. She prayed and then the children dug in.

"I'm going to watch and learn everything I can," Frank said. "Maybe someday I can be like my pa."

Susanne's chest muscles clenched. She must make it clear that the children had to stay away from the horses, but first, she had to reassure Frank. She squeezed his shoulder. "You remind me of him already. He'd be very proud."

Frank looked pleased.

If only she didn't have to tell him the rest. "Children, I want you to listen to me." She leaned forward, waited until she had the attention of all four. "Those horses are wild and unpredictable. Dangerous, even. I want you to stay away from them. I have only allowed them here because Tanner said he would put in the crop in exchange for using the corrals."

Frank's jaw tightened. "Pa said I could help with the horses."

"These aren't your pa's animals. Tanner isn't used to watching out for children. Frank, I'm sorry, but I must insist you stay away from them."

Frank looked straight into her eyes. He didn't speak a word but he didn't need to. She knew he did not agree with her decision.

Would he disobey her?

Liz leaned forward. "Auntie Susanne, maybe we can invite them to share a meal with us. It would be the neighborly thing to do. I could help you make something."

Susanne's shoulders sank. She could warn Frank about the horses, but how did she warn Liz about the dangers of giving too much of her heart to those men?

"I really like that vegetable barley soup you make," Liz continued. "Maybe we could make that for them."

Susanne tried to redirect her. "Why don't we make some for supper?"

Janie got a faraway look in her eyes, not unusual for the child. "Mr. Tanner is the best-looking one of his brothers, isn't he?"

It felt as if someone had kicked Susanne in the middle of her chest. She struggled to get in enough air to speak. She'd seen the adoration in Janie's eyes and been concerned she'd develop a fondness for Tanner. But she hadn't expected it to occur so soon. How was she to nip this in the bud without hurting the child?

She reached for Janie's hand. "Honey, it doesn't matter if he's good-looking or not. What matters about a man is whether he is honorable and trustworthy. We don't know if that is the case with Mr. Tanner. Please keep that in mind."

Janie's mouth pressed into a defiant line. She blinked twice then sucked in air. "He is so. Why don't you believe it?"

Susanne knew the futility of trying to reason with a stubborn six-year-old. "Maybe he is. Maybe he isn't. Only time will tell."

Janie crossed her arms over her chest. "I know it already."

Susanne sighed. Her agreement with Tanner might become a bigger problem than she could have anticipated.

Robbie pushed away his fork with a clatter. "I'm going to ask him if I can ride his horse."

Alarm bells clanged in Susanne's brain. Had he not listened to a word she'd said? "Robbie, you'll do no such thing. Those horses are wild and dangerous. You stay away from them, you hear?"

Robbie gave her a look of surprise. "Auntie Susanne, I only meant Scout, the horse he rides all the time."

Her breath whooshed out. "Still, you shouldn't bother the man." Not that he was around to bother. He'd been quick enough to take advantage of his side of their agreement, but then he'd left once his horses were in the corrals. When did he plan to plow her field?

They finished the meal and as they cleaned up, she heard a horse ride into the yard. The children crowded to the window.

"It's Mr. Tanner. He brought Pa's horse in."

Susanne joined them at the window. He had indeed

brought in old Pat, the plow horse. She had been trying for days to drum up the nerve to bring the big animal in from the field. Frank insisted the horse was as gentle as a kitten, but she couldn't quite bring herself to believe it. He was far too big to be compared to a kitten.

Tanner waved at them and she ducked back. She didn't want him to think she watched him. If he'd noticed her, she hoped he'd thought she was eager to see her side of the agreement fulfilled. Indeed, it was the truth.

"He's coming to the door," Janie said, and rushed to open it for him.

"Janie, wait." The child ran headlong into danger. She trusted strangers, expected nothing but kindness. Not that Susanne could fault Jim for teaching the children to think the best of everyone. Too bad life would teach them otherwise.

Janie opened the door. "Hello, Mr. Tanner."

"Hello, little miss. What a nice smile."

Janie about melted at his feet.

Susanne hurried to the door to rescue Janie. She needed to warn the man to be careful of the child's tender heart.

"Ma'am, before I start on the crop planting, I figure to plow a vegetable garden for you today. I see the fences for a spot, but do you want to show me your preferences? Maybe tell me how big you want it, and what direction you want the rows?"

She couldn't keep up with his questions. Plow the vegetable garden? This was not part of their agreement.

A war raged within her. The voices of Aunt Ada, Mr. Befus, Alfred Morris and even her own battled against the necessity of feeding four hungry mouths.

She looked at the children clustered around her.

"If you don't mind?" His voice carried a note of caution.

Necessity won. "Not at all."

He held the door open and she stepped out to stand at his side. Then she realized she'd forgotten the children. "Come along."

They followed eagerly. Every step took her further into her fears.

He led the way to the garden, measuring his steps so she walked at his side. The children ran ahead, scrambled over the garden fence and began chasing each other through the dry, dusty weeds. Their laughter and screams filled the air and made her smile despite the tension crackling along her spine.

Tanner chuckled. "Nice to see them enjoying themselves. Reminds me of me and my brothers when we were young."

They reached the garden gate and paused.

A hundred old memories flooded her mind. "I remember helping my mama plant her garden." She sucked in air. "Before she died."

"Your mother is dead? I'm sorry."

She kept her attention on the crop of weeds before her. "Both my parents drowned when I was twelve. A flash flood." She hoped her voice remained flat and emotionless though her insides ached with the memory. She couldn't stop the shudder that rocked her shoulders.

"I was seven when my ma died. Her name was Seena. I still miss her." His voice deepened and she understood he fought the same pain she did.

"I guess the missing never goes away." She looked at him.

He looked at her, sharing—at least, in her mind—a common bond of loss. His dark eyes held a world of sorrow and sympathy that called to her lonely heart. The idea made her insides feel they could break into a thousand pieces with the slightest jar.

"Auntie Susanne, look at me," Janie called, saving her from her silly thoughts. Lonely heart, indeed. She'd never be lonely with four children to raise. "I'm a queen." Janie had woven some kind of vine into a coronet on her head.

"You sure are," Susanne said, her voice surprisingly calm.

"Do I look nice, Mr. Tanner?" the child asked.

"Just like a queen." He chuckled as he turned to Susanne. "I guess these kids keep you on your toes."

"I admit I'm never bored. In fact, I feel bad that I'm so busy I don't get a chance to do special things with them."

"Maybe you'll be less busy now that I'm here to help."

She wished he hadn't reminded her of the situation. Her nerves twitched. Accepting help equaled obligation and losing the freedom to make her own choices. It allowed someone to demand something in return. Something she couldn't or didn't want to give.

Now was the time to insist on boundaries around the children. But before she could speak, he opened the gate and ushered her through. "Show me what you want." He crossed his arms and waited.

She'd have that discussion later, after the garden had been worked. The children and their needs must come first.

She'd walked as far as the fence several times, planning how to plant the garden if she ever got the ground tilled. She'd even started digging it with a spade but made little progress. The garden spot had seemed as big as the oat field when she'd turned over one clod at a time. She'd not refuse his help if it meant providing for the children.

"If you wouldn't mind, you can plow the entire area and run the rows this way." She indicated the direction with a wave of her hand.

"It will be ready in a couple of hours. You go prepare your seeds while I take care of it."

She hustled back to the house as her inner war continued. Her vows, her fear and caution against the pressing needs of the farm.

Her throat burned knowing she had little choice but to accept his help. But she would not be obligated. Somehow she had to make that clear to him.

She lifted the cellar lid and climbed down the ladder to get the box of seeds she'd stored there, and brought them up. In addition, for weeks she'd been saving the eyes from the potatoes as she peeled them and storing them in a bucket.

She fairly danced as she organized the lot. The garden would be planted today. With God's good blessing she would have food to feed the children through the winter.

She wanted to monitor Tanner's progress without appearing to be watching him, so she took the seeds to the edge of the garden.

He followed after the horse and plow, the reins loose in his hands. Pat appeared happy to be working, plodding along at a moderate pace. Did horses express emotions? Tanner grinned and waved. Seemed he was happy, too.

The idea should put her at ease, but it had quite the opposite effect.

Aunt Ada would act as if she enjoyed something only to turn on Susanne with sudden criticism and harshness, stealing away any idea that her aunt had been pleased in the least.

Susanne hurried away to get a hoe, a rake, twine and stakes.

When she returned, Tanner had his back to her as he plowed the other direction and she felt free to watch. There was something about his posture that suggested he was relaxed. Could it be true that he enjoyed this task? Would that make him less demanding of repayment? He was using the corrals. Would that be enough?

He finished plowing the garden and guided Pat back to the yard.

Susanne grabbed the rake intending to smooth the furrows.

"No need to do that," Tanner said. "I'll be right back." He drove the horse to the barn and unhooked the plow, then backed Pat to another implement. In minutes he drove the horse across the yard dragging harrows that lifted a cloud of dust in their wake.

"I didn't even know they were in there," she said.

"They were kind of buried in the grass." He returned to the garden. The children chased after the harrows. They'd soon be dirty from head to toe, but she didn't have the heart to call them away. They were enjoying themselves far too much.

Tanner glanced over his shoulder, saw them playing in the dirt and laughed. He turned to Susanne and called, "There's nothing sweeter than the smell of freshly turned soil." His smile faded. "Except maybe the smell of sage and pine." He looked at the mountains for a moment before he returned his attention to the garden.

She leaned on the garden fence. If only she could enjoy watching the land being prepared for planting, but it was impossible. Her gaze drifted again and again to the man doing the work. His muscles bulged beneath the fabric of his shirt, emphasizing his strength. He stopped, wiped his brow with a handkerchief and rolled his sleeves to his elbows, exposing bronze skin the color of an old penny. Jim had told her the Harding boys' mother had been a full-blooded Indian. She knew only fragments of the story. Just enough to know the woman had been injured and rescued by Tanner's father. It seemed very romantic and caring.

Which meant nothing in the scheme of things. All that mattered to her was providing for and protecting these children. And her own heart.

Tanner turned the horse and harrows around and faced her. Their gazes caught. She couldn't pull from his look. Couldn't draw breath. Couldn't make her brain work. The children played, their happy sounds but a melody in the background.

He tipped his head slightly and drove the horse from the garden.

She breathed again and sagged against the fence, feeling as if her protective walls had been threatened.

His footsteps thudded across the yard and she jerked to attention and gathered up the twine, but before she could pick up the stakes, he did. He reached for the twine and she relinquished it without a thought.

Sucking in a deep breath, she told herself to refuse his help. But, while she gathered her thoughts, he trotted to the garden and drove the stake in on one end, affixed the twine and hurried down the length to drive in the second stake, pulling the line taut.

He returned and picked up the hoe.

He meant to help plant the garden.

"You don't have to do this. I can manage."

He stopped. The air stilled and the children grew quiet. "Do you object?" Something in his voice made her pause and consider her answer. It wasn't exactly fear she heard; she was quite certain Tanner would never admit fear. Did he think she objected on the basis of his mixed heritage? She'd already informed him it was the least of her concerns.

As she'd often said, actions proved one's words.

She had to prove her words by her actions, as well.

"I have no objection." She tried unsuccessfully to quell the turmoil in her heart.

She prayed she wouldn't live to regret this arrangement.

Chapter Four

Tanner's muscles had turned to stone. He'd waited for her response, and when she said she had no objection he relaxed so suddenly he welcomed the hoe to lean on. He'd sensed her apprehension all day. Part of him wanted to assure her she had nothing to fear from him. A larger part knew he should walk away from this family before anyone could take exception to his presence on the farm of an unmarried white woman. Two things kept him from leaving. First, the desperate need of this family. And, to a lesser degree, his plan to tame the horses.

Ma would have approved of him helping this family.

What would Seena Harding have said if she'd seen the way he stared at Susanne as he paused at the end of the garden with Pat's reins slack in his hands? Maybe she could have explained to him why the whole world had ground to a halt as their looks went on and on.

He gave a little snort that he hoped sounded like he might be dislodging something caught in the back of his throat. Like maybe dust or fluff off the weeds. Who'd have thought plowing a garden could confuse a man so thoroughly? Then he finally spoke.

"What are you going to plant?"

"I'm going to plant peas and beans and potatoes and carrots over here. And over there lettuce and radishes and chard. And turnips." She laughed as if the idea pleased her immensely. The look she gave him about turned him to mush.

What was wrong with him? He'd never felt this way before in his entire life. Well, except for the time that Rosneau girl had batted her eyes at him when they were both about fifteen. Right before her father had grabbed his daughter, pushing her behind him and saying, "You stay away from the likes of him." Tanner should have understood how unwelcome he was at that point, but he'd persisted until both Jenny and Mr. Rosneau had made it abundantly clear with more than words.

At the reminder of that humiliation, he pulled his senses back where they belonged—in his head. "No beets?"

"Oh, yeah. Beets, too."

"Sounds fine. What are you starting with?"

"Peas. Lots of peas."

He dug a trench along the taut cord and she followed, bent over at the waist as she dropped pea seeds in the trench.

"Can we help?" Liz asked. Her brothers and sister stood behind her waiting for his answer.

"You certainly can." He moved the twine and dug another trench. He got pea seeds and gave some to each of the children, set them at various places along the row and showed them how to carefully drop in the seeds. They all bent over, intent on the task.

He lifted his eyes to see Susanne watching him.

Her gaze shifted to the children and her expression hardened.

He tried to think what it meant, but he could only find confusion in his thoughts. She'd agreed to let him help, but he sensed a reluctance in her. Because of who he was? Or rather what he was?

Seeing she had almost reached the end of her row, he moved the string and dug another trench. The whole time he avoided looking directly at her, trying to keep his thoughts in order.

He quickly filled in her row, checked the children's row and covered it, as well.

Susanne straightened to look at what she'd completed, but when she took a step backward, she stumbled on a lump of dirt and fell on her rump. Her breath whooshed from her.

He dropped his hoe, prepared to run to her rescue, but he forced his feet to remain where they were. Not everyone would welcome a hand up from a half-breed.

Her burst of laughter froze him to the spot.

She jumped to her feet, dusted her skirts and laughed again. "That will teach me to watch where I'm going."

The children clustered about her.

"Are you okay?" Liz asked, her voice full of concern.

She gathered them in a group hug. "I'm fine.

Robbie broke free. "Aunt Susanne, show us how to watch where you're going when you go backward."

She laughed again. "I can't show you 'cause I can't do it." Her gaze hit Tanner. Her eyes danced with happiness and pleasure in these children, and perhaps in life in general.

He thought he was frozen in place before. Now it threatened to become a permanent state. What would it be like to be part of such joy and acceptance? Then he stopped himself. His family accepted him. It was all he needed.

Susanne looked away, shifting her attention back to the children. "I see you're done with your row. What shall we plant next?" She led them to the stack of seeds and offered them their choice.

His body remembered how to work and he covered in the rows and moved the stakes.

"They decided on beets," she declared.

"I like beets," he said. "You ever make beet pickles? Maisie, that's my stepmother, makes great beet pickles. They taste mighty fine in the middle of winter. So spicy sweet." He rattled on like a loose wagon wheel, but he couldn't seem to stop. It beat staring at her as if he'd lost his senses.

"Auntie Susanne, you ever make beet pickles?" Janie asked. "They sound good."

"They do, indeed. Maybe Tanner will ask his stepmother to give me her recipe." She faced him with an expression of horror. "I'm sorry. I should have said Mr. Harding."

It was his turn to enjoy a laugh. "Think I already said Mr. Harding is my pa, though most people call him Big Sam. I prefer you call me Tanner."

She nodded, lowered her gaze, then slowly brought it back to his. "I'd be pleased if you'd use my Christian name, as well."

Little did she know, he already did in his thoughts. "Thank you."

"Can we call you Tanner?" Robbie asked.

Tanner looked at Susanne, wondering whether she would allow the familiarity. He knew that many folk didn't approve of children using the Christian names of adults, but on the ranch they'd never held to such rules. "I don't mind, if it's okay with you."

She nodded. "If you aren't offended."

"Not in the least. My ma didn't hold with children and adults being treated differently."

"Then, yes." She spoke to the children. "But you must remember to be respectful."

Suddenly the children were shy and wouldn't look at him.

Janie giggled. "Tanner is just like us."

Susanne shook her head, but her eyes brimmed with amusement. "No. He's an adult."

"I know." Janie gave her aunt a look rife with impatience. "'Cause he's big and strong like my papa."

The children studied him.

He let them make their assessment. "I'll never be like your papa. 'Cause no one can ever be like him. Your papa was special to you and always will be."

Four little heads nodded.

"You ever meet him?" Frank asked. "Papa would have liked you."

Tanner couldn't believe the boy's words. His throat tightened at the suggestion. "I met your pa a few times in town." It was a fair ways to Granite Creek so trips were infrequent. He tried to recall the few times he'd seen Jim Collins. "I recall last summer he was in town waiting for the stagecoach to arrive. A pretty young lady climbed down and got into his wagon." By the time he finished he realized that young lady must have been Susanne. Would she be offended at his brash comments? He stole a glance at her, saw her cheeks had grown pink, though he might put that down to the effort of her work.

"A pretty lady?" Janie asked, innocent and curious.

"He means Auntie Susanne," Liz said.

"I suppose I do. Sorry, ma'am. Didn't realize until after I'd spoken that I was talking about you."

"Why are you sorry?" Robbie asked. "She is pretty, isn't she? I think so."

"Me, too," Frank said, and his sisters added their agreement.

Susanne's cheeks grew pinker by the moment. Tanner should think of a way to change the subject but he could only stare and smile. She certainly was pretty.

What was wrong with his head that he stood here like a dunce thinking about how pretty this white gal was?

How had the conversation led him so far astray? They'd been talking about Jim Collins. His thoughts settled into their proper place.

"I also met your pa a time or two while I was out riding the range. One time he helped me move a bunch of cows that were stranded by a little rock slide in a draw. He didn't seem to mind pitching in to move the rocks." He paused, wishing for a way to ease the children's sense of loss. "He was a good man. Sorry to see him go."

Frank nodded. "He *was* a good man."

Tanner knew he had to distract the children from their grief. "What do you say to getting the rest of this garden in?"

The children eagerly shifted back to the task at hand. As Tanner measured out the next row, Susanne came up to him.

"Thank you for your kind words regarding my brother. They mean a lot to me and the children."

He slowly brought his gaze to hers, telling himself the whole time that he could look her in the eye without getting all muddled in the head. As soon as their gazes connected, he knew he was wrong.

Something about the way she looked at him made him forget who he was and think only of who he might be...except for his mixed heritage.

"You're good with the children," she added when she realized he had nothing to say.

Her comment eased his stubborn mind. "Even though I was young at the time, I remember my ma explaining to one of the cowboys why she allowed her young sons to explore so freely." At the memory a smile started in his heart. "She said we'd learn best by trying things and seeing if they worked or not. Like the time I tried to rope a bull. I got the rope over his head and he jerked me off the fence. I hung on. I'm not sure what I thought I'd do. The bull dragged me along, bumping across every rock and lump in the ground. But I wouldn't let go. Might still be there if Pa hadn't rode up. He grabbed me. Had to pry my hands open to release the rope." He chuckled.

Susanne looked shocked. "Were you hurt?"

He looked at the palms of his hands as if checking for the rope burns and rubbed his stomach, remembering the bruises. "Nothing serious. You know what I said to Pa?"

"You thanked him for rescuing you?"

"Nope. I said, 'Guess I won't do that again.'" He leaned back on his heels, the memory ripe with so many good things. His pa's concern, his ma's pride in how hard he tried and the knowledge that they both cared about him in their different ways.

She laughed. "I would hope not."

They returned to putting seeds in the ground. After the beets, beans and corn were planted, Susanne said, "I'll have to do the carrot seeds. They need to be sprinkled carefully."

The children stood to one side, watching. Robbie shoved Frank hard enough to make him fall down. Janie kicked at the dirt sending up puffs of dust.

"Stop doing that!" Liz said.

The children were getting restless. "Let's do potatoes," Tanner told them. "They're fun."

"Yeah!" Robbie yelled. He ran to the bucket holding the eyes.

"Whoa, there." Susanne ran after him to save the potato eyes. Her bonnet fell down her back and her brown skirts flicked back and forth with each step. Her laughter filled the air as she caught up to Robbie and swung him off his feet. "What's your rush?"

Tanner leaned on his hoe and enjoyed the scene.

"Tanner said it was fun."

She set him down. "And so it shall be."

Tanner's inside warmed as he watched the pair laughing together.

Susanne found tin cans for each of the children and divvied the potatoes among them. They returned to his side where he waited with the hoe.

"Wait one minute," Susanne said, and raced away.

Tanner again admired the view.

"Where's she going?" Liz demanded.

"I don't know. I guess we'll find out when she gets back." For his part, he was content to watch.

She ducked into the barn and he heard a clatter come from inside. Had she fallen over some of the farm implements strewn about? He started to toss the hoe aside so he could go after her when she marched out, triumphantly carrying another hoe.

"Let's work in teams," she said as she reached the garden. "That way the work will go twice as fast. Who wants to be on my team?"

To Tanner's utter amazement, all four said they wanted to be on his.

Susanne tossed one hand in the air in what he hoped meant surprise. A part of his mind worried she might be offended. "You're going to make me plant by myself? Does that seem fair?"

"I'll help you," Liz said, and went to her aunt's side.

Tanner edged backward. He had no desire to come between Susanne and her charges. But perhaps he could offer a solution. "Tell you what." He addressed the children. "We'll make teams and plant one row then make new teams for the next row. Agreed?"

They nodded.

"Liz and Robbie are on your aunt's team for the first row. Frank and Janie are on mine."

The children sorted themselves out and got into place at the end of the first two rows. Susanne and her team beside Tanner and his team.

He tried not to be aware of her. Not to feel her elbow bump him. Not to want to close his eyes and breathe in her presence. He cleared his throat. "Ready?"

"Yes!" they chorused.

He secretly smiled at Susanne's eager participation. "On your mark. Get set. Go." He dug a hole, one of the children dropped in an eye. He scooped the dirt over it. He dug another hole. The other child dropped in an eye and Tanner covered it. Beside him, Susanne did the same thing. He kept himself to a slow, steady pace so they worked side by side.

They reached the end and turned about. Liz and Frank traded places and they planted two more rows. At the end, Janie and Robbie traded places.

All too soon they were done and the six of them stood back and admired their work. He wouldn't mind staying there the rest of the afternoon, but that was impossible.

"What's next?" he asked.

"Just lettuce and small stuff. I'll finish up. I want to plant some flowers, too." Her voice grew dreamy.

He stole a look at her. She looked at the garden, a slight smile on her lips as if she saw it in full bloom.

She held out her hands to draw the children close. "Let's thank God for the garden and ask Him to bless it." She raised her eyebrows as she looked at Tanner.

He shook his head and backed up. "This is your garden."

She seemed to understand and, with the children clustered about her, she bowed her head. The children followed her example.

He snatched his hat off, at the same time smiling at how Janie held her hands together in prayer.

"Dear Heavenly Father," Susanne said in a reverent yet trusting tone. "Thank You that our garden is planted. Bless it with rain and sunshine. Provide us with food from the ground. Thank You that You hear our prayers and always, always meet our needs and take care of us. Amen."

For a moment they remained huddled together, then the children ran to play.

He didn't put his hat back on, feeling as if he stood on holy ground.

She faced him, a gentle smile on her lips. "Thank you," she said. "I've been worried about the garden since the snow melted. I know God will take care of me, provide for our needs, but it's easier to trust when I see things happening."

He nodded, not knowing how to respond. Then words escaped him. "It's difficult to trust when you can't see God or know if He's listening."

Her eyes widened. "He's always listening. He's always near. We have His promise and I have but to look about to see His presence in all that He's created."

Tanner needed proof in this aspect of his life as he did in every aspect. When he didn't respond she smiled though her eyes remained guarded.

"Anyway, thanks again for your help. You made it fun for the children."

"It's the way I was raised. Maisie always says there's no point in looking at work as drudgery when it can as easily be joyful." He had to clear up something that lingered at the back of his mind. "I hope you weren't upset because the children all wanted to be on my team." He had no desire to earn her disfavor. On the heels of that thought came another so foreign it was surely a mistake. He'd enjoyed working with her and had allowed himself to believe she didn't mind working with him. He knew it couldn't be so. He'd known most of his life both on the ranch and off that he was neither white nor Indian. Some of the cowboys called him *injun* and tormented him. Or at least they had until Tanner got strong enough they feared crossing him.

In town—well, he wasn't going to dwell on the many times he'd been shunned at a social event or young ladies refused to sit by him or even crossed the street to avoid him.

It was enough to enjoy one sunny afternoon when he didn't feel that disapproval. He wasn't in a hurry to end it, but he must before she did.

He moved away six feet, paused to speak his piece. "Tomorrow I'll return to take care of plowing the field for the crop. I won't bother you again."

Susanne stared after him as he rode from the yard. It seemed he couldn't wait to get away. Her cheeks warmed. Had she said too much? Given him reason to think she expected him to be ready and willing to take care of chores other than the crop? But she wanted nothing from him other than the fulfillment of their agreement.

She returned to the garden, planted a patch of lettuce and then marked out several round areas for flowers next to the fence so she could enjoy them from the kitchen window.

Maybe Tanner had a young lady he was interested in. That would explain his eagerness to let Susanne know he would be avoiding her. The young lady should consider herself fortunate. Tanner would certainly make a good husband and father if the way he'd acted this afternoon was any indication.

She'd enjoyed the afternoon, perhaps more than she had a right to. But the lessons learned from Aunt Ada had not been in vain. Every pleasant moment ended poorly, so she wasn't surprised that Tanner had suddenly withdrawn and made it clear he wanted to avoid her in the future. However, she would not let it ruin her day. Another Aunt Ada lesson.

She finished her planting, put away the tools and supplies then went out to the pasture to get the cow.

The walk gave her time to settle her thoughts and bring them back to where they belonged. *God, I'm trying to be grateful that Tanner seems to be the answer to my prayer for help, but in truth, I'm perhaps not as grateful as I should be. I'm sure You understand how cautious I am about this. You are the only one I can count on. You love me unconditionally. You will never leave me or forsake me.*

Since God could read her thoughts there was no point in being less than honest, so she admitted it had been fun working alongside Tanner. She even admitted she sometimes had yearnings for something more in her life. Those yearnings would not be given a name. They must be denied. Her job was to raise the children and do it in a way that they would never feel they were a burden to her. She'd never put them in a position of obligation.

She'd tell Tanner she meant to end their agreement but then how could she get the crop in on her own? Besides, he already had his horses there.

She couldn't tell him not to come. But she'd make certain to accept nothing more from him.

She put the cow in the barn, then as she headed for the house she noticed the children peering through the bars of the corrals watching the horses. "Please stay away from the horses."

Frank faced her. "We're only looking. No harm in that, is there? We're safe on the outside of the corrals. After all, Pa built them solid as a rock."

To suggest otherwise would be too close to inviting all-out rebellion. "So long as you stay outside the fence."

"Of course, we will." Frank's look accused her of foolishness.

"Liz, do you want to help make soup?"

Liz followed her. Several yards behind, Janie trudged after her sister, her bottom lip quivering.

Susanne knelt to hug her little niece. "What's wrong?"

"He left without saying goodbye."

Susanne knew she meant Tanner. She also understood how difficult it was for Janie to watch people leave. She'd lost her mother and father and it had created a need to hold on to people. She hugged the child tighter. "Sweetie, he's only coming to put in the crop."

"And work with his horses," Liz added, as if that made a world of difference.

How could she make them understand it was a temporary arrangement? Already the child had grown to see Tanner as part of her life. Anything she said would likely bring a fresh onslaught of tears. "Janie, I'm not going anywhere, nor are your brothers and sister."

The child clung to Susanne, silent sobs shaking her. Tears pooled in Susanne's eyes, and she again vowed that she would provide a permanent home for these children and protect them from hurt. How was she to do that if Tanner hung about? Already they expected more from him than they should.

After a bit, Janie shuddered and tipped her head back to look at Susanne. "I love you, Auntie."

Susanne kissed the soft cheeks. "I love you, too." She reached for Liz's hand. "You, too."

"What about Robbie and Frank?" Janie asked.

"I love them, too."

Satisfied, Janie allowed Susanne to get to her feet and, holding the girls' hands, she continued to the house. As she worked with them preparing the soup and biscuits, she often glanced out the window to the garden and smiled to see it planted. Soon they would have fresh vegetables and she'd enjoy the flowers she'd planted.

And she owed Tanner nothing. He had the use of the corrals in exchange for his help.

Her smile deepened. Once the crop was in the ground, she could manage on her own.

When they heard Tanner ride into the yard the next day, Frank and Robbie slipped out the door before she could stop them.

"I want to go, too," Janie said, tears pooling in her eyes when Susanne halted her.

"Sweetie, he's working with a big horse. We need to stay out of his way."

Tears trickled silently down the child's cheeks.

Susanne's heart bled a little. "Why don't I put a chair by the window and you can watch from there?"

Janie nodded and waited for Susanne to position a chair in place, then stood on it, her nose pressed to the window.

Susanne returned to cleaning the kitchen. She'd promised herself she would do more than wash the dishes and wipe the table. As she worked, she stole glances out the window as Tanner hitched Pat to the plow and headed for the field. Not once did he look in her direction. Not that she expected him to. He'd been abundantly clear that he would be avoiding her. Which was exactly what she wanted.

She sighed, then, realizing Liz watched her, she stretched as if needing a change of position.

What she needed was—

She didn't know. Wouldn't say. Because God would provide what she needed. And she must not expect to get everything she wanted.

"Why don't you clean the lamp chimneys?" she suggested to the older girl.

Liz nodded.

Susanne prepared a basin of warm soapy water and gathered all the chimneys and put them on a cloth in the middle of the table.

She left Liz with the task, filled a bucket with hot water and got down on her hands and knees to scrub the floor. She rose halfway through to change the water. How could she have let the floor get so dirty?

Liz polished a glass chimney, but the chair where Janie had stood was now empty. Susanne glanced about. "Did Janie go to her bedroom?"

"She went outside."

Susanne's heart thudded against her chest. Surely she wouldn't—

She dashed outside. "Janie, where are you?"

There was no reply, though Robbie and Frank leaned back from watching the horses through the fence and looked about.

Susanne scanned the yard, looking up into the tree branches where Janie often went, but there was no sign of the child. She went into the yard where she could see farther afield. Her gaze went reluctantly, fearfully to the field where Tanner worked and she screamed. "Janie."

Tanner would never hear or see the little girl sitting on the ground just feet ahead of the horse.

Chapter Five

"Giddyap," Tanner called, but old Pat shook his head and refused to move. Odd. The horse had been placid and cooperative until now. Tanner hollered again and flicked the reins.

Old Pat dug in his hooves and stood immobile.

Thinking perhaps his harness rubbed wrong, Tanner dropped the reins and walked to Pat's head. In two strides, his heart hit the roof of his mouth and he ground to an abrupt halt.

"Janie, what are you doing?" How had she gotten there without him seeing? She must have slipped past while his attention had been on driving the horse.

His knees wobbled at the thought of what might have happened if Pat wasn't so wise. He patted the horse. "Good boy." Then Tanner squatted in front of Janie. Her face was streaked with tears and dust. He pulled out his handkerchief and wiped her cheeks dry and somewhat clean.

"What's the problem, little one?"

"You…you…you never said hello. Or goodbye. Don't you like me?" A tear spilled from each eye.

"I like you fine." It hurt clear through to think his desire to avoid the family had been misinterpreted by this child. "I didn't mean to hurt your feelings. From now on I'll remember to say hello and goodbye. Okay?"

She nodded.

He held out his arms and she came to him and hugged him about the neck, practically choking him, not that he'd complain. It felt too good.

"Janie!" Susanne raced across the field.

Tanner caught his breath, expecting her to trip and fall any moment. At the same time, he set Janie aside. He shouldn't have hugged her, but he didn't regret it. The little girl needed his reassurance and he was prepared to give it, even if it would lead to being reminded of his place.

Susanne reached them, dropped to her knees in the dirt and pulled the child into her arms, rocking back and forth. "Shh, shh, shh," she said over and over though no one made any other sound.

After several minutes, she held Janie at arm's length. "You scared me out of ten years. I thought—" She swallowed loudly and hugged the child again then pushed to her feet. "Off you go to your brothers."

The boys stood at the end of the field, their eyes wide.

Janie plodded to them and the three returned to the yard.

Now Susanne would speak her mind. Tanner prepared for the dressing-down he expected.

She shuddered then faced him. "I can't thank you enough."

Did he hear her wrong?

"For what?" He could think of nothing.

"For stopping in time."

"Don't thank me. I didn't see her. Thank the horse."

She went to Pat, hesitated a good eighteen inches from the animal and wrung her hands.

Tanner's thoughts stuttered. She was afraid of the horse. How had she hoped to ever get the crop seeded on her own?

She remained an arm's length from Pat and patted his neck gingerly. "Thank you. You're a good old horse."

Tanner grinned. "I'm not sure he knows what all the fuss is about."

"Sure he does." She studied Tanner.

Now she'd scold him for hugging the little girl. The little white girl.

"I don't know how to say this," she began.

He stiffened, preparing for the words that he shouldn't care about anymore, but even after all these years they would sting. They always did.

"Janie adores you. She was heartbroken when you left last night. I don't care to see her hurt."

Those were the words she found difficult to speak? They were like honey to him. "I don't care to see her hurt, either. I promised her I would say hello and good-bye from now on. If it's okay with you?"

"I think she would like that."

In the awkward silence that ensued, their eyes darted to the half-worked field. Then to the mountains to the west and the clouds scuttling across the sky.

When he finally brought his gaze to hers, his heart gave a peculiar leap at what he saw…or rather, what he thought he saw. Or perhaps wished he saw. She looked at him as if he was a man and she a woman. Nothing less. Nothing more.

He wiped his handkerchief across his face and pulled his thoughts back into order.

"I thank you for being so gentle and understanding with Janie." Susanne smiled and it went clear to the far, cold corners of his heart and warmed them.

This had to end. He could not let his thoughts run wild, like unbroken horses. If he hoped to be able to control those untamed animals, he must first learn to control his thoughts. She was smiling only because she was grateful Janie was unhurt. There was nothing more to it.

"I would never intentionally hurt her," he said. "Or any of the children." *Or you.*

"I hope not. Now I'll leave you to finish my field. I know you're anxious to get it done so you can work with your horses."

She walked back across the field and into the house. He grabbed the reins and returned to plowing—a job that left him far too much time to think.

Susanne had said nothing about Tanner touching Janie. Quite the opposite. She seemed grateful for his kindness to the child.

He looked at the back of his hand. Looked at the skin on his arms where the sleeves were rolled up. He didn't have a mirror but he didn't need one. He was dark skinned with black hair and black eyes. Ma had always called him a handsome little man. Maisie had often patted his back and told him he was handsome. But apart from those two—and they were supposed to think he was a decent fellow—the only comments he ever got were quite different.

How would Susanne respond if he told her the things he'd been called, the things he'd overheard? He wasn't about to say anything, so he'd never know. Besides, he had no intention of inviting frank comments from her. Yes, she'd said it was his actions that mattered, not his skin color. Did she really mean it? Had sparing Janie been action enough?

He scoffed. If anyone deserved credit for that, it was Pat.

He rolled his shoulders back and forth and forced his thoughts to dwell on the horses in the corrals. He'd get the crop planted as quickly as possible, then he'd devote his time to working with the animals. He measured how much he had accomplished against how much remained. It would take him most of a week to finish plowing and most of another to plant the crop. Whoever had suggested that farming was for weaklings? It was downright hard work.

It would be some time before he could get at the horses, though giving them a spell to settle down wasn't a bad idea.

Judging the time by the position of the sun in the clear blue sky, he stopped at noon and took Pat in for water and a rest. Tanner ducked his head under the stream of cold water from the pump and shook his head. He straightened, opened his eyes and stared into a pair of blue eyes.

Susanne stood before him.

"Hot and dusty," he said, as if she couldn't figure that out for herself.

"It's dinner time. I made you a meal." She handed him a plate with biscuits and a bowl of soup. The smell brought a flood of saliva to his mouth. Maisie had sent him with a package of food but he was hungry enough to eat both, and a third if someone offered it.

"Thanks." He backed into the shade of the barn.

She didn't move.

He tried to think if he'd forgotten something. But nothing came to mind. He wished she'd either speak her mind or leave, because he was about hungry enough to eat his own arm.

She opened her mouth. Closed it. Shook her head. "Enjoy your meal." She fled to the house.

He downed three biscuits with butter and jam as he watched her go. He ate every crumb and spoonful of what she'd brought and all four sandwiches Maisie had sent, then leaned his head back against the barn wall.

What had she wanted to say and didn't? Perhaps he didn't want to know and should be grateful she hadn't spoken.

Except he wasn't. Some demanding part of him wanted to know what she really thought of him even though he knew it might tear his heart to shreds.

What did Maisie say on occasion? Better to know the truth than believe a lie.

The only lie he had ever believed was to think Jenny saw past his mixed blood. He drank another dipper full of cold water and stared toward the field.

Seems he knew the truth but didn't quite accept it. In the deepest pit of his stomach there lay a faint hope that someone outside his family would see him for who he was.

Who was he? He tried to shake off the question. Who he was in his thoughts and who other people judged him to be were separated by a bottomless gully.

It would be as easy to stop the earth from turning as to cross that chasm.

* * *

"Auntie Susanne, are you done?" Liz's words jerked Susanne from her thoughts.

"Just about." She washed the last pot and handed it to Liz to dry, but she couldn't stop the question that echoed in her mind. Why had she taken a meal out to Tanner? Certainly it was the hospitable thing to do, but hadn't she intended to ignore him as he worked on the farm?

When he'd rescued Janie, she'd been so overcome with gratitude she almost hugged him. Now, wouldn't that have given him the wrong idea of what to expect in the way of gratitude? Taking him biscuits and soup seemed far safer.

But seeing him lift his head from the water trough, droplets shimmering on his black hair, muddy streaks brushing the sides of his face, had unsettled her. What was there about him that affected her so?

She silently scoffed. She was only feeling gratitude at his rescue of Janie and at the promise of getting the crop in.

Shaking off thoughts of Tanner, she focused on her chores. With instructions to stay away from the horse pen, she sent the children to play. Then she turned her attention to the flower beds along the front of the house. Last year they had been a riot of color and she hoped for the same this year, but it wouldn't happen if the weeds choked out the flowers.

The afternoon passed, the heat intensified. She finished weeding and went to the well to wash and get a cold drink. Her gaze sought Tanner in the field. He must be parched by now.

"Come on, children. We're going to take Tanner some water." They needed no second invitation and left the fence, heading immediately for the field. "Wait for me," she said, filling a bucket with water and taking along a dipper.

They went to the field and waited for him to reach the end.

He dropped the reins and joined them. "Water. I've been dreaming of a cold drink for half an hour."

"You could always stop and get one." Or she could take him water. That seemed an even better idea. It would get the crop in more quickly. She'd bake cookies and tomorrow bring him a snack as well as a drink. It was the least she could do.

"I'll stop soon. Pat's put in a long day. He needs to rest."

"The day's been just as long for you." She wanted to say so much more. The children played a ways off so she felt she could talk freely. "I appreciate your help but I don't want you to do more than is fair. This seems like a lot of work in return for using the corrals." She sought words to explain herself better. "I don't want to take advantage of your offer."

He drank another dipper of water and lifted his hat to pour water over his hair. He shook his head, sending a shower over them both.

She wiped a drop from her eye, her gaze following the droplets of water on his cheeks even though she warned herself to look elsewhere.

He adjusted his hat on his head, the feather in the hatband a cocky flag.

"Susanne, I suggested this arrangement and I am happy with it if you are." He crossed his arms and waited for her reply.

She fluttered her hands as she tried to find a way

to explain her reservations. Why not tell him the real reason?

"Eight years ago, after my parents died, I went to live with my aunt Ada. She never let me forget that I was under obligation to her, and because of that I had to jump to her every order. I felt I meant nothing to her but someone to work. And she worked me hard. I promised myself I would never again be in that position. I'd never be obligated to someone and thus give them the right to own me as though I was some horse they'd purchased." She waved a nervous hand at Pat. "Truth is, most people treat their horses better. It was only my faith in God and His goodness that saw me through those days."

"I'm sorry you had that experience. I understand how unfair life can be at times." He clamped his lips shut as if he regretted his words, then hurried on before she could respond. "But I'm not putting you under any obligation. I'm benefiting from this agreement as much as you are."

She nodded. She liked what he said, but no words had the power to erase her fears. Nor her caution. There seemed nothing more to say except one thing. "I'm sorry to unburden myself to you."

"I'm glad you told me." He touched the brim of his hat and returned to work.

She called to the children to join her as she turned her steps toward the house. They scampered after her except for Janie, who stood looking after Tanner.

Susanne went back, took her hand and led her gently away.

"He promised he'd say goodbye," Janie said.

"I know." She hoped he wouldn't forget.

The afternoon passed and Susanne went to get the

milk cow. The rope no longer secured her to the tree but had caught under the water trough, so she hadn't wandered. She had yet to figure out how to tie her in such a way she wouldn't get free.

She brought in the milk cow, milked her and then left her in the stall with some oats. She strained the milk. *Thank You, God, that there's milk for the children.*

She started to prepare a meal for the children. Again, only potatoes and eggs, but it filled their stomachs. *Thank You, God, for the eggs and potatoes. And for the promise of more garden produce.*

Throughout dinner, another silent prayer hovered in the background. She didn't want to give it words but God knew her thoughts. *Thank You for Tanner's help. And help me to keep the books between us balanced.*

"Here he comes," Janie called as they cleaned up after the meal.

"Stay here." Susanne caught the girl before she could run out the door. "He has to take care of Pat."

She stopped Frank and Robbie from leaving, too.

"I could help," Frank protested.

"Maybe you can." Because it would be good for him to watch or just enjoy the company of a man, she allowed him to go.

Janie dragged a chair to the window so she could see. Robbie climbed up and shared the chair.

Susanne had no need to look out the window to know Tanner's every move, because Janie kept her informed.

"Pat is drinking lots. Tanner is taking that thing off his neck." Janie leaned her elbows on the window ledge. "He went into the barn. Frank did, too."

Robbie jumped down and began rolling a marble back and forth across the table.

"I can't see them now." Janie's voice wobbled. "What are they doing?"

"They'll be brushing Pat and feeding him," Susanne explained.

"How long it's gonna take?"

"Sweetie, I don't know." She imagined Tanner brushing Pat, perhaps giving Frank a brush and the two of them working together. Maybe they'd talk. Frank would talk about his pa. They'd give Pat oats and put away the harness.

Then what? Seems that should be done by now, but they didn't come out.

"Are they still there?" Janie fretted. "Maybe they left."

"You would have seen them."

"Can I go look?"

"You can wait a bit longer."

A soft keening sound came from the child and Susanne clenched her muscles. It was the same sound the child had made after her mama died. She'd barely stopped making it when Jim died and it started again. Susanne well remembered the lost feeling causing her niece's distress.

How often had she asked how her parents could die and leave her, and why Jim didn't take her with him? But he was married with two children at the time and looking for a place where he could start farming.

Susanne went to Janie and wrapped her arms about the child. "I'll stay here and help you watch. I'll make sure he says goodbye like he promised."

Janie pressed her head to Susanne's shoulder, but her eyes never left the window. Liz and Robbie joined them at the window, both seeming as anxious and tense as

Janie. Susanne wanted to warn them that Tanner was not going to become a permanent part of their lives. She was about to reassure them of God's continuing presence when Frank stepped out of the barn.

Janie jerked away from Susanne and pressed to the window glass.

Tanner came out, leading his saddled horse.

"He's gonna leave," Janie wailed.

"He's only leading his horse." *Please, please, please don't forget one uncertain little girl.*

Tanner and Frank crossed the yard. Tanner handed Frank the reins and continued alone toward the house.

Janie was off the chair and running out to meet him while he was still five feet away.

He squatted to the child's level. "I've come to say goodbye."

She flung herself at him, almost unbalancing him. "I thought you'd forget."

His eyes found Susanne's over the little girl's head. She knew she wasn't mistaken in seeing a world of sorrow in them and recalled his words about life being unfair. His own ma had died, so he understood the loss of a parent. But his loss was in the distant past while Janie's was recent and raw. *Please remember how insecure she is right now.*

He held Janie. She held him. After a bit he said, "I thought this was goodbye."

"You coming back tomorrow?" Janie asked.

"Got to. Got horses to tend to. Got a crop to plant and got a little girl to say hi to."

Janie released him. "Me?"

"You're the only little girl around here." He patted her head. "I'll be back."

The child almost glowed with pleasure at his promise.

He pushed upright, adjusted his askew hat. "Goodbye to you all." His gaze touched Robbie, then Liz, and both said goodbye.

Then his gaze hit her.

She suddenly felt like Janie and wanted to prevent him from leaving. What a foolish thought. But to a lesser degree she shared Janie's knowledge and fear of people departing from her life.

"Goodbye," he said.

"Goodbye." She forced the word from her mouth.

He touched the brim of his hat, stepped outside and took the reins from Frank. "Goodbye," he said to the boy. Then he swung into his saddle and rode away.

Silence descended. Lonely, empty silence.

The children stared after him until he disappeared from view. Still they stood staring at the place where they'd last seen him.

Not just the children remained rooted to the moment. Susanne did, as well.

"Will he really come back?" Robbie asked. All the children turned to Susanne for reassurance.

"His horses are here, so I expect he'll return."

Their little heads nodded. It wasn't the answer they needed. They wanted to know he'd come back because of them.

She ached inside. How was she to make them understand that people you cared for could be snatched away in an instant? But they already knew that and yet clung to the hope that this time it would be different. Had she made a huge mistake in agreeing to this arrangement with Tanner?

Her nerves twitched. The children were going to be seriously heartbroken when he left them. What could she do to prevent it?

Chapter Six

Tanner did not slow down or turn around until he was well out of sight of the ranch. Then he pulled up and stared in the direction he'd just come from.

Poor little Janie. Wanting to keep everyone close. He understood the feeling.

His thoughts shifted to Susanne and what she'd told him about life with her aunt Ada. He shook his head. One thing he would never understand in this life was how people could treat others with such disregard. No wonder Susanne didn't want to accept any charity, or even neighborly help. To her it meant providing the giver a reason to demand repayment.

He thought of her prayer over the garden and her calm assurance of God's care. How could she be so certain of it after the way her life had gone?

Envy stung his heart. He longed for the same kind of assurance. Instead, he had such doubts. Seemed to him that God must look at him the way most people did. As a misfit.

How many times had he expected Susanne to say something to indicate how she viewed his half-breed status? He'd waited for a warning, some sign of her negative opinion of him.

He'd not seen it. Not once. Not even a hint.

Dare he hope she didn't see him as a misfit? No. He was being foolish. Yet a smile straight from a lonely place in his heart remained on his face as he rode home to join the others for supper. They ate late this time of year, getting as much done in the daylight hours as possible.

As he approached the ranch, he tried to think what he'd say when Maisie asked about his day.

No one was in the barn as he unsaddled Scout and took care of his horse's needs. He appreciated the time alone as he struggled to sort out his thoughts.

The dinner bell rang and he stepped into the evening air, still warm but with a cooling breeze that would make sleep more comfortable. This afternoon had been hot. He smiled as he recalled Susanne bringing him water. Why hadn't he gone to the well and gotten a drink when thirst first came? Because he wanted to see if she'd take pity on him. He was testing her. And testing himself to see if his wishes held a whiff of possibility. He shoved aside the foolish thought. He did not expect anything from her but neighborly politeness.

He'd watched her working around the house. She'd kept up a steady pace, never taking a break until the job was done. Perhaps she'd learned that at the hands of Aunt Ada.

Levi fell in at his side. "What are you grinning about?"

Johnny joined them. "If I didn't know him better I'd say he looks like he's in love." He drawled out the last word.

"What? You think it's impossible for me to fall in

love?" He favored his brother with a fierce frown. "Or do you mean you think it's impossible someone would fall in love with me?" It was an echo of his own doubts and reverberated through his brain. He looked the most native of the three so heard the most unfavorable comments.

"Didn't mean either. Fact is, you stay as far away from young ladies as humanly possible. And wearing that chip on your shoulder is gonna give you permanently poor posture."

Johnny's words were accurate, but Tanner would not give him the benefit of acknowledging it. Besides, a man had to preserve a little dignity before his younger brothers. "You don't know what you're talking about."

They reached the house, preventing further words on the subject, but Johnny's words clung. Yes, he avoided people. He had no desire to hear their assessment of him. But a chip on his shoulder? Uh-uh.

Tanner was still musing over the idea when Maisie said to him, "How was your day?"

"Started plowing today." What he'd planned to say was, *The horses are settling down.*

Levi shook his head sadly. "Never thought to see my big brother become a farmer."

"Little enough to do in exchange for using the corrals," Tanner said. "You saw them. They're ideal."

Levi gave a crooked grin. "Wasn't the only thing I saw." He directed his words at Maisie. "Miss Collins is a fine-looking young woman. She's—" He jerked his gaze back to Tanner. "How old would you say she is?"

"She's twenty."

Levi's eyes widened. "She told you that or you asked?"

"I just figured it. She said her parents died when she was twelve and that was eight years ago."

"Huh."

Not often he saw Levi at a loss for words and he grinned his pleasure.

Johnny held his fork in one hand and pointed it at Tanner. "Sounds like a lot of talking going on."

"What? One sentence?"

Maisie intervened. "She's lost both parents and her brother and sister-in-law. That poor child."

It was on the tip of his tongue to say Susanne was no child, but he kept the thought to himself.

"And now with four children to raise." Maisie shook her head and turned to Big Sam. "I need to go visit her."

Sam nodded. "I'll take you myself as soon as I can."

"Or I might go on my own. It's been a long time since I had an outing," Maisie murmured, and the three boys grinned at each other. Maisie would manage to get her way.

Maisie turned again to Tanner. "I had no idea she was so young. Maybe it isn't a good idea for you to be over there."

Tanner stared at his stepmother. "Why on earth not? She'll never get the crop in on her own. For one thing, she's afraid of the plow horse."

"I understand. But what will people say?"

Heat stung Tanner's neck. "Because I'm a half-breed and she's a white gal?" His voice was low and emotionless while his insides rolled enough to make him dizzy.

"Of course not. I've said it before and I'll say it again. You'd be a good catch for any woman. You're kind and gentle and thoughtful."

Levi and Johnny rolled their eyes.

"What I meant is she's a young woman alone. I'm concerned about her reputation. And you should be, as well."

Tanner looked about the table. They all watched him to see what he'd do. "A good reputation won't feed four hungry children." He drank his glass of water and hoped the conversation would end.

The others shifted their attention to other topics, though he often caught Maisie watching him and read the concern in her eyes.

Perhaps she was right. But what could he do about it? He'd made an agreement and he meant to keep it.

The best he could do was stay away from her.

The next morning, he discovered how difficult it was going to be to keep his distance.

First, he had to say hello to Janie. She came running as soon as she saw him.

"Hello, little miss." He swung her into the air, bringing happy giggles from the child.

He greeted each of the children.

"Hello, Liz. Your hair looks nice this morning." She returned the greeting but ducked her head, perhaps a little embarrassed at the attention.

"Hello, Frank. How are the horses?"

"Morning. The horses are fine. Getting more and more used to us. 'Course I only watched them from the fence."

"Good to hear. Hello, Robbie. How are you?" He ruffled the boy's hair.

"I gots a marble." He pulled out a cat's-eye aggie from his pocket.

Tanner inspected it. "Why, that's a dandy."

"Pa gave it to me."

"Then you take real good care of it."

Susanne had the cow by the lead rope, taking it out to tether for the day.

"Hello," he said. "Let me do that."

"I can do it."

He understood her message. She didn't want him to do one thing more than their agreement stipulated. Rather than argue, he fell into step beside her. So much for staying as far away from her as possible, he thought. But he knew the cow could put up a struggle.

She stopped and gave him a challenging look. "I can do this on my own."

Maisie's words echoed in the back of his mind, as did his decision to stay away from Susanne, but even louder was the desire to help. To test and judge her reaction to him.

Perhaps she objected to him, not his help. How could he get an answer to the question? He could come right out and ask, but he sensed she would say the right words. Only way to judge if she had the right feelings was to spend time with her and see if she objected, either outright or subtly. He shut the door on Maisie's concerns, even knowing they would return to accuse him. Maisie's words had a way of doing that.

"Pat's still eating his oats," he told Susanne by way of explanation. "I got nothing else do to at the moment."

"Our understanding was you were going to work with your horses."

Ah, yes. He'd almost forgotten. "They need a few days to settle in and feel comfortable. I intend to break them gently."

"I see." She continued onward. He saw her destination. A big old tree in the middle of the pasture. The water trough was already there and water glistened in it.

The cow ambled along between them. They reached the spot and he stood back as she tied the rope around the tree.

"There," she said with obvious satisfaction.

He jerked the rope and it came free. "Don't think Daisy is going to stay here long." Already the cow eyed the far fence, no doubt thinking of greener, more distant pastures.

Susanne spared Tanner an annoyed look and again tied the rope.

He jerked it and this time it stuck.

She laughed.

He jerked it again, harder. The end flew around the tree and plopped at her feet. He said nothing, revealed nothing in his face, even though he enjoyed this immensely.

She picked up the rope and stared at the end. "You're going to make me ask, aren't you?"

He shrugged.

She sighed. "Mr. Harding, would you please be so kind as to show me how to tie the rope so it will stay?"

"Don't mind a bit." He showed her how to knot the rope so Daisy couldn't escape but so Susanne could grab the end and free Daisy when the time came to take her home. Then he undid it. "Your turn."

She tried, and failed. "Oh, bother," she muttered, and tried again. This time she got it right. She faced him. "Thank you. It's a lesson I won't forget."

"My ma was right. You learn best by doing it yourself." He grinned, wanting nothing more than to pat her on the back and congratulate her, but Maisie's words shouted through his head. Even without his stepmother's warning, he would not touch her. He had no desire to see her flinch. But he had to cross his arms to keep the urge under control.

He looked toward the yard. "Pat will be done by now." He would have stridden away and left her standing there, but it would be rude so he again walked at her side back to the barn.

The four children waited for them and watched as he harnessed Pat. They followed him as far as the edge of the field and observed him back Pat to the plow. Finished, he called, "Goodbye. Go help your aunt."

He watched them return to the yard. Frank went to the barn. Yesterday, Tanner had suggested that the boy sort through the stuff scattered about and given him a few directions.

Robbie and Janie wandered off together and Liz went to the house, probably to help her aunt.

Tanner turned to plow the field but he kept an errant eye on the children, watching them come and go.

Susanne didn't appear. Was she avoiding him so completely that she wouldn't even leave the house while he was there?

He glanced at the sun. Would noon never arrive so he could go to the yard?

Maisie's words sounded in his head. She was right. Tanner needed to be concerned about Susanne's reputation. He would not look toward the house again.

The heat inside the house intensified even though the doors and windows were all open. Susanne wiped her apron across her brow and pulled the last tray of cookies from the oven. She might have waited for a cooler day to bake but she'd convinced herself she must do it today, her excuse being there were no cookies in the house and the children especially loved the boiled raisin ones.

Her desire to bake had nothing to do with Tanner, she insisted. Certainly she would take him some at dinnertime. It would be inhospitable to do otherwise.

She transferred the cookies to a cooling rack. Whom did she think she was fooling? Not herself. The desire to have something to feed Tanner had been the main impetus for baking today. Tomorrow she'd make bread, never mind the temperature inside or out.

"You think Tanner will like these?" Liz asked.

Had Susanne's thoughts communicated themselves to Liz? Of course not. Liz and all the children simply enjoyed having a change in their boring routine.

"If he doesn't, it will mean all the more for us to enjoy."

She glanced at the clock. The morning usually flew by, but today the hands on the clock seemed to have stopped. Had she remembered to wind it? The second hand moved, but was it slower than normal? She found the key and wound it even though she knew she had done it the previous evening. It was one of the last things she did every night before she went to bed.

Every other morning she had felt overwhelmed with the work that awaited her but not today. The garden was in, the crop would soon be in, and the cow was tethered so she couldn't wander. Now she would turn her attention to the household needs that had been neglected for many weeks.

She'd wait until Monday to do the laundry, but the children's two bedrooms needed to be cleaned today.

She entered the boys' room and gasped. How had it gotten so dirty?

She provided her own answer. Neglect.

She added to that answer. Perhaps she'd been a little rebellious, as well. At first, Aunt Ada's orders were a constant reminder of all Susanne needed to do, and she had worked as hard as Aunt Ada would have required. Then one day she realized she didn't have to do what her aunt said any longer, and she'd quit.

Now she realized both ways were controlled by Aunt Ada. It was time to end that control. She would do what needed to be done and clean the rooms for her sake, as well as the children's. They deserved to be better taken care of than this. The chore would keep her mind occupied so she wasn't constantly thinking of Tanner, of what he was doing and how his help might incite him to make other demands. She sighed. Would she ever truly be able to put Aunt Ada's harsh lessons behind her?

She stripped the two beds and hauled the mattresses outside to air in the sun.

Liz followed, holding a broom. "I'll beat the dirt out of them."

Leaving her to the task, Susanne returned to the bedroom. She gathered up the clothes scattered about, sorting the ones that needed laundering from those that didn't, readying them for Monday's chore.

Squeals and giggles came from outside the window. She looked out and saw Janie and Robbie jumping on the mattresses. Aunt Ada would have bawled Susanne out for such foolishness, probably had her whipped. Susanne watched for a moment, couldn't see they were hurting anything and left them to enjoy themselves.

A glance at the clock revealed she had lots of time before she would slip the biscuits into the oven.

She scrubbed the walls, washed the windows, cleaned out the drawers and finally drew a deep breath. The house smelled so much better. She stepped outside. "Who wants to help me carry the mattresses back in?" She stood the mattress on edge and Liz swept both sides, then, with Liz and the two little ones at one end and Susanne the other, they carried each mattress in and back to the beds.

Liz looked about. "It's so nice and clean. Can I do our bedroom now?"

"I'll help you after dinner." She put the biscuits in the oven and while they baked, she made the beds with clean linens—thankfully. Alice had a spare set of bedding for each of the beds. She smoothed the quilts then stood back and admired her work.

"Here he comes," Robbie yelled, and raced out the door.

Janie followed on his heels.

"Stay back from the horse," Susanne called. She watched out the window to make certain the children were safe, but once she saw they stood a respectful distance away her gaze went to Tanner. He wore a thin layer of dirt, which did nothing to mar his looks.

His looks? What did they matter? All she cared about was getting the crop in. But, despite her mental scolding, she couldn't tear her gaze from him. He moved with fluid grace, perhaps inherited from his Indian forebears. His dark skin gave him a more masculine appeal than the fair-skinned men she usually saw. He was a strong, kind man. She'd seen that evidenced many times in the past few days.

He let Pat drink his fill and turned him into the barn for feed.

He and Frank came out together. What had kept Frank occupied in there all morning? She should have checked on him, but he was so responsible she never considered the need.

Tanner stopped at the pump. He poured the bucket of water over his head and came up dripping. He shook his head sending a spray of water about him that caught the sun.

Liz saw it, too, and gasped. "He's wearing a rainbow."

The water dropped to the ground before she finished speaking.

"It's gone."

Gone. The word drilled a hole through Susanne's thoughts. She stared at the clock, the second hand ticking the passing of time. Why had she suddenly been hammered by one word? Gone. Yes, her parents were gone. Her brother was gone. She'd learned to live with the emptiness of her parents' death and would eventually accept Jim's as a part of her life, too.

Her concern wasn't about people leaving. It was about being under obligation. But the word *gone* echoed through her insides. She shook it away, focused on her need to keep the books balanced with Tanner. Taking him biscuits and cookies could be added to her side of the ledger.

She prepared a plate. For two ticks of the second hand of the clock, she thought of sending Liz out with the food but, no, she would take it herself. She wasn't going to let the fear instilled in her by Aunt Ada control her.

"Come along, Liz, let's take this to him."

Liz walked sedately at Susanne's side.

Tanner had sunk to the ground in the shade of the barn but scrambled to his feet at her approach.

"Brought you something to eat." She handed him the plate. Their fingers brushed as he took it and her heart fluttered like a trapped butterfly. Only because she was too hot. Nothing more.

"How did your morning go?" she asked.

At the same time, he asked, "Did you have a good morning?"

"You go first," he said.

"I cleaned the boys' bedroom and made cookies." She indicated the half dozen on the plate. "I hope you like raisin cookies."

"Love 'em. I could smell them halfway across the field and hoped I might get to taste them."

"How did the plowing go?"

"Good. Old Pat is no problem to handle."

"He's so big."

Tanner grinned. "I already figured out you were scared of him."

She knew there was no point in denying it, but did he have to look so pleased with himself? "I'm not a farm girl, you know."

"Really?" He seemed genuinely surprised, or else he teased her. She kind of liked the idea of the latter.

"Nope. Never lived on a farm until I came out here."

"Last summer when I saw you get off the stagecoach— that was your first visit?"

She nodded.

"You've been through a lot of changes." The children were a distance away, watching the horses, but he lowered his voice so they couldn't hear. "So have they. Are they okay?"

"For the most part. It's hard, of course. But not as bad as at first."

"Hard for you, too."

She'd never acknowledged it before. The pain and helplessness and uncertainties of those early days hit her. Tears rushed to her eyes before she could stop them. She turned away and sniffed.

He lifted his hand as if he meant to reach out and comfort her but dropped it without doing so. "I'm sorry. I didn't mean to cause you pain."

She sniffed again and swiped at her eyes. "Sometimes the emotions swell unexpectedly."

He nodded. "I have only to see the yoke from Ma's two-hide dress to feel like a lost seven-year-old again." He got a distant, sad look in his eyes.

"Two-hide dress? What's that?"

She breathed easier when he smiled.

"It's a dress my mother's people made from two hides. The yoke contrasts the rest of the dress and is decorated in some way. My mother's has some beads on it. She was wearing it when Pa found her. Most of the dress was torn and ruined, but she saved the yoke. I have it now."

"Tell me about your mother. How did your pa meet her?" He'd said his pa had found her. She wanted to know more.

"My ma was with the Lakota Indians at the Battle of the Little Bighorn." The children had clustered about to hear his story. "She ran from the soldiers, but one chased after her and shot her. She fell and pretended to be dead, and as soon as he left, she crept away. She was seriously injured. A bullet through her side." He touched the spot on his own body. "She survived three days and nights by eating berries and roots and drinking from little streams. Always she kept to the streams, following them north and west. She said she knew it was the only way of escape. She packed the wound with moss, but it continued to bleed."

He paused, a faraway look in his eyes.

The children sat quietly beside Susanne on the ground. Tanner crossed his legs and lowered himself to the ground in one smooth motion. He continued his story.

"Finally she was too weak to go on and found a place by the river where she could die in comfort."

Liz gasped.

Tanner smiled at her. "Don't worry, it turns out fine. You see, my pa was out riding, hunting game and enjoying the country when he came upon her. She was so frightened. White men meant death in her mind, and she tried to fight him off, but she had no strength left. He made soft sounds to try and reassure her. She was too weak to resist him, and he carried her back to his camp and tended her until she healed. They fell in love and married and he moved to the farthest corner of the territory in hopes she could live in peace."

"Did she?" Liz asked.

"For the most part, yes. Until she got sick and died."

Liz nodded. She understood about illness and death far better than a child her age should.

"Is Sundown Ranch where he brought her?" Frank asked.

"It is. And they were both very happy there. My brothers and I were born there."

"It's both a sad and happy story," Liz decided.

"Mostly happy, I'd say," Tanner assured her. "Ma and

Pa were very happy together. Then Pa married Maisie and they're very happy."

"Are you happy?" Liz asked.

It was an inappropriate question but the same one Susanne wanted to ask so she didn't scold the girl.

"You want to know a secret?" He leaned closer to the children and they all tipped their heads to hear. Susanne made sure to lean close enough so she'd hear, too.

"It's this." He spoke very quietly so they all had to strain to hear. "A person is about as happy as they make up their mind to be. And I've decided to be happy." His voice returned to normal. "So yes, Liz, I am happy. Are you?"

She nodded. "Except sometimes I miss my mama and papa and that makes me sad."

Janie started her keening again.

Susanne pulled her to her lap, but Janie wouldn't sit there. She went to Tanner. He understood her need and pulled her to his lap. His sorrow-filled eyes met Susanne's and something wrenched inside her...a sensation of both fear and freedom.

She wondered if she would ever breathe again.

Robbie looked thoughtful. "I guess a person can be sad and happy almost at the same time."

Tanner chuckled. "How did you get to be so wise at such a young age?"

Robbie shrugged. "Just am."

Tanner laughed and the tension eased.

The plate of food remained untouched by Tanner's side. "Oh, my. We've kept you from your dinner and I have to feed the children." She scrambled to her feet.

But she couldn't leave so abruptly and she let the children run ahead. "Tanner, thank you for telling us about your family. And for reminding us all we could be happy if we choose to be."

He'd risen, too, and she looked into his eyes. His dark, bottomless eyes. She could lose herself in his gaze, forget every hard lesson she'd learned and all her good intentions. Why did she get the feeling he invited her to do so?

She struggled to pull her thoughts back under control.

She had no intention of repeating any of her hard lessons or forgetting what mattered in her life, though, at the moment, she couldn't say what those things were. Then Tanner shifted his gaze, freeing her from its power. Being independent. Depending on no one. Taking care of the children. That's what mattered. That's all that mattered. She'd best remember that.

Chapter Seven

Tanner ate his dinner, then returned to plowing in the hot sun. The work required little thinking, which left him lots of time to watch the goings-on in the yard and hope Susanne and the children might bring him a drink and some more of those cookies.

He figured out how many passes up and down the field he must make before he could expect their visit. At any other time he would have kicked his horse into a gallop and raced to his destination, but there was no hurrying a big horse pulling a plow. A man who meant to be a farmer had to have the patience of Job.

Finally Susanne and the children crossed toward the field. He smiled clear through. Janie carried a plate gingerly and Susanne hovered at the child's side in case the plate tipped. Frank carried a bucket, water splashing on his boots. Robbie held the dipper aloft. Liz walked at Frank's side and the two chatted quietly. Robbie, though, wasn't quiet. His voice carried to Tanner.

Tanner reached the end of the row and he eagerly joined the family.

"I brung cookies," Janie said, holding out the plate.

"I've been thinking of how good they tasted for about two hours now. But first let me get a drink." His smile encompassed the five of them but lingered on Susanne. She wore a blue bonnet that made her eyes even bluer. Her hair was pulled back in a tidy knot, but strands drifted across her cheek, tugged free in the breeze. She smiled.

Maisie's words plagued him. He must be careful of her reputation, though he wondered who would know or care. Except he'd grown up in this area and understood things had a way of getting around. The town of Granite Creek was a good distance off, but that didn't mean the occupants wouldn't delight in a little gossip about those who lived out in the hills.

He washed and drank his fill of water, then savored the cookies. As he chewed, he studied the field. Seemed the safest place to look. "Smells good, doesn't it?"

Susanne drew in a deep breath. "Sure does. Smells like a promise of life and abundance."

He'd never thought of it that way. "I kind of prefer the untamed spaces, but a family needs to eat."

She shifted her attention to him. "I guess you feel torn between the two worlds of your parents."

Her words jolted through him and his eyes met hers. "I suppose I do."

She looked away. "Change is hard but it seems necessary."

"Do you mean about the white man driving out the Indians?" He doubted he kept the bitterness from his voice.

"Of course not. I simply meant a person must adapt to change. It's as you said about being happy. We choose how happy we are. I meant the same about change. We choose to adapt or be miserable."

He considered her words. "Do you know how many times I've considered joining the few Indians roaming free?"

"What keeps you from doing so?"

"Lots of things. My pa and stepmother. My brothers. The ranch. I love it. And maybe, deep down, I know I could never undo the past and re-create the life that had once been." He realized at some point he'd made a choice to deal with the facts of his life. "Besides, I don't belong in the native world."

"No, you belong right where you are."

He'd never believed that and wasn't sure he did even now, but her words made him want to.

He ate the half dozen cookies they'd brought and had another drink of water before he returned to work. He mulled over her words as he spent the rest of the afternoon following the horse up and down the field. By suppertime he wondered if Susanne meant what she'd said, because he had half begun to believe her.

When he took Pat into the barn, Frank was still sorting and cleaning the tack room. The harnesses hung from nails, the wood was stacked against one wall and brushes filled a little shelf. The tools were lined up neatly in one corner and garbage swept into a pile. "Wow. You've done a lot of work," Tanner said. "It's looking so much better. Did your aunt see it?"

"Not yet. She hasn't brought the cow in. Won't she be surprised?"

"I'd love to see her face when she sees what you've done."

"Maybe you will. She's gone with the others to bring Daisy home."

Tanner knew that. He'd purposely quit when she went

out. His noble intention was to be ready to leave as soon as he said goodbye, but his selfish intention had him taking his time caring for Pat, brushing him longer than necessary, then spending time cleaning the harness.

His nerves jangled as he heard them approach.

Frank stood by the tack-room door, his arms crossed, a pleased expectation on his face.

Robbie ran in first. He saw Tanner and yelled, "He's still here."

Janie was right on his heels. "I told you he wouldn't go without saying goodbye."

Liz followed her sister and gave Tanner a shy smile.

Behind them, Susanne led the cow in. She paused to let her eyes adjust, and then found him in the shadows and smiled. "You waited."

He nodded. "Promised Miss Janie I would always say hello and goodbye." He swung Janie up and perched her on one hip, then seeing the longing in Robbie's eyes, he lifted him to the other.

Susanne watched him. For a heartbeat he wondered if he should put the children down. Then she smiled.

"You two are quite a load for Mr. Tanner."

"Not at all," he said. He liked the way they clung to him. Almost as much as he liked the fact she didn't tell them to get down.

She looked about, saw the neatened barn and gasped. "Is this what you've been doing, Frank?"

"Do you like it?" He waited anxiously for her reply.

She smiled and nodded. "It looks wonderful." She went to Frank and draped an arm about his shoulders. "You've done a fine job. Your ma and pa would be mighty proud."

The boy's chest swelled enough to strain his shirt

buttons. As Frank showed Susanne every detail of what he'd done, Susanne praised his efforts. She touched Frank's shoulder often, patted his back, chuckled at something he said.

Tanner stood rooted to the spot, the children in his arms. Though it was time to leave, he enjoyed watching Susanne and Frank too much to rob himself of the pleasure.

When they returned to the others, Susanne noticed the cow waiting in the doorway.

"Oh, Daisy. I forgot all about you." She grabbed the rope and led the cow to the stall.

Tanner set the children down. "I have to go home."

Janie clung to one side, Robbie to the other.

He squatted down and took a chin in each hand. "I can't say hello if I don't say goodbye."

"You'll come back tomorrow?" Janie asked.

The barn had grown quiet. Frank and Liz stood to one side, watching and waiting for his answer.

Susanne stood beside Daisy, also watching. Likely she just wanted to protect the children.

He returned his gaze to Janie. "Tomorrow is Sunday."

Susanne gasped. "I plumb lost track of the days. Good thing I didn't miss it altogether. Sunday is my favorite day. Janie, people don't work on Sunday."

Janie's lip quivered. "You're not—" she sniffed "—coming back?"

He slowly pushed to his feet. "I'd like to see to my horses if that's all right."

"It's all right," Janie said, and the other children nodded approval.

"It has to be all right with your aunt."

The two youngest rushed to Susanne's side and pulled on her arms. "It's okay, isn't it?"

She laughed. "Of course, he can come tend his horses."

He hoped the look of welcome on her face was for him and not just for the benefit of the children.

He saddled Scout and, as he led him from the barn, he glanced over his shoulder. Susanne stood in the doorway with the children. He sketched a goodbye salute to her, then said goodbye to each of the children.

He rode away, pausing just before he could no longer see the farm. He turned. The children stood where he had left them and Susanne remained in the doorway. He waved and they all waved back. Even Susanne.

A feeling of satisfaction such as he seldom felt filled him as he rode home.

Tanner drank his morning coffee in a leisurely fashion though his insides were taut with a desire to rush away. "Guess I'll ride over and check on the horses."

Big Sam didn't allow unnecessary work on Sunday; however, the animals must be tended so he simply nodded. "Are they settling down?"

"Having the kids around is teaching them not to be so skittish. They're getting used to Robbie's yells."

"Maybe we can all go over," Levi said, his voice twice as innocent as his intention. "She might invite us to join them for a meal."

"Maybe you should give Miss Collins warning before you show up expecting to be fed," Tanner said, his voice as deceptively innocent as his brother's.

Maisie watched them closely. "Wouldn't be fair to

drop in on her without warning," she said after studying them both for a moment.

"Guess not." Levi shrugged.

Tanner grinned. His brother had only been teasing, but Maisie had reined him in. Still, Tanner made sure he didn't hurry to leave the ranch. No point in doing something to invite more teasing from Levi and Johnny.

He took his time wandering to the barn as if he had nothing particular in mind.

Levi and Johnny followed, nudging each other and grinning.

Tanner pretended to get sidetracked by one of the other horses. Then he spent several minutes in the tack room, rearranging things and fussing with a tangled set of reins.

Levi and Johnny stood in the doorway, lounging on either side of the doorjamb.

"Thought you were going to check on your horses," Johnny said.

"Aren't you afraid they might be out of water?" Levi said in his most innocent voice.

"Seems he isn't all that concerned about them," Johnny added.

Levi shook his head. "Appears to me he's lost interest."

Tanner continued to ignore them.

"Don't suppose he's found something he's more interested in, do you?" Johnny scratched his head as if puzzled.

Tanner grunted. "Ain't you two got something to do today?"

They shook their heads.

"Well then, why don't you try and find something?"

Johnny shrugged. "Don't mind doing what we're doing."

"So long as you're having fun." He grabbed his saddle and pushed past them.

They followed him to Scout's stall and watched his every move.

"You'd think the two of you had never seen a horse saddled before."

Levi leaned against the stall and grinned. "Seen it lots of times."

"What we ain't seen," Johnny said, pointing a blade of grass at Tanner, "is our big brother going to visit a lady friend."

The two of them grinned at him.

He'd known all morning it was coming. He'd decided he wouldn't respond but denial burst from his lips. "I am going to see ten mares. I'd hardly call them 'lady friends.'"

Neither of his brothers responded nor did they stop grinning.

He led Scout from the barn, Levi and Johnny crowding after him. He swung into the saddle.

"Give our greetings to Miss Collins," Levi said.

"Surprised you can talk around that grin on your face," Tanner muttered. Louder, he added, "Don't plan to see Miss Collins today." He rode away before either of them could say another word.

He didn't *plan* to see Susanne, despite hoping she'd be around.

He leaned forward as he neared the Collins farm, even as he told himself he wasn't anxious to see them. His eyes scanned the property and lit on them. They were knotted together under a tree. The girls wore gray bonnets and dark blue dresses and the boys held their hats against their chests. But it was Susanne who drew his attention. Her blue dress fluttered about her legs.

Janie and Robbie took a step toward him before Susanne could restrain them.

He could feel their anxious waiting as he swung off Scout and draped the reins over the saddle horn. Scout would not leave so long as Tanner remained.

Five pairs of eyes watched him cross the yard toward them.

Susanne released the younger two and they ran to him whooping loud enough to cause the wild horses to race to the far side of the enclosure.

"Hello, you two." He squatted down and let them fling themselves into his outstretched arms. It sure felt good to be so welcome.

Susanne and the two older children waited under the tree. If he wasn't mistaken they looked as eager for his greeting. At least Frank and Liz did. Susanne's expression revealed less.

He let the younger ones ride his legs as he closed the distance to the others. "Good morning." He squeezed Frank's shoulder and tugged a lock of Liz's hair. It hit him then. How would they manage to grow older without a father to guide and protect them? He couldn't imagine how he would have turned out as capable and self-sufficient as he was without Big Sam's guidance. Who would guide these little ones? Susanne for certain, but who would exert the male influence? And why was he so concerned? It wasn't like there weren't a dozen eligible men in the area who would almost certainly welcome a ready-made family.

Like Alfred Morris. He'd figured he was the man he saw visiting the first day he came to the farm.

He wondered at the pain behind his ribs.

Finally, he let himself look fully at Susanne. He managed a fairly normal sounding "Good morning."

"Good morning," she said, her blue eyes filling with sunshine. "We were about to have church."

He looked around. Had he missed something? He sure could have, his attention focused on the children and Susanne, but he saw no church, no benches, no gathering of people. "Church?"

She laughed softly as if pleased with his reaction. "Every Sunday we have our own little service. We sing a couple of hymns and read from the Bible. You're welcome to join us." Her eyes flashed with warmth and welcome, or was it just what he wanted to believe?

He darted a glance past her shoulder at the corrals. He'd come to check the horses. He surely didn't belong in a tight-knit family, pretend-church gathering. "Thanks, but I don't think I'd fit in."

Pink stained her cheeks and she ducked her head.

Had he said something wrong? If so, he surely had no idea what. "I'll see to my horses."

"Aw," Janie protested. "I want you to stay."

"Maybe another time." He got as far as the corrals, but it didn't seem right to create a distraction while Susanne had church, so he leaned against the fence and watched them pray. Of necessity, he also listened.

The children sat on the ground in a semicircle facing her. She, likewise, sat on the ground, her skirt fanned out around her like a large blue flower. "Remember the hymn we've been learning?"

The children nodded.

"All together now." Susanne waved her hand to guide them and they sang, "'My faith looks up to Thee, Thou Lamb of Calvary.'"

It was the best choir Tanner had ever heard.

He half snorted. Like he'd heard a lot of musical performances. The Hardings made it to church for special occasions—Easter and Christmas and July Fourth— and as often as possible during the summer months, but not regularly. It was too far and if they went to town it made more sense to go Saturday or a weekday when they could conduct business.

Maisie lamented the irregularity of their attendance, though it had suited Ma fine. She'd sooner worship in the great outdoors than with those who often resented her.

The words of the hymns caught at his heart. "'Hear me...my zeal inspire...a living fire.'"

A living fire. If only he could feel God's love that way.

"That was fine," Susanne said. "I'm sure God is pleased. Now let's try 'Nearer, My God, to Thee.'"

Tanner gulped. It seemed God had heard his longing and created a hymn to answer it. He couldn't move as he heard the words, "though like a wanderer...yet in my dreams I'd be nearer, my God, to Thee." The lyrics drilled through him. He had considered wandering and had rejected the idea. But still his heart wandered, searching for a home.

He closed his eyes, reminding himself he had a home. He had parents and brothers. Yet there remained an aching absence inside him.

He opened his eyes and let the enjoyment of watching Susanne and the children fill the void.

"Today I will read Psalm 139." Susanne opened the Bible on her lap.

He'd heard the psalm before, but this time the words nested in his head.

You know me... Where can I go from your Spirit... You knit me together in my mother's womb... Know my anxious thoughts...and lead me in the way everlasting.

The yearning in his heart grew.

After a few moments Susanne must have dismissed the children, for they ran to play and she joined him at the fence. She seemed so peaceful despite her losses and burdens.

"I love Sundays." She smiled at him, easing his troubled mind. "It was the one day at Aunt Ada's that she didn't bother me. I guess she considered it against her religion to act badly on Sunday." Susanne chuckled.

It was on the tip of Tanner's tongue to ask how she could laugh when she said, "We went to church. I loved it."

He imagined she would. At church she could sit idle and not expect to get her ears boxed for doing so.

"I loved the hymns and the Bible lesson," she said. "In my church there were stained glass windows that showed Jesus the Good Shepherd." Her voice grew dreamy. "God felt so close there."

She faced him. "Do you oppose going to church?"

He shook his head. "I go when it's possible." He'd almost said when it was convenient.

"Do you go because you love God? Do you belong to Him?"

She was very direct. He owed her an equally direct answer.

But what could he say?

* * *

She had been too bold. Still, she couldn't pull the words back, nor did she want to. She needed to know. What were his beliefs?

He gave a vague wave of his hand as if he didn't care to discuss the matter, then he released a breath that must surely have been pent up for several seconds.

"I recall a time when Ma and Pa took us boys to a grove of trees that Pa said was like a cathedral. The branches arched overhead, so thick the sky poked through in few places. The air inside was very still, with birds singing in the branches."

Susanne focused on his words, mesmerized by the soft tone of his voice and the faraway look in his eyes.

"Ma bowed her head and sang a song I'd never heard before. She said it was her own song, from her heart. Words to tell God how much she loved Him, the world He'd made and the husband and sons He'd blessed her with. I could feel God in every breath she took." He shrugged a little and gave a half-mocking smile.

"That's beautiful."

"I was about Janie's age. God felt so close, too."

"Have you gone there often since then?" She could picture him worshipping God in that place much as she and the children had recently worshipped under the generous branches of the elm tree.

"No." The skin around his eyes seemed to tighten.

She couldn't say what the expression meant, only that it made her want to comfort him. However, he wasn't one of the children she could hug, so she locked her fingers together. "Why not?"

"Ma died before summer came again and I've never wanted to return."

She could not deny him—or herself—the right to comfort and she pressed one hand to his forearm. "I'm sorry."

"Guess I'll never feel that close to God again."

She sucked in a barely audible gasp. "But God hasn't changed. He is still as near as our next breath, and His love is as warm as the sun overhead. He promises to never leave us or forsake us."

He turned toward the horses, shifting away from her touch. "I'm happy that you have found that so. I have not."

She dropped her hand to her side, longing to ask him for an explanation. What didn't he find so? God's love? His faithfulness?

Was she right in thinking she glimpsed the root of his feeling distant from God?

"Perhaps you are confusing God's faithfulness with people's faithfulness or lack of it."

He jerked about to face her and yanked up one sleeve to expose his dark skin. He jabbed his finger at it. "I'm a half-breed. Some people prefer to call me a dirty Injun." He grunted. "Not that I'm Indian, either. At least not in the eyes of my relatives and their friends. I'm neither. I belong nowhere."

"Do your brothers feel the same?" It was awful to think of three little boys being treated so unfairly.

He lifted one shoulder. "It doesn't seem to bother them as much as me."

Susanne sniffed and widened her eyes to keep them from filling with tears. She'd glimpsed the depth of his pain and it ripped through her like a knife. Ignoring his earlier rejection of her touch, she pressed her fingers to the bare skin of his arm. His muscles twitched. Warmth flowed through her but she ignored her reaction. It was far more important to convey to him the truth she felt deep in her heart.

"You are not a mistake. God made you in your mother's womb. He placed you here on earth for His purposes. I know I'm grateful you're here to help. Think about it. How is it you captured your horses and needed corrals and here I have corrals waiting just when I also need the crop planted? Seems more than coincidence to my way of thinking."

His gaze lingered on her fingers still resting on his arm. Slowly he looked up. "You realize not everyone will agree with you."

She understood he meant about his birth not being a mistake. "Not everyone matters."

"That's so, isn't it?" He withdrew and leaned his forearms on the fence as he watched his horses.

She stood next to him, imitating his pose.

"I didn't tell you that some of these mares are offspring of my mother's mare, who was turned out after her death to join the wild herd." He explained how the mare would allow no one else to ride her.

Susanne studied the horses more closely, then turned to Tanner. "I can see why they're so important to you."

He didn't say anything as his eyes held hers unblinkingly. She wasn't sure what he sought there, but she knew what she needed to do. She needed to see him accept and be glad of his mixed heritage.

"Do you know what else I see?" she asked.

His eyes begged for more, but he pushed back from the fence. "I came to take care of the horses." He vaulted into the corral.

She sighed. Perhaps he was right. She hardly knew

him. How could she expect him to believe what she'd been about to say? That he seemed to be a strong, kind, thoughtful man who kept his word whether to children or adults. That his heritage didn't matter. Only his actions.

But she never got the chance to say all that.

He set about looking after the horses and she turned to spy the children playing a game some distance away. She returned to the house. At some point today she meant to spend a few minutes writing in her diary—something that happened so infrequently it didn't deserve the name diary. Now was the perfect time, she reasoned.

She sat at the table, but her gaze went often to the window, where every now and then she caught a glimpse of Tanner in the pen with the horses. All too soon, he jumped over the fence, looked around and spied the children.

He went to them. Saying goodbye no doubt.

He made his way back to his horse. Would he say goodbye to her? Not that it mattered. He had no obligation to do so.

Obligation. The word seared through her. Had she so quickly forgotten what it meant?

Surely wasting his time at the corrals would count against her in the ledger she kept in her head. Yes, she'd been trying to convince him of God's love. But perhaps he was right to distrust people. She certainly shared a sense of caution around people. But trusting God was different.

She needed to bear that in mind and not get so easily drawn aside by her attraction to a man who only wanted to exchange work for the use of corrals.

She forbade herself to look out the window to watch Tanner depart.

She had returned to her writing when a knock at the door jolted her from her chair.

He'd come to say goodbye.

Or maybe he'd come for some other purpose—maybe even to say he had changed his mind about their agreement.

She purposely slowed her steps as she crossed to open the door. "Yes?" Surely her tone of voice conveyed nothing but politeness.

Tanner removed his hat. "I've come to say goodbye."

"Goodbye." She offered him nothing more. Not even a smile.

"I'll get back to the plowing tomorrow."

"Thank you."

He jammed his hat on his head and swung onto his horse.

She closed the door and leaned against it, quelling her foolish longings to be more than a business deal to Tanner. She mustn't let herself forget to keep the ledger balanced so that she'd never be owing him.

Taking a deep breath, she pushed away from the door, gathered up the pen, ink and diary, and put them away. She had nothing she wanted to write on the pages. Not today.

She picked up a book to read but it didn't appeal. She sat in the rocker in the front room and pulled the Bible to her lap, then closed it after realizing she hadn't understood a word. She looked out the side window to where the children still played a game of tag.

With a deep sigh she went to her bedroom, opened the top drawer and pulled out the velvet box that held her mother's brooch. She tipped back the lid and touched it with a fingertip. She missed her parents with an ache that still stung. Today she had let those feelings influence her response toward Tanner. From now on she knew she had to guard her heart and mind before she let herself forget what mattered—taking care of the children and being free to make her own decisions in life.

A sound from outside drew her attention. Did she hear horse hooves?

Had Tanner returned?

She dropped the jewelry box into the drawer and hurried to the kitchen.

No. She must control her thoughts. She slowed her steps and waited for a knock. Only then did she cross the room and throw open the door.

She stared at the man before her. "Mr. Morris." There wasn't a person in the whole world she'd rather not see, with the exception of Aunt Ada.

"You could invite me in for tea." The man didn't even bother to remove his hat.

Susanne narrowed her eyes. "I don't think that would be appropriate." She eased past him to step outside and pulled the door closed after her.

"Fine. Fine."

She walked away from the house, not wanting him to think she could be persuaded to change her mind and invite him inside.

One of the horses whinnied.

Alfred Morris stopped and cocked his head, then made a beeline for the corrals. "Where did you get these horses?"

Not that it was any of his business. "They belong to the Hardings." He need not know any more details.

"Big Sam's, you say?"

She hadn't, but saw no need to correct him.

"I recall his first wife had a horse so wild no one else could touch it. Some animals, like some people, can't be tamed."

Susanne could not bear to look at him. She suspected there was another reason besides ill manners for him not removing his hat. He had very little hair left. His lips, too, were thin, she noticed. Or perhaps it was the way he always pulled them into a frown. Come to think of it, he reminded her of Aunt Ada, with that constant look of disapproval.

"Like Big Sam's first wife. She was—" His voice carried the same note of disapproval.

She cut him off. "You must not speak poorly of the dead."

He stiffened as if objecting to her correction, then relaxed, though it seemed to her it took a great deal of effort to bring a half smile to his lips. "You're quite right, of course. She left him three wild sons to deal with, though."

Susanne would not justify his remarks with a response.

After a moment he cleared his throat. "Perhaps we can go for a little walk."

She nodded. "I'll call the children."

"Never mind. That's not what I had in mind."

How well she knew it. "Then I'm afraid I must decline your invitation." All she wanted was for him to leave, so she stood ill at ease in the middle of the yard and made no effort to be hospitable.

As soon as they saw him, the children had ceased

their play and disappeared behind some bushes. "I must check on the children."

He caught her arm, making escape impossible.

Ice flowed up her veins and she jerked away. "Have a care."

He showed not a speck of repentance for what he'd done. "Susanne—"

She'd rebuke him for freely using her name but didn't want to listen to his arguments. No doubt he would tell her that if she'd simply agree to marry him he'd have the right to use her name. No doubt, he'd think he also had the right to order her about as he pleased. Only because she knew there was no point in saying anything did she refrain from chastising him.

"You know you can't manage this farm," he told her. "You can barely manage the children. What about your crop?" He jerked his thumb in the direction of the field. His gaze went there, too, and his jaw dropped. "You've started plowing?"

Let him make whatever assumption he wished.

He shook his head sadly. "That is not woman's work. Stop being so foolish and stubborn. Marry me and move into town. I'd certainly never expect you to plow."

She gave him a long, hard study. "I'm sure you'd have some expectations."

A feral gleam came into his eyes. She'd seen the same look on Mr. Befus's face just before Aunt Ada had left them alone in the parlor, just before the man had tried to exert his ownership over her body. She shuddered.

"I would expect you to be a good wife. Fair enough trade for providing you with a pleasant home."

"I'm sure." He'd never understand the sarcasm dripping from her voice. "However, as I've said before, I intend to keep the farm. It belongs to the children. It's their future."

His brows practically knit together. Strange how they were so bushy when his head was so bald.

As he spoke she'd shifted from foot to foot and looked over her shoulder many times, hoping he would think she had pressing concerns in the house and take himself home. But he stood as solid as a stubborn boulder in the middle of a field. And he talked.

She'd never known anyone—man or woman—who could use so many words to say so little. She stopped listening almost as soon as he started.

"Did I tell you?"

Her attention jerked back to him. "Tell me what?"

"Mother is coming to live with me...with us."

Susanne shuddered. There would never be *us*. Why couldn't he understand that?

"She can't wait to meet you. She's not well, you know, and will require care."

"Care? Really? Are you hiring a nurse?"

He waved a hand dismissively. "No need. I'm sure you can manage quite nicely."

If she was bigger and had fewer manners, she would have physically removed him from the place. Instead, she drew herself up tall and straight. "Mr. Morris, I'm afraid you'll have to find someone else to care for your mother. As you so often point out, I have my hands full with the children and I have absolutely no intention of marrying you. Good day to you." She lifted her skirts from the dust, marched into the house and slammed the door.

She waited to hear the horse ride away, but the sound

didn't come. Had she missed it? Listening carefully, she jumped two feet when a knock sounded on the door.

"Susanne, we need to talk."

"Mr. Morris, we do not need to talk. Please go away." What if he insisted on coming in? She looked about for something to protect herself with and edged toward the stove and the sturdy poker.

"Fine, if that's how you want to be." A silent moment passed, as if he held his breath as hard as she held hers. "But I'm not prepared to accept your rejection. I understand you expect to be courted. I'm a patient man."

Her heart thundered in her ears as she waited for him to leave.

Finally his footsteps thudded away and she collapsed into a chair. But not until the horse clopped from the yard could she breathe without the air catching in her chest.

The door flew open and the children rushed in.

Robbie scrambled to her lap. "Frank said we would chase the man away if he didn't go."

She smiled at Frank. "Thank you." Good to know he was prepared to defend her. If Mr. Morris persisted, she might be in need of his help. She closed her eyes a second. Mr. Morris wanted a nursemaid for his mother. Did he suppose "rescuing" her from the farm would obligate her to fulfill that role? How could she persuade the persistent man that she had no desire whatsoever to be rescued, much less obligated to anyone?

To think, just before Mr. Morris knocked, she'd been thinking how lonely she felt. How she ached to be viewed by Tanner as something more than a business deal. Mr. Morris's visit had reminded her that she must not let those feelings influence how she spoke and acted with Tanner. She'd come perilously close to doing so earlier in the day when he visited.

She hugged Robbie so tightly he squirmed. "Auntie Susanne, I can't breathe."

It took a great deal of effort to loosen her arms. Seemed she needed something, someone to hold.

She opened her arms to the other children and pulled them into one big hug.

Her arms were full. Her heart was full. And she was free to choose her own way. Taking care of the children, protecting them and maintaining her freedom constituted all she wanted.

All she'd ever want.

She needed to remember that. Especially around Tanner.

Even after he got the crop in the ground, he'd still be on the farm working with his horses. Not for the first time she wondered what she'd gotten herself into. Somehow she had to keep her emotions and reactions under control.

No matter what Tanner Harding said or did.

Chapter Eight

You aren't a mistake. The words went round and round in his head. He wished she meant it as more than a truth she believed from the Bible.

God regretted making some men. Isn't that what the Bible said about the people in Noah's day? Tanner stubbornly refused to acknowledge the flaw in his reasoning—that their horrible sins and refusal to repent had led to their destruction.

Do you know what else I see? He didn't want to know what she meant to say, although a childish part of him longed for words of approval. There was no reason to expect that's what she had in mind. Could be she meant to say he belonged somewhere else.

He was too big a coward to risk hearing the words.

He galloped up one hill and down the next with no mind to his destination until the wind had blown away some of the tangles in his brain. He slowed down. Time to give Scout a break.

The discussion with Susanne had brought a sweet memory of his ma. How close he'd felt to her and to God that day as they worshipped in the trees.

He looked about. Without planning it, he had ridden to the valley where those trees still stood. He reined in and stared at the spot.

Did the branches still form an arched canopy overhead?

Would God still feel as close as He had back then?

There was only one way to find out. He could get off Scout and find the path leading to the inner sanctuary of the trees. His ma's faith called him. Susanne's assurance of God's love strengthened him.

Do you know what else I see?

Instead of dismounting, he nudged Scout forward, urged him into a gallop and raced away from the spot.

The next morning he rushed through breakfast.

"Anxious to visit the Collins place?" Levi asked in his seemingly innocent voice.

"Got to finish the plowing so I can get at the horses."

"Yup. I would be, too," Johnny said, and Tanner's brothers looked at each other and laughed.

Big Sam asked for the jam. "You'll have your hands full all summer."

For some silly reason that struck Johnny and Levi as funny and they laughed again.

"He's already got his hands full," Levi said when he'd sobered enough to speak.

Maisie gave the three of them loving looks, then her brow furrowed. "I can't help but worry about the propriety of the situation."

"Don't you worry, girl. Tanner would never do anything to damage her reputation," Big Sam said, and earned himself a look of such love that Tanner turned his attention to his plate.

Maisie, with her dark blond hair and light brown eyes, Maisie, with her honey-colored skin and honey-flavored voice, would never acknowledge that, simply by speaking to Susanne, Tanner posed a threat. Not because he was a man but because of the fact that he was a half-breed.

"Just bear in mind her reputation," Maisie said.

"I've never forgotten it." Though to be completely honest he might have for a few seconds while standing at the corrals with her yesterday. *You aren't a mistake.* He'd wanted to believe it even though he understood she didn't necessarily mean it as he took it. She likely didn't mean she herself felt that way about him…only that she believed God did.

He slowed his eating lest anyone think there was more to his hurry than the plowing.

The others finished while he still had half a cup of coffee left.

"Come on, brother," Johnny said. "There's work to be done."

Tanner gulped the rest of his coffee and followed his brothers to the barn. Big Sam, Johnny and Levi were riding out to check on the new calves. Tanner was careful to make sure he took longer saddling up than they did. He waved goodbye to them, then finished the task in seconds. He kept Scout to a gentle canter until he knew no one from the ranch could see him, then urged him into a gallop.

His only reason was to exercise Scout. He had no reason to hurry other than to get the crop in before it rained so he could, as he said, work with the horses.

He slowed as the farm came in sight. Sheets billowed on the line. Next to the house, Susanne had her sleeves rolled up past her elbows and was bent over a washtub, scrubbing something. He sat back to enjoy the scene.

Then he shifted his gaze to find the children. They sat huddled together a few feet from Susanne. Something about their posture sent tension into his spine. He leaned forward. Was Robbie crying and was Liz trying to comfort him?

Within seconds Scout carried him forward in a gallop. As soon as he reached the yard, he jumped from the horse, his feet at a run.

Robbie looked at him, his eyes full of tears.

Remembering his promise, Tanner called a general good morning, then hunkered down before Robbie. "What's the matter?"

"I—I—" The boy couldn't choke the words out.

"He losted his marble," Janie said, a sob following her words.

Tanner's heart tightened, knowing how precious something was when it came from a dead parent. He had only to touch the yoke of his mother's dress to be filled with pleasant memories.

Robbie sniffed. "It's gone."

"But you'll find it." It surprised him that Susanne showed so little concern.

As if reading his mind, she shook the water from her hands and stood beside him. "We've looked everywhere."

Tanner pushed upright. "Then we'll look again."

She met his look, her expression going from discouragement to hope before she closed her eyes. When she reopened them, caution and refusal filled her eyes. "It's not necessary for you to help. You'll want to get the plowing done."

"His marble is important."

She pressed the back of her hand to her forehead as if weary of the subject. His eyes went to the sheets on the line. How early had she started the laundry that six sheets already billowed in the breeze? Maybe she was weary because of her work.

"I'll make sure Pat has enough feed and while he eats, we'll have a look." He didn't give her a chance to oppose him but trotted to the barn. The children scrambled to their feet and followed him.

"When did you first notice it was gone?" he asked Robbie.

"This morning. I put my hand in my pocket—" Robbie illustrated. "But no marble." He pulled his hands out to show him they were empty.

"Is there a hole in your pocket?"

Robbie's hands went back to his pocket. He felt around. Then shook his head. "No holes."

Tanner threw another scoop of oats into the manger for Pat, who remained placidly unconcerned as the children gathered round him. "Did you have it yesterday?"

Robbie's brow knotted. "I don't remember."

Tanner looked to the others. "Did any of you see him playing with it?"

They shook their heads as their eyes locked on him, full of trust and expectation. They counted on him to find it. It was a mighty big responsibility. The marble could have fallen anywhere. How could he hope to find it?

"Where have you looked?"

The four of them talked at once. Seems they'd looked in the house, in the barn, in the garden, under the trees.

"Not many places left, are there?"

They shook their heads. Already he'd disappointed them.

"Let me think. There has to be some clue. Robbie, when do you last remember having it?"

His forehead furrowed like an old man's. Then he brightened. "I remember," he shouted. "I had it in my hand when that old Mr. Morris came. Then we went and hid in the bushes."

Mr. Morris had come again? Was he courting Susanne? Tanner's gaze went to the doorway. He blinked at Susanne standing there. He hadn't heard her join them. With surprise—and something he didn't care to analyze or admit—he met her cool blue eyes. Was her silent look meant to inform him it was none of his business who came calling? He tipped his head in acknowledgment. It *was* none of his business and none of his concern.

He shifted back to Robbie. "Did you have it when you were in the bushes?"

Robbie's bottom lip trembled. "I not remember."

Feeling overwhelmed by the boy's distress, Tanner's gaze went again to Susanne. She lifted her hands in a gesture of helplessness and her eyes looked wet. Tanner's lungs froze. The whole family was on the verge of tears and he feared he would not handle it well if they all started sobbing.

"Show me where you were when Mr. Morris came." He reached for Robbie's hand. It was small and warm in his big paw. Robbie shuffled toward the tree by the garden.

"There." He pointed.

"What bushes did you go into?"

He indicated the ones several feet beyond the tree.

If Robbie had dropped the marble as the children hurried away, it might have bounced or rolled away. Tanner studied the lay of the land. A marble wouldn't roll through grass but—his eyes narrowed—if it happened to land on a bare spot... There was such a bit of ground not ten feet away. He went to it and bent over, combed his fingers through the dirt. He touched something round and smooth. Could it be?

"Robbie, check this out."

Robbie had followed hard on his heels, as had the others. "Did you find it?"

"Can't say for sure. But there's something here."

Robbie scrambled forward on his hands and knees and pawed through the dirt. With a whoop of joy, he lifted his marble. "I found it!"

The children gathered around him, and Tanner leaned back, as pleased as any of them.

Susanne came to his side, wiping her eyes. He dared not look at her for fear that seeing her tears would undo him completely. "I owe you for this," she said.

Tanner felt his muscles tighten. Owe? Was everything about payback with this lady? "You needn't worry. You are under no obligation." He strode away to get Pat.

The children hurried after him, surrounding him so he couldn't move. "Thank you," they all chimed.

"You're welcome." He hugged each of them, feeling Susanne's gaze on him the whole time. Why couldn't she be like the children and accept the act for what it was—a kindness, not an obligation?

Susanne returned to her neglected laundry tub and kept her back to Tanner as he took Pat to the field to plow. She scrubbed the girls' dresses hard enough she risked leaving holes in the fabric. She wrung the dresses to within an inch of death, but her efforts did little to ease her mind.

She'd unintentionally offended Tanner. She'd meant her words to indicate gratitude and he'd taken them to mean regret.

She arched her back to relieve the tension from bending over. If she was truthful she had harbored a little bit of regret, wondering where his actions belonged in her balance ledger.

Under no obligation, he said. But she was. She had agreed for him to use the corrals but that cost her nothing. They stood idle; she had no use for them. He, on the other hand, would sacrifice days working her land and seeding her crop.

Her insides turned and rolled. She pressed a hand to her stomach and moaned. Would she never be free of the resentment she'd learned at Aunt Ada's? How many times had she listened to her aunt rail on about obligations and vowed she'd never allow herself to be in that position again? She knew this was different. So why didn't she *feel* it was?

God, help me. I am so trapped by my fear of being controlled by someone. Yet I must accept help. Tanner seems satisfied with our agreement. Why can't I be?

She fought the question as she washed the boys' trousers and hung them to dry. The fight continued as she dumped the water on the plants around the house. The battle raged as she prepared a meal for the children.

Should she take some food to Tanner? She knew Maisie packed him a lunch, but he had always seemed grateful for what she gave, as well.

What would she say to him? How could she explain when *she* didn't understand?

She fed the children, listened to their chatter though she heard not a word. Still Tanner did not stop for dinner. Would he stay out all day simply to avoid her?

She could hardly swallow the last of her food and washed it down with a glass of water.

As the minutes ticked past, her guilt shifted to worry. Something might be wrong. But when she glanced out the window Pat still moved forward with Tanner behind the plow. Neither of them appeared to be injured.

But something *was* wrong. And she must make it right.

"Children, I want you to stay here while I go see why Tanner hasn't come in. Liz, watch the little ones, please. And, please, stay in the house." She did not want an audience to what she must do.

She donned her bonnet, tied it tight, wishing she could hide behind its protection. But hiding wouldn't fix this. She stepped outside and closed the door behind her. Sucking in air to fortify herself, she marched across the yard to the field.

He was halfway up the row. Close enough she could see his mouth tighten, but too far to see his eyes and hope for clues to his thoughts.

She waited.

He didn't rush Pat; nor did he pull him back. They plodded forward at a maddeningly slow pace. Now that she had made up her mind about what she must do, she wanted to get it done.

Finally he reached the end. He nodded a greeting but spoke not a word. Nor did she. She'd bide her time until she did what she must.

He unhitched Pat and drove him toward the barn.

She kept pace. "I fear I have offended you and that was not my intention."

"Uh-huh."

He was not going to make this easy. Not that she blamed him.

"I would like to say Aunt Ada is responsible for my bad behavior, but I can't. She isn't even here. Yes, she taught me that accepting favors carried a dear price. Do you know that she once gave me an old dress of hers? I had outgrown all of mine. The dress was out of style and inappropriate for my age, but I took it gratefully and remade it to fit. It looked quite fine, I thought. What did Aunt Ada do?"

Tanner didn't stop to guess. He continued walking Pat to the barn and she kept up beside him, rattling on.

"You'd never guess. I don't think anyone would. She demanded it back. Said I had no right to ruin it. What if she'd wanted to wear it again? I bit my tongue to keep from saying she'd have to lose fifty pounds before she'd ever wear it again." She would never have said anything so unkind, even to Aunt Ada.

"I didn't mind giving it back except it left me in rags, but that wasn't all. She said I must pay for ruining it. How was I to pay when she gave me no allowance and kept me so busy I could never hope to work for someone else? Seems she had it all figured out how I would repay her. She gave me a pile of mending and said I would have to do it after I'd taken care of my other work." She realized she twisted her hands together and made herself stop. "I'm sorry. That isn't what I came to say." She drew in a slow breath to calm her nerves. Why had she babbled on so?

They'd reached the barn and he led Pat to water. As the horse drank, Tanner asked, "What did you mean to say?"

She took courage from his calm voice. Perhaps he wasn't as offended as she thought. Nevertheless, she had an apology to convey.

She stood tall. "I'm sorry I wasn't more gracious about you helping Robbie find the marble. It was very kind of you and meant a lot to Robbie." A beat passed in which she realized she needed to say more. "And to me. Thank you."

He faced her then, and his black eyes revealed nothing. He waited as if he wanted more. The mere idea made her hands twist again. She hung her arms at her sides and made her fingers be still. "Are you still angry with me?"

"I was never angry."

"You weren't? Then what?"

"Susanne, you aren't the first person to act as if they didn't care for my help. Don't suppose you'll be the last." His voice was flat, but she sensed a whole world of pain in them.

"Tanner, it has nothing to do with you. It's me. My problem." She waited. He didn't answer, simply led Pat into the barn and gave him a good feed.

She followed and stood back until he was done. Somehow she had to convince him. "Your mother was a Lakota. You're proud of that. Your father is Big Sam Harding. You're proud of that, too."

"I am."

"Then why aren't you proud of who you are? Seems to me you have good reason to be, what with a noble woman as your mother and a strong man as your father. But you're not. Why?"

He failed to hide his surprise.

She did not blink but held his gaze, silently demanding he answer her question.

He shifted his attention to something over her shoulder.

Still she waited.

Finally his gaze came back to her. "Does it matter what I think of myself? Others are happy enough to tell me what they think of me. And it's not good."

"Not everyone would agree with that assessment. What about your parents and your brothers? What about friends?" *What about me?*

He shrugged. "I guess not everyone."

"There you go."

He managed a tight smile. "Maybe you and I are alike in that we are both trying to shake off bad things in our lives that seem to hold us."

She smiled at the idea of them being alike. "Then maybe we can help each other." She was partial to that idea.

He took a moment, as if considering her suggestion, then gave her a smile that reached his eyes. "No obligation?"

She nodded, pleased clear through. "No offense taken?"

He chuckled. "You got yourself a deal." Then he sobered. "We both might find this deal harder to fulfill than our first one."

Harder for sure, she thought, but likely a lot more satisfying.

"I'll bring out some dinner for you." She went happily to the house.

"You're smiling," Liz said as Susanne entered the kitchen. "That's good. That means everything is okay."

"Everything is fine. Why don't you all go see Tanner while I prepare a plate for him?" She had made a spicy stew with tomatoes and it hadn't turned out too badly.

The children rushed out the door with a great deal of laughing and whooping.

She smiled. She'd take this food out to Tanner and not put it down on her mental ledger. No more obligation. They had an agreement that suited them both. She would no longer let Aunt Ada make her life miserable or keep her from trusting people.

Ironic how both their problems came down to trusting. Could she help him learn to trust people? Could he help her learn to trust the kindness of others?

She tried not to think of how much it had cost her to do so in the past.

The past was gone. It was time to face the future, to confront her fears. Even if things didn't turn out well, at least she would have tried.

With that, she mentally looked to the days ahead and closed her mind to the pain of the past. Surely things could be different this time.

Chapter Nine

Tanner finished his dinner and handed the empty plate to Susanne. "Thank you. It was delicious."

"I tried to make something a little more interesting than the eggs and potatoes we've been surviving on."

They studied each other. He had no idea what she saw but squelched his initial reaction of thinking she saw a half-breed. He meant to stop judging her based on what others said and did. Come to think of it, he never should have done so in the first place. A person should be judged on their own merits and actions. It was what he wanted for himself. If he hoped to get it, he had to extend the same courtesy to others.

"Best get back to work," he said, standing up. He drove Pat to the field, the children on his heels.

"My pa used to play with us," Robbie said.

Tanner finished hitching Pat to the plow and turned to consider the four children. "You miss your ma and pa, don't you?"

Four heads nodded.

"What kind of things did they do with you?" he asked.

"Played chase," Robbie shouted.

"We went on picnics," Liz said.

"Pa said he would let me help him train horses." Frank tried so hard to be responsible and act like a man though he was only a boy.

"He tickled us." Janie giggled.

Tanner scooped her up. "You mean like this?" He soon had her screaming with laughter. He set her down and acted as if he was about to return to the plow; instead, he grabbed Robbie and tickled him.

The boy laughed and yelled, "Help me, help me." In seconds, Frank and Liz tackled him. He could have held them off, but he pretended they pushed him to the ground. They all piled on him except for Janie, who held back, perhaps a little fearful of the commotion. He lifted her to his chest and grabbed the other three, pinning them to the ground.

They struggled without getting loose. "Gotta say you give up."

Liz was the first to speak. "I give."

He let her go and she backed away, remaining on her knees at his side.

"I'll never give up." Frank intensified his efforts.

Tanner shifted the two younger ones to Liz's side and got serious about wrestling with Frank. He let the boy pin him to the ground, let him tickle him, pretending he couldn't throw him off. After a bit, and a great deal of apparent struggle, he managed to get Frank to the ground, pinning the boy's arms over his head.

Frank wriggled and squirmed but could not unseat Tanner.

"Give up?" Tanner asked.

"No."

He'd give the boy marks for pure stubbornness.

He looked up when he heard Susanne coming toward them. She would think he wasn't doing his job according to their agreement.

Their first agreement. Remembering their second agreement, he let Frank go and stood up. He grinned at Susanne. "The boy's tough."

He could read the hesitation in her face and waited for her reaction.

When she smiled he almost forgot he stood in the middle of a patch of grass. It seemed the world had shifted.

"He takes after his father," she said.

Frank flexed his muscles. "Pa was strong."

Tanner and Susanne shared a secret smile.

"Now let's leave Tanner to do his work," Susanne said, and shepherded the children away. She glanced over her shoulder and waved goodbye.

Tanner grinned. There was a time he would have taken her words and actions to mean she didn't want the children hanging around him. But he wouldn't allow such thoughts to form in the light of the glorious sunshine.

His smile lingered well into the afternoon. His gaze went often to the activity around the house. Susanne took laundry off the line. Then she checked the garden. He could have told her it was too soon for anything to be coming through the ground, but he understood her impatience. Seeing those first shoots push through to sunlight renewed most anyone's belief in the world.

He tried not to appear too pleased when she brought him cookies and water, the children helping carry everything. After all, she'd done so from the first day.

But today it felt different. The boiled raisin cookies were sweet to his tongue, the water cool to his throat, and her smile as bright as the sunlight pooling around them.

Robbie checked his pocket for his marble. "Not gonna lose it again."

Tanner wanted to tell him he should keep it in the house if he didn't want to lose it, but he understood how Robbie found comfort from being able to touch it any time he wanted.

Janie hung at his knees, wanting to be picked up.

"Can you sit for a bit?" he asked Susanne.

"Don't mind enjoying the sunshine." She sat, her skirts fanned out about her.

A thought flared in his mind. Did she truly enjoy spending a moment with him, or was she only proving she could relax and not think of obligation?

He sat and pulled Janie to his lap. Robbie crowded close and Tanner patted his knee to indicate there was room for them both. Robbie sat—or rather squirmed— beside his sister.

Tanner had two cookies left. "Anyone need a cookie?"

Two little mouths came open.

He laughed. "Do you expect me to feed you?"

Their mouths still open, drool pooling at the corner of their lips, they nodded.

So he held the cookies and let the children eat from his hands.

It sent Susanne into a fit of laughter. "They're like little birds."

"I don't mind."

"I know you don't." Her blue eyes filled with what he allowed himself to believe was approval. He let the idea percolate in his mind. It grew sweeter with every second. Nice to think someone outside his family might view him with approval.

Her eyes darkened, causing his heart to fill with yearning, and longing. A vast ocean of things he couldn't admit to.

Robbie's lips closed about Tanner's fingers bringing his gaze back to the children.

"All done." He set them aside. "Thank you. See you all later." He allowed himself a glance at Susanne as he returned to work.

The rest of the afternoon passed pleasantly enough as he watched Susanne and the children in the yard and contemplated how different it was to stop being defensive about every comment.

Later, Susanne and the children went inside for supper.

She stepped out of the house and tented her hand over her eyes as she looked in his direction. Was she concerned because he worked later than usual? He meant to finish the plowing so tomorrow he could start planting.

He lifted one hand in a little wave that he hoped she would understand meant everything was fine.

He plowed the last furrow. "Pat, that part of your work is done." He didn't unhitch the horse until he had parked the plow by the barn.

The children erupted from the house and ran to him, Susanne in their wake. "You finished plowing?"

"I'm done."

"I'm glad," she said, her voice full of pleasure.

He leaned back, his hands on his hips, happy to be done and pleased at her eager smile.

"You want me to take care of Pat?" Frank asked, pulling Tanner back to his duties.

"I'm coming, and you can help."

He allowed the boy to lead the big gentle horse to the trough and let Frank help take off the harness. "Pat deserves a good feed tonight." He watched Frank put out oats, making sure the amount wasn't more than was good for the animal. When Frank finished, Tanner squeezed the boy's shoulder. "Good job."

He was in no hurry to leave, but it was time. "Goodbye, I'll see you tomorrow." He tried to make it a general, all-inclusive comment, then his gaze skimmed the children and skidded to a halt when it met Susanne's. Who knew how long he would have stared into her eyes if Janie hadn't pulled on his arm. "Goodbye, Mr. Tanner."

He ruffled her hair and Robbie's, touched Liz on the head and shook Frank's hand. He nodded at Susanne, wondering if his eyes said more than he meant for them to. Regret at leaving, desire to believe she accepted him. He murmured a farewell, swung to Scout's back and rode away.

He arrived at the ranch just as Big Sam headed for the house.

"Better hurry. Maisie's already rung the bell." He looked Tanner up and down. "Try and get some of that dirt off before you come to the house."

Tanner ducked his head in the water trough, scrubbed his hands up to his elbows, then dried them on an old towel Maisie kept nearby. He trotted to the house, kissed Maisie's check and went to his chair.

Levi and Johnny barely waited for him to sit before the pair of them leaned forward.

"How come you're so late?" Johnny demanded.

"You been plowing all this time?" Levi asked.

"Levi," Maisie warned. "Have a care for Miss Collins's reputation."

"Sorry, Ma." Levi was the only one who called Maisie ma. But then, he barely remembered Seena, the Lakota woman who had birthed all three of them.

Tanner didn't bother explaining his tardiness. They could wait.

Big Sam told an amusing story about one of the cowboys being chased by a cow. "Tried to warn him to get out of the way, but he weren't in any hurry." He chuckled. "Once he saw the cow bearing down on him, he hurried all right. Never seen a bowlegged cowboy move so fast."

As she laughed, Maisie shifted her attention to Tanner. "How was your day?"

"I finished plowing." He grinned widely. The others would think that was reason enough for his pleased look. He wouldn't be telling them of his new agreement with Susanne. Not that they'd understand anyway.

"I believe tomorrow would be a good day for me to visit our neighbor," Maisie said. "Tanner, please inform her of my plans when you get there."

Maisie was going to visit? What would she see? A beautiful young woman. Four delightful children. What else?

Tanner had no reason to be concerned and yet he was.

Maisie had suggested he have a care for her reputation. After she saw Susanne's beauty and the way Tanner's eyes were drawn to the young woman, she'd be even more concerned.

* * *

"Maisie said to tell you she'd be over for a visit first thing this afternoon."

Susanne stared at Tanner. "A visit? Here?" Yes, it was the neighborly thing to do, but why now? "What will I serve her?"

"Got any more of those boiled raisin cookies?"

"Only a few. I must bake. What does she like? What will she think?"

"Susanne, calm down. Maisie is not going to judge you."

She rolled her eyes. "Shows what you know about women."

He laughed. "I know my stepmother. She's patient and kind. After all, she puts up with my brothers."

"And you?"

"I've never been a problem."

She laughed at his teasing. "I'll take your word that she's sweet." Then she brushed at her skirts and swiped at her hair. "And I'm… I'm…"

He crossed his arms over his chest and waited.

She fluttered her hands. "I don't know what I am."

"Why not just be yourself?"

"Guess I don't have much choice."

"I kind of thought you wanted me to believe being myself was enough."

His words shattered her worries. "It is."

"Then believe it for yourself."

"I do." Except when she had company coming.

"Then what's wrong?"

Her shoulders sagged. "I'm letting Aunt Ada make me feel incompetent and insignificant again." She squared her shoulders. "I'm not going to allow that any longer. I'll make cookies and welcome a visit from Maisie."

He continued to study her. What did he see? Spurts of insignificance and incompetence bubbled to the surface of her thoughts.

"I thought you'd be longing to see another woman."

His words smoothed her thoughts. The idea was new and yet it fit. "I am."

"Good." He put his hat on, adjusted it and took Pat out to the field. Today he was starting to put the seed in the ground.

Today she was entertaining company.

Today she would put Aunt Ada's negative influence out of her mind.

Today was going to be a good day.

"Liz, do you want to help me make cookies?"

The others wanted to help, too, except for Frank. He returned to cleaning the barn.

They spent the morning baking. By the time they were done, the kitchen was in shambles, and she scurried around cleaning up the spilled flour and cookie dough and washed the floor.

She made a hurried dinner of pork and beans that she'd set to cook the night before. Thankfully, biscuits only took a few minutes.

"Here comes Tanner," Robbie shouted, and tore out the door.

Susanne finished washing the dishes from their meal, allowing Tanner time to take care of the horse, then she took out a generous serving of beans, four biscuits and half a dozen freshly baked molasses cookies.

"Mmm. This looks good. Thank you. The aroma from the kitchen drifted my way all morning." He eyed her as if wondering if she had settled down after her morning outburst. "Are you ready for Maisie's visit?"

She nodded. "Cookies baked, house clean." She considered the children. "I decided against putting them in their good clothes—at least they're clean."

Tanner chuckled. "Maisie knows what it's like to have children. She got three wild boys when she married Big Sam."

Susanne tried to imagine Tanner as a boy. "Can't say about your brothers, but it seems she succeeded in taming you very well."

His eyebrows went toward his hairline.

She could almost hear him composing a denial. "No more expecting offense," she gently reminded him. "Especially when none was intended."

His eyebrows returned to where they belonged and he smiled. "She did her best at taming us though some would question her success."

"Some would, would they?" She hoped her grin informed him she meant to tease him.

He nodded. "But then some people still believe the world is flat."

She burst out laughing at his droll comment. "I'll leave you to enjoy your meal in peace."

"I don't mind company."

Normally the children hung around, but today they lined up along the corral fence, watching Pretty Lady come to Robbie.

Susanne sat down, her back against the wall, and Tanner sat beside her. "Go ahead and eat," she said when he hesitated.

He ate everything she'd brought, plus the sandwiches Maisie had sent.

"I need to bake bread," she said. "Been planning it for days and it still hasn't happened."

"Nothing wrong with biscuits."

He stretched out his leather-clad legs. She liked seeing a man in leather. The feather in his hat gave him a rakish look that quite intrigued her.

Her cheeks warmed at her inappropriate thoughts.

"I don't want to be caught sitting in the shade." She scrambled to her feet and took his dishes.

"No, your aunt Ada would not approve of that."

She stopped, turned and met his gaze. "This time it's about me, not Aunt Ada."

He nodded though his eyes questioned her statement.

She sighed. "It's not easy to forget years of listening to her voice inside my head."

"Just be yourself."

"You, too." She hurried to the house and washed the few remaining dishes.

Just be yourself. It had sounded so easy when she'd told Tanner. But now doubts fluttered through her head. When had being herself ever been enough? Not since her parents died. But today she'd show Mrs. Maisie Harding that she was enough.

She found Alice's white tablecloth and spread it over the table, smoothing out the creases as best she could without ironing it. Alice had some nice china in the back of the cupboard and she brought out two cups and matching saucers and washed them.

By the time she heard the sound of an approaching buggy, she was ready.

The children clustered at the door while Susanne stepped outside to welcome her guest.

Maisie tied the horse to the nearest post and turned

to greet Susanne. "I'm Maisie Harding—please call me Maisie."

Susanne gave her name and introduced the children. Frank and Liz were polite, but the two younger ones hid their faces behind her skirt.

"Come in." She studied the woman without staring, taking in her dark blond hair in a tidy roll at the back of her head and light brown eyes that seemed kind and friendly. She wore a spotless black skirt and pale blue blouse.

"May I serve you tea?" Susanne welcomed something to keep her hands busy, even as her mind scrambled for something to say to this woman. Would she fail again in some way? She pushed the fear from her mind and forced herself to relax.

Maisie looked about. "You have a very pleasant home." Then she turned to the children, who stood in a row behind the chair where Susanne would sit. "I haven't seen any of you since Christmas."

They stared wide-eyed.

"I remember you," Liz said. "You sang a song at the Christmas program."

Susanne remembered, too, though at the time she hadn't realized the woman was mother to three grown sons. "I enjoyed hearing you," she said.

"Thank you. I am always so grateful for a chance to attend church."

Susanne's hands grew still. "I miss church."

"But, Auntie, we have church here," Janie whispered.

Susanne chuckled and explained what Janie meant.

"That's a nice thing to do," Maisie told her.

Susanne served tea and passed cookies to their guest, then to the children.

"Aunt Susanne, can we go outside?" Liz asked.

She nodded. Then she realized she was alone with Maisie and wished she hadn't granted the children permission to leave.

Maisie ate a cookie she pronounced delicious, then gave Susanne a serious look. "How are you managing?" she asked.

"Fine," Susanne answered automatically.

"How are the children dealing with their loss? So sad for them."

"They have good days and bad days." How much should she tell this woman?

Maisie chuckled. "I remember when I married Big Sam. He'd been doing his best, but the boys had been left on their own much of the time. They were...well, shall we say, a little untamed." She looked a bit regretful. "Some would say they still are." She took a sip of her tea. "Tanner, especially. That poor boy felt his mother's loss the worst of the three." She shrugged. "Each one handles their grief differently."

Susanne's heart accused her. "I mostly let the children run wild and I certainly have neglected their lessons."

"You have your hands full trying to be mother and father and farmer here. I'm glad Tanner is able to help you. For his sake, as well as yours."

Susanne stared at Maisie. "His sake?"

"Surely you realize how much he enjoys helping here?"

Susanne schooled her face to reveal nothing. What did the woman mean? Finally she found her voice. "He's anxious to get working with his horses. Say, would you like to see them?"

"I would. Thank you."

They walked to the corrals and stepped up on the bottom rail to watch the horses. One of the mares had been at the fence by Robbie but raced away at their approach.

Maisie admired the mares, then left the fence. "Let's walk a bit."

Susanne had the feeling she was about to be scolded.

"You must get lonely here on the farm." Maisie sounded so understanding that Susanne's steps faltered. She'd just been caught thinking as Aunt Ada had taught her—expecting to be corrected on some matter—when this kind woman was offering her sympathy and understanding.

"I have the children," she said.

"And I'm sure they're a blessing." They walked three feet. "No one has bothered you?"

There was Mr. Morris but she'd never been afraid of his visits, not until this last one. Surely he wouldn't get any more bothersome than that. "No, ma'am."

"Do be careful."

Did Maisie mean to warn Susanne? Were there men in the area, perhaps cowboys on the Sundown Ranch, who would take advantage of her situation?

Or—she almost stumbled at the idea—was she warning Susanne that she'd done wrong in accepting Tanner's help. Did she think Susanne was taking advantage of his good nature? That she had no concern for his feelings?

They turned and headed back to the yard. This direction gave them plenty of opportunity to watch Tanner in the field. He glanced in their direction.

After that, Susanne kept her gaze straight ahead.

She'd give the woman no reason to think there was reason to judge her concerning Tanner's visits.

When they reached the house, Maisie asked, "Are you able to get to town for supplies?"

"I have a horse and wagon." Never mind she was too afraid of Pat and too inexperienced to get the horse and wagon hitched together let alone make her way to town. She was getting desperately low on supplies. She would manage to restock...but how?

"Don't hesitate to ask for help if you need it. Just tell Tanner what you need and he'll see to it. Now I must head back. Thank you for the nice visit." She waved to the children and Tanner.

Susanne stared after her long after she left. Maisie was right. It would be easy to take advantage of Tanner's kindness. She would be careful not to do that.

With a final glance toward Tanner she ducked into the house.

No obligation. It sounded so simple when they'd agreed. Now it seemed anything but. Maybe Aunt Ada was right.

She stared at the cookies on the table. She should take some cookies and water to Tanner, but her thoughts were so tangled.

Was she ever going to be able to put her past behind her?

Chapter Ten

Tanner watched Maisie drive away and Susanne go inside. What had the women talked about? Had his name
entered the conversation? He'd never know, because
he'd never ask.

At the time for his usual afternoon snack and drink,
he saw the children in the yard, but as he reached the
end of the field, neither they nor Susanne brought him
water and cookies. He turned and made another pass
at the field, but still no one headed his way.

His insides knotted. Could Maisie have warned her
to stay away from him? For the sake of her reputation,
she'd say. It wouldn't take much for Susanne to decide
she should allow no friendship, nothing beyond what
their first agreement called for. It would take little to
convince her to believe their second agreement was ill
conceived.

On his third pass he noticed the children raced about
the yard, but this time Susanne stood in the middle,
calling out.

His nerves twitched. They weren't acting quite right.
Was something wrong? He knew for certain there was

when Susanne ran from tree to tree, looking into the branches. How odd. Had some piece of laundry blown away and she only now realized it?

She looked his way, the concern on her face evident even at this distance. She picked up her skirts and ran toward him.

He left Pat standing there and crossed toward Susanne in double-quick time.

She grabbed his arms to steady herself and gasped for air. "Janie..." She gulped. "She's gone."

"Gone? Where?"

"I don't know," Susanne wailed. She wavered and he had a feeling she would have collapsed had he not held her.

He patted her back as she leaned into him. "Now start at the beginning and tell me what's going on."

"I sent the children out to play when Maisie was here."

Now the children had caught up to them and they hovered beside Tanner. Frank held Robbie.

"I thought she'd stayed in the house," Liz said, tears streaming down her face.

"But now we can't find her and we've looked everywhere." Susanne shuddered and clung to him. She lifted her face to look imploringly into his eyes. "Please help me find her."

"Of course, I will." She'd asked without concern about obligation. Certainly it might be because of her concern over Janie. Still, it felt mighty fine that she trusted him enough to simply ask for help.

"Come on. Let's have a look." He'd often seen the little girl hunker down into tiny enclosures—in the bushes, under a spreading branch, behind the wagon. He assured himself the others had simply overlooked her in their panic.

Susanne followed as close as his next breath, with the children hard on her heels.

He checked every tree, examined every bush, scoured the inside of the barn. With every move the tension in his body increased.

Susanne clung to his hand. "Where can she be?"

"We've somehow overlooked her." He did his best to sound reassuring. "Liz, would you look in the house again? Look everywhere."

"I'll help," Frank followed, still carrying Robbie.

With the children gone, Tanner gritted his teeth and went to the corrals.

Susanne pulled him to a stop. "Janie never goes to the corrals except with her brothers and she always stays at the fence." She blinked back horror that darkened her eyes. "If she did…"

No words were necessary. They both knew what they might find beyond the protective fence. After all, these were wild horses. He should never have brought them here. If they'd hurt Janie, he would turn them loose and never again dream of taming part of the wild herd.

He gathered up his courage and took the last three steps toward the fence. He forced his lungs to work and eased his hand from Susanne's grasp though it was the last thing in the world he wanted to do. He clenched and unclenched his fists before he reached for the top bar of the fence, the wood warm and rough beneath his palms. He planted one booted foot on the bottom rail and then the other foot. He tightened his grasp and heaved himself up to stare into the corral. Two mares grazed in one corner, paused to look his way and returned to eating. Four grazed along the far side. Only one of them looked up. He studied the ground around them. Nothing but grass. He swung his focus toward three horses gathered at his left. They nodded slowly as if having a conversation. No little girl near them. Pretty Lady stood alone by the fence where Robbie often played with her. Tanner's eyes remained on the horse's head, refusing to look lower. He simply couldn't—

"Is she there?" Susanne's voice shook with fear that echoed in Tanner's head.

He jerked his attention to the ground, to the fence, scanned every inch of the enclosure. His lungs emptied in a whoosh. He dropped to the ground and leaned against the fence as his bones melted with relief. "She isn't in there."

Susanne grabbed his hands and squeezed hard. "Thank God."

He pulled her to his chest. "Amen to that." He wasn't one to ask God for much, but at this moment his heart filled with gratitude that his horses had not injured the little girl.

He scanned the surrounding area, the grassy hills, groves of trees, a coulee that led up to the place where he'd captured the horses. "Where is she?"

Susanne sucked in air. "God can see her. We need to pray He'll show us where she is." She took a step back, leaving him feeling empty, but retained her grip on his hands. She bowed her head. "Dear God, show us where Janie is. Keep her safe until we find her. In You we trust."

It had been years since Tanner had prayed. But now seemed a perfect time to start again. "God, help us," he whispered.

"I'm going to have a look around." He called Scout and swung to his back without bothering with a saddle.

Susanne pressed to Scout's side, reaching for Tanner's hand. She squeezed it hard. "Please, find her."

"I'll do my best." He rode slowly in widening circles around the farm, hanging down over Scout's neck as he searched the ground for signs of Janie having passed this way. He dismounted at every grove of trees and looked into every canopy of leaves. Janie was small and an expert at hiding. But he found no little girl.

Horrible pictures raced through his mind. A wild animal prowling about or worse, a wild man. But he saw no signs of either and trusted his tracking skills well enough to know he hadn't missed anything.

He reached the top of a little hill and turned toward the farm. Susanne stood in the middle of the yard, her hand tented over her eyes as she watched him. He shook his head. Although he couldn't see her clearly, he studied her for another moment, feeling and sharing her distress.

He rode on to the next hilltop and studied as far as the horizon in every direction. Toward the ranch, he made out a familiar horse and buggy. Maisie. Shouldn't she have reached home by now? He squinted and saw she was headed in the direction of the farm. What would bring her this way after she'd just visited? And she was coming fast.

Tremors raced up and down his spine. He kicked Scout into a gallop on a path that would intercept her.

Maisie didn't slow down until he was almost upon her. There was no mistaking the worried look on her face.

"What's wrong?" he called, slowing Scout so he could hear her reply.

She pulled to a stop and waited for him to reach her. "I thought you might be worried." She pointed over her shoulder.

Tanner followed the direction she indicated. "Janie." She sat on the floor behind Maisie, her eyes wide.

Tanner dropped to the ground and reached the buggy in two racing strides. He scooped the little girl from the back and hugged her as tightly as he dared. She clung to his neck and started to cry in heaving gulps.

"How… Where…?"

Maisie gave one of her sweet, gentle smiles. "When I got home I found her hiding under the robe I keep in the back of the wagon. I knew Susanne would be awfully worried when she couldn't find the child so I headed back again."

"Are you okay?" he asked Janie, who nodded.

"Then let's get you back to your aunt." He paused at Maisie's side. "Thank you."

"I'm glad she's safe."

"You'll be okay?" he asked Maisie.

"I'm fine. Take the child back to Susanne. And, Tanner?"

"Yes?"

"I like Susanne."

He nodded. He did, too, but he wasn't about to say so. He swung onto Scout's back a little more awkwardly than usual with Janie hanging from his neck. Not that he minded. He'd keep her there always if it would mean she was safe.

She sobbed for the first mile back to the farm. Then she sighed and snuggled into his arms. "I knowed you'd find me," she murmured. When she said nothing more, he looked at her. She'd fallen asleep.

Tanner rode home at a moderate pace so as not to disturb her.

On the slope of the second hilltop he saw the farm. There Susanne walked along the thin trail in his direction, her head down, searching the ground. He should have known she wouldn't be content to wait. Waiting was so hard.

He was about to call out when she glanced up and saw him. He waved his hat in a victory circle.

She picked up her skirts and raced toward them.

"Here comes your aunt."

Janie wakened and he turned her about so she could see Susanne. He galloped toward her. As soon as he was close enough, he dropped to the ground, with the girl clinging to his neck.

Susanne flew into his arms, crushing Janie between them. She laughed and cried as she patted Janie and smoothed her hair. Then she patted Tanner's cheeks. "Thank you, thank you, thank you." She smiled at him with such joy he felt ten feet tall. "You are a good man." She patted his cheek again.

He didn't know why finding a child should mark him as a good man. Any person would have sprung into action, but he liked hearing it and buried the words in his heart.

They turned their steps toward the farm, where the other children waited anxiously. When they were all gathered round he set Janie on her feet and told them what happened.

Susanne knelt before Janie. "I'm so glad you are okay but, sweetie, please promise me you won't get into any wagon or buggy but our own."

Janie clung to her aunt. "It was such a nice place to

hide but then I fell asleep and then the buggy started moving and I was scared."

Susanne hugged her. She looked up at Tanner, her eyes awash. She needed a hug every bit as much as Janie did, though now was not the time or place. He squeezed her shoulder hoping she'd understand.

She gave a tremulous smile that warmed his soul.

He hugged the other children, his heart overflowing with gratitude and affection. His gaze sought the distance, seeking a place where he belonged in this picture. Was he the man who planted the crop? Was he a neighbor, a friend? Could he be more? Was it possible for a half-breed with one foot in the white world and the other in the native world to fit into a white family? To be accepted?

"Pat!" The poor, patient horse stood in the middle of the field where Tanner had abandoned him. "I need to bring him home."

"I'll help," Frank said.

Although he didn't need help, he and Frank strode side by side to the field. He let Frank do a good half the work of unhitching and then driving the horse to the barn. Pat drank deeply and gave a hefty snort when they led him to his stall. "Feed him extra well tonight," Tanner said. "He deserves it."

He and Frank brushed the horse and fussed over him.

"I was a little scared," Frank said from the other side of Pat.

Tanner couldn't see him, and perhaps that's why Frank felt comfortable enough to confess his feelings. "Me, too."

"She's so little."

"Yes, she is."

"I don't think I could stand it if something happened to her." Frank's voice broke.

Tanner edged around Pat. What could he say to help the boy? Then something Maisie had said often as Tanner and his brothers were growing up came to mind. "God's job is to help and guide us. Our job is to follow and trust Him."

Frank looked at Tanner, his gaze probing deep. "Do you believe that's true?"

The truth hit him in the gut. "Yes, I guess I do. But sometimes our job is hard."

Frank resumed brushing Pat. "Sure hope I learn to do it soon."

"Me, too. Maybe life would be simpler if we did."

"Hmm."

The two of them finished grooming Pat and as they left the barn Tanner draped his arm across the boy's shoulders. Maybe it was time to learn to trust more, if only so he could help Frank.

The hour was late. Maisie would be wondering how everyone was. But he hated to say goodbye, hated to leave them. It wasn't so much they needed him, he realized with a start, as he needed them.

When they reached the house, Frank stepped inside and Tanner remained at the doorway. "Come here, Janie." The child flung herself into his arms. "Goodbye until tomorrow."

He held her as he said goodbye to each of the children.

"Goodbye," he said then to Susanne, his gaze clinging to her. He did not want to leave but he knew he had to. He put Janie down and backed out the door.

Susanne followed him outside and pulled the door

closed. "Thank you again." Her eyes were filled with gratitude and so much more, though he couldn't say what. She lowered her gaze. "I hate to see you go." Her voice was a mere whisper. "I feel safer with you here."

It was on the tip of his tongue to say he would stay in the barn. He'd even sleep in the middle of the plowed field if it made her feel better. But Maisie's warning to consider Susanne's reputation wouldn't allow him to offer. "I'll be back tomorrow."

He couldn't say who reached for the other first but their hands clasped. Their gazes locked and his heart welcomed her.

She broke away. "Goodbye. Safe trip."

He swung to Scout's back and rode away. The afternoon had been overcharged with emotion and it was causing him to have feelings and thoughts that had no basis.

He told himself he wouldn't think how good it felt to be included in the family scenario, to be hugged by everyone including Susanne, but he did anyway.

How could he ever hope to belong in either world?

Susanne returned to the kitchen and the waiting children. "We'll stay together from now on." She assigned them each a chore that kept them in the house until after supper and dishes. Then they trooped out to bring the cow home. Not until they were all in bed was she forced to face her thoughts.

She'd acted like one of the children, clinging to Tanner. Looking for someone bigger and stronger to hold her.

And he had.

But what must he think? She'd revealed too much.

Opened her heart to the realization she would like to share her life with someone.

The depth of her longing frightened her. Letting someone into her life filled her with dread. Wasn't it the greatest risk of obligation?

Now there was only one thing she could do. She would be very careful in the future to keep her distance from Tanner.

She went to bed early hoping sleep would ease her troubled thoughts. But her mind refused to be lulled to sleep for a long time.

A noise jerked her awake. She sat up, straining to hear the sound again. When she heard nothing, she fell back on her pillow. It had only been her imagination, fueled by Maisie's words to be careful and then the worrisome disappearance of Janie.

She closed her eyes, ready to welcome sleep once more.

Again something wakened her. Her heart raced, her pulse beat against the top of her head. This time she heard the sound. *Thump.* Something banged into the outside of the house. Suddenly she felt so alone and vulnerable.

A small sound eased past her clenched teeth. She swallowed it back, and slowly, her limbs trembling, she slipped from the bed and grabbed a wrapper. But it was not enough protection. Instead she grabbed one of Jim's coats that still hung in the wardrobe. She slipped it on, buttoned it to the neck and silently tiptoed from her room.

The sound grew louder, more frequent. More insistent.

She edged noiselessly across the kitchen floor and grabbed the poker. Her mouth was so dry her throat tickled and she feared she might cough. But she couldn't make a sound. Her best defense was surprise. The thumps progressed along the wall, coming closer and closer to the door.

She gritted her teeth. Jim's rifle. Where was it? She had hidden it behind the coats and boots and extra bedding in the closet between the two bedrooms where the children slept.

Praying she could find it without bringing the contents of the closet crashing to the floor, she slid her feet slowly in that direction. The door creaked as she opened it. She froze, waiting to see if the outside sounds would cease. *Please, God, send away whatever it is.*

She heard another thump, accompanied by a grunt. It sounded human and Susanne pawed frantically past the coats for the rifle. When her fingers touched the cold steel of the barrel, she eased it out gingerly. She'd never shot a gun. Never loaded one. All she knew to do was point it and yell "bang." Hardly effective self-defense.

She could only hope the intruder would not know of her deficiencies.

She faced the door and lifted the weapon to her shoulder as she'd seen Jim do. She waited, her legs vibrating with tension, her heart pounding so hard she feared she would faint.

The intruder found the door. Rattled the handle. Thudded against the wood. Muttered.

The door wasn't locked. She'd never felt it needed to be. They lived twenty miles from town, ten miles from the Sundown Ranch and even farther from any neighbors. In the time she'd been here, there had never been more than a handful of visitors.

The handle rattled again and then the door creaked

open. A sliver of moonlight sliced across the floor and was immediately blocked by the outline of a man.

"Stop right there," she ordered, boldly and loudly though she felt more like whimpering and hiding in a corner. "I've got my rifle aimed at you and I'll use it if you come one step closer." The faint moonlight glistened off the barrel.

The man swayed back, both hands up. "Don' shoot."

Even without his slurred words, the stench of alcohol and sweat made Susanne grimace. Bad enough an intruder but an intoxicated one! "Back away from the door."

The man took a step but swayed sideways.

"Get back." She edged forward, mindful of how unsteady the man was on his feet. How easily he could lurch at her. All she wanted to do was get the door closed between them.

"Tanner. I wanna see Tanner."

"Tanner doesn't live here. You have the wrong place."

The figure swayed back and forth as he backed up. "I seen him here. Where ish he?"

"Go to the Sundown Ranch. You'll find him there."

The man collapsed six feet back from the open door. "I wait for him."

Susanne pushed the door shut, barred it securely and stood before the window where she could make out the now unmoving dark shape on the ground.

How long until morning? How long before Tanner came?

The clock above the door ticked away the seconds, each as long as a normal hour. Never before had she realized how loud the clock was. Her legs quivered, her arms ached, but she would not leave her position. She would not take her eyes off the intruder. What if he got up? What if he sobered up? Would he be angry? Intent on getting into the house?

Susanne held her position until the sky turned gunmetal gray, then pink streaks heralded the sun's arrival. Behind her she heard the children stir.

Frank came to his bedroom door. "Auntie Susanne! What are you doing?"

"Stay in your room," she whispered. "Keep Robbie there, too. Tell the girls to stay in their rooms."

"What's wrong?" Frank whispered back.

"You can get dressed, but be as quiet as possible." She feared any noise would waken the man outside. Now that it was light, she saw he had tangled black hair and wore the same kind of leather trousers that Tanner wore.

The four children clustered in their doorways, curious and afraid.

"There's someone asleep out there. I don't want him to wake up. But if he does, I want you children in your bedrooms with the doors closed."

They didn't move.

She tore her gaze away enough to glance at them. Seeing their expressions of fear, she wanted to comfort and assure them. But how could she when her own nerves rattled so loud she could barely think? "We'll wait here until Tanner comes."

The children relaxed visibly.

"He'll know what to do," Frank said.

"He'll take care of us," Janie said with such conviction the four of them turned back to their rooms and closed their door silently. The faint rustle of them dressing was the only sound they made.

Susanne wished she didn't feel like Janie—waiting

for Tanner to take care of her. Seemed he was always helping and rescuing her. And despite last night's vow that she would not open her heart up to longings and needs that frightened her, she could hardly wait to see him ride over the hill.

"Here he comes," she whispered, not knowing if the children could hear her.

He crested the hill, stopped and eyed the place. Did he see something amiss?

Then he reined about and rode out of sight.

Her heart thudded to the soles of her feet. Was he leaving her to handle this on her own?

Chapter Eleven

Tanner knew it the moment he crested the hill. He saw the door closed and no sign of activity, and knew something was wrong. Then he saw the figure of a man outside the house. Every nerve in his body kicked into a frenzy. A dozen different possibilities filled his imagination, none of them good.

Had some ruffian discovered Susanne alone and defenseless and taken advantage of her?

Were the occupants of the house injured? Or worse?

He waited, his heart thumping an irregular rhythm against his ribs. He studied the house, the yard, the surrounding area, finding nothing to indicate what had happened. Still he waited, assessing every possibility. He did not mean to ride in there without a great deal of caution. It could be a trap.

He turned away from the farm and guided Scout along the line of hills that hid him from the farm. His heart pounded and his breath scraped from his lungs. While he was out of sight all sorts of things could happen. He forbade his imagination to provide pictures of the dreadful possibilities.

At a grove of trees he tied Scout. "You stay here." He half crouched, half ran toward the yard, keeping to what little cover he could find. At times, there was nothing but grass, and he squirmed forward on his belly, pausing often to strain for any sound, any clue. All he heard was his own ragged breathing and the whistle of his heartbeat in his ears.

He approached the farm from behind the cover of the barn, and remained motionless behind a scraggly bush as he studied every detail of the yard. He saw no one lingering in the shadows, peering from the loft or hiding behind the chicken house. He waited and listened until his ears burned, then eased forward. He clung to the rough wall of the barn as he edged around to see the house.

It came into view. So did the man on the ground.

He studied the shape several seconds until recognition dawned. Then, anger flooding his veins, he strode forward and nudged the figure with his boot. "Charlie, wake up."

Charlie grunted and groaned. He rubbed his eyes against the sunlight and slowly sat up, his head hanging down. He pressed his hands to the sides of his head. "Hurts."

"You got a hangover." He had little sympathy for his cousin. He was a half-breed just like Tanner. But the kind of half-breed that gave them a bad name. "What are you doing here?"

"Came to see you." He squinted up at Tanner. "Where was ya?"

"I don't live here." He looked toward the house. Susanne peered out the window, her face wreathed in worry. "It's okay," he called. "Are you all right?"

She nodded, her eyes far too wide. Even through the wavy glass, the tension around her mouth was evident.

He left Charlie clutching his head and walked to the door. When he turned the handle he met resistance. She'd barred the door. Had Charlie tried to enter the house? Had he succeeded? Every breath contained a thousand knives.

"Susanne, open the door." He had to assure himself she and the children were all right.

He barely waited for her to do so before he pushed the door open and stepped inside. She faced him, wearing a man's heavy coat that almost smothered her. Sticking out from a too-long sleeve, one hand held a rifle. His eyes sought hers and he saw her colorless face, her trembling lips. She looked ready to collapse and without another moment's hesitation he reached for her.

She crumpled against him, sobbing softly.

"Are you okay? Are the children okay?"

The children burst from their rooms and crowded around him. He held the quivering Susanne with one arm. With the other, he drew the kids close.

They all talked at once so he could not make out what any of them said. "One at a time. What happened?"

Frank stood back, the official spokesman. "When we got up Auntie Susanne was guarding the door with Pa's rifle. She told us someone was out there and we should stay in our rooms and be quiet."

"The man is Charlie, a cousin of mine. You can go out now. He won't harm you. But to be on the safe side, stay away from him. I need to talk to your aunt."

Four fearful children edged past Tanner. They left the door open so he could watch Charlie, who sat in a miserable heap where Tanner had found him. The children slipped by him and raced to the barn. They hurried inside, where Tanner could see them hovering in the shadows, watching and waiting.

He helped Susanne to a chair and pulled a second chair close and held her hands and rubbed her back. After some moments, her breathing steadied and he felt he could ask the questions burning in his head.

"Did he come in? Did he hurt you?"

She lifted her gaze to his. Slowly she shook her head. "He scared me." She shuddered. "I don't even know how to use a gun. What if he'd come in and tried to hurt one of the children?"

Or you? "I don't think he would." Not when he was sober, at least, but who could foretell what a drunk Charlie would do? "How long was he there?"

"I don't know." She crumpled into a sobbing heap.

Tanner wanted nothing more than to hold her and comfort her, but she cradled her arms about her and seemed lost in her own turmoil. He continued to rub her back.

"I'll send him on his way, then I'll show you how to load and fire the rifle." Hitting a target did not matter as much as being able to persuade an intruder that she meant business.

She sucked back a sob, wiped her eyes and nodded. "Thank you. Again." She sat up straight. "I'm really quite all right." She pulled the sleeves of the big coat over her hands and gave a chuckle that caught in her throat. "I'm not even decent."

He didn't want to leave her; nor did he want to make her uncomfortable by sitting in her kitchen while she was still in her nightclothes, though they were well covered by the coat.

He patted her back one last time and pushed to his feet. "I'll take care of Charlie." He strode from the house, grabbed Charlie by the back of his shirt and heaved him to his feet. "Where's your horse?" He'd not seen any sign of the animal.

Charlie jerked his head up the coulee. "Left 'im in the pen you built up in the coulee."

"Then take yourself up there and ride on out. If you ever come back and bother this family again, I'll be forced to deal most severely with you." He would not say what he might do. Let Charlie fill in those details.

"But, Tanner, it's a long walk."

"You made it this way. I'm sure you can make it back."

"But ain't you and me friends? I thought we could throw in together. Go into the mountains and live like our ancestors did."

There had been a time when the idea would have appealed to Tanner. It no longer did. He wasn't sure where he belonged but he didn't want it to be on some faraway mountain valley where he'd live like a recluse. "Which ancestors would you mean?" The question brought the man upright.

Charlie squinted at him, as if trying to see past the befuddlement in his brain. "You're changed. You going white?"

"Can't see how I can, do you?"

It was a question he knew many of his half-breed brothers shared. Can't be white. Can't be native. Who could they be? He meant to find out.

"Now go get your horse. If you want to visit me, come to the ranch. Not here. You understand?"

"Yeah." Charlie made a crazy zigzag path up the coulee.

As Tanner turned to the house, the children stepped slowly from the barn.

"Is he going to leave?" Liz asked.

"He won't come back." Tanner understood how frightening the incident had been for them and wanted to reassure them. "Your aunt would have defended you. Now go have your breakfast."

Frank stayed back as the others hurried to the house. "She didn't have a shell in the rifle."

"I know. I'll show her what to do. First, I have to go get Scout."

Frank nodded but his shoulders remained hunched. Frank was old enough to realize the danger Charlie posed and the inadequacy of an aunt who didn't know how to use the rifle to protect them. Tanner meant to resolve that problem before the day was out.

He walked back to the trees to untie Scout and rode him to the farm. Then he got Pat ready to go to work, waiting and hoping Susanne would come out to speak to him. She didn't. He delayed as long as he could, then went to the field. The crop still had to be planted.

As he worked, he watched the yard for a glimpse of Susanne, but she stayed in the house. The children stayed close by, too, except for the little while it took Frank to tether the cow and Liz to gather the eggs.

Tanner glanced up the draw. No sign of Charlie returning.

By noon, his nerves were so taut he could hear them strumming as he inhaled.

He fed and watered Pat, but Susanne did not come out with a plate of food and cup of water for him. Was she more frightened than he realized? Or did she blame him because Charlie was someone he knew?

Minutes later Frank came over carrying a plate of food. "Auntie Susanne is busy with some baking so she sent me."

"Thanks." Tanner sank down by the barn to eat. The food was like sawdust in his mouth. Was it really because she was too busy? Or was she so badly offended she wouldn't speak to him again?

He finished his tasteless meal and handed the plate back to Frank. "Tell her thanks."

"I will." Frank didn't move. He looked as if he was about to say something, then gave a little shrug and left.

Tanner returned to seeding. It was a good thing Pat knew what to do because Tanner's mind was only half on his task. He was preoccupied with Susanne and his eyes sought a glimpse of her at every pass. Finally he saw her. She came out to dump dishwater on the plants by the house, then bent to pull an errant weed, but she hurried back inside without so much as a glance in his direction. Once he thought he saw her watching him out the side window. He blinked and the image was gone. Likely his imagination. It seemed a thick, invisible wall had been erected around her.

By midafternoon, he could hardly breathe. Somehow he had to make things right between them again. If only she would bring out the snack. His hopes died when Liz headed his way with a plate and Frank followed with a bucket of water. Weren't the little ones coming, too? Were they forbidden to speak to him?

He stopped at the end of the field and waited for the pair to reach him. "Where's Robbie and Janie?"

Liz handed him cookies. "Auntie Susanne is cutting

Robbie's hair and Janie has been confined to the house for the afternoon."

"Oh?" Though he wouldn't pry, he'd sure like to know why.

"Yeah." Frank's voice carried either disgust or discouragement and Tanner wasn't sure which. "She had a temper tantrum, threw a plate on the floor and broke it."

"Doesn't sound like Janie."

Liz and Frank exchanged glances, then Liz said, "She's upset 'cause she thinks Auntie Susanne is mad at you."

"Is she?" Tanner hoped he appeared relaxed and only mildly interested when he was aching to know the answer.

"I don't know," Frank said. "But she's awfully quiet. I said you wanted to teach her to shoot and she said to tell you no thanks. That sounds kind of mad to me."

"I guess all we can do is give her time to get over it." Secretly he wondered if she would. He knew why she was angry at him. Charlie was his cousin, a half-breed just like Tanner. No doubt she blamed him. Just as she was likely having second thoughts about being associated with a half-breed if Charlie's behavior was an indication of what they were like.

He'd give her time. Surely she would realize that he and Charlie were not alike, aside from their mixed heritage. That was something they couldn't help. Their choices and behavior were things they could control, and Tanner had done nothing except help her.

By the end of the day, she'd not made any sign of having changed her mind.

He stopped by the house to say goodbye, but she hung back. "Goodbye, Susanne. I'll be back in the morning."

"Goodbye, and thank you again."

Did pink flood her cheeks? Why would she blush?

He asked himself the same questions the next day when he encountered more of the same. She avoided him and when he spoke to her—*good morning* and *goodbye*—her cheeks blossomed like a wild rose.

He pondered the reason day and night. He tossed and turned until his brothers said they could hear him in their rooms and threatened to make him sleep in the barn.

It was on the ride over on the third day that it hit him. She blushed because she was embarrassed for clinging to him both when he found Janie and when he rescued her from Charlie, even though there was really no rescuing. Of course, she did not know that. She'd clung to him in trust.

Perhaps her reaction had frightened her. After all, she tried so hard not to need anyone.

Or…a new thought surfaced…maybe she thought he'd be offended by her actions.

He grinned from ear to ear. He liked the way she'd clung to him. Liked having her lean on him in times of trouble. If he could, he would always be there for her to run to.

How was he to make her understand that without coming right out and saying it? For a moment, he considered doing exactly that—telling her how glad he was to hold her and comfort her. But he wasn't ready to risk being misunderstood. There remained a very real doubt that she saw him as another Charlie.

He must do something to open the door to better feelings between them.

* * *

Robbie perched at the window, waiting for Tanner to appear. "He isn't coming. What if he never comes again?"

Susanne wanted to assure Robbie that Tanner would come. He'd said he would seed the crop. His horses were here. But she was beyond trying to convince them when she couldn't convince herself.

Janie kicked the chair and wailed when it hurt her foot.

The children had been difficult the past few days.

"He's not going to come," Janie yelled. "'Cause you don't like him anymore."

Susanne felt four pairs of eyes on her. "Is that what you think?" She meant all of them.

Liz shrugged. "Why are you still mad at him?"

"Mad? What makes you think I am?"

Frank spoke up. "That's what he thinks. He said we had to give you time to get over it."

"I'm not angry at him. I never was."

"Then why don't you talk to him?" Liz asked.

Why, indeed? To avoid embarrassing him? To prevent further humiliation if she should run to him for support and he not give it? To punish herself for wanting so much?

Whatever the reason, she knew what she had to do.

"I'll talk to him," she promised, much to the delight of the children, who sighed and smiled.

Robbie returned to his perch at the window.

Susanne knew she wasn't the only one who held her breath waiting for his announcement. And it came almost at once.

"Here he comes."

The children rushed outside to wait for him.

Susanne remained inside. She pressed her hand to her breastbone in a futile attempt to ease away the tightness that gripped her chest. *Dear Father in heaven, help me find a way to ease the strain between us without throwing myself into his arms.*

She listened to him greet the children, then heard the sound of his footsteps thud toward the door. She opened it and her eyes filled with an unexpected sight. A huge bouquet of wildflowers—white daisies and bear grass, blue harebells, pink paintbrush and elephant head.

"For you." He handed it to her.

She buried her face in the blossoms. It must have taken him an hour or more to pick all these. No wonder he was later than usual. "Thank you." He'd done this for her and she was touched.

She'd practiced what she would say to him to explain she wasn't angry, but now she could think of nothing.

She glanced up and saw the uncertainty in his face and her heart went out to him. He feared rejection almost more than anything. How else would he interpret her withdrawal but as rejection? And yet he risked incurring more by bringing her this offering. Her tight throat made it impossible to say anything, but she must find a way to let him know she'd never hurt him.

"Thank you," she said again. "They're lovely."

"I wanted you to know—" He stopped.

"Yes? What did you want me to know?"

"About the other day. You know, about Janie and Charlie. I understand how upset you were. How upset we both were. But be assured I have no intention of reading more into things than that."

She'd hugged him, leaned into his arms, gone to him

for courage, strength and comfort. She'd found them all in his arms, and her heart had ached for more.

Tanner, though, had seen it as simply her being upset. She should have been relieved at his words—she was not.

If there had been a physical wall between them he had just slammed shut the only door she could hope to go through.

To hide her disappointment, she again pressed her nose to the flowers. A bee escaped the confines of the bouquet, buzzing angrily. She squealed and tried to bat the insect away.

When it landed on her neck she turned toward Tanner. "Get it off." Her voice was thin. "Ow. He stung me."

Tanner grabbed the bee and squashed it in his palm, then wiped his hand on his trousers. "Let me have a look at that."

The children rushed in. "We heard Auntie Susanne scream. What's wrong?"

"I'll take the flowers and put them in water," Liz said, bending to gather up the dropped bouquet.

"Leave them." Tanner scooped up the flowers and tossed them out the door. "There might be another bee in them. Your aunt got stung." He returned to Susanne's side and gently lifted her hand from the spot where the bee had stung her. "Let me look at that."

She tipped her head and exposed her neck. He trailed gentle fingers over the area. "No stinger. That's good. Liz, can you find me the baking soda?"

While Liz went to the cupboard for it, Tanner guided Susanne to a chair. She sat, her thoughts alternately frozen to a standstill at his touch and then a whirlwind of confusion at her reaction. A thousand wishes and dreams sprang to life. When had she stopped longing for love and belonging? When, and more importantly, why, had she decided neither were within her reach?

Liz brought the baking soda and with a little water he made a paste and applied it, his fingers massaging her neck, sending delightful tremors up and down her skin. How would it be to be touched in such a way for no reason—not because of a bee sting, not because of a fearful reaction—but simply because he wanted to touch her? She closed her eyes against the rush of emotion that left her shaken to the core.

"Are you okay?" he asked.

She nodded even as she forced back the overwhelming tide of longing and opened her eyes. "I'm just—" She couldn't finish. She cleared her throat before she started again. "I'm fine. It's just a little bee sting."

The two youngest ones stared at her, their eyes wide, their mouths pursed in worry. She pulled them both to her.

"I don't like bees," Janie said, a sob catching her final word.

Robbie clung to her. "Are you going to die?"

"Oh, sweet child. I'm not going to die from a bee sting." She pressed a kiss to his cheek and another to Janie's, then turned to the older children. They tried to hide their concern and failed.

Liz looked about ready to cry. "Are you mad at Tanner for bringing you flowers with a bee in them?" The question hung in the air, deadening every other thought, stealing the breath from everyone in the room.

Susanne looked into each child's worried gaze. She could speak to each of them or she could ease everyone's mind by speaking to Tanner. She faced him. "Tanner, I appreciate the flowers and your effort to ease things between us. I assure you I am not angry at you. I never was. I only—" She took a deep breath and forced herself to say the words. "I feared I had taken advantage of our friendship."

His gaze held hers in a demanding, challenging manner.

She couldn't free herself from his look and was only vaguely aware that Frank and Liz took the younger children and went outside, pulling the door closed behind them.

He shifted his chair so they sat almost knee to knee. "Let's be clear about something. I did not think you were taking advantage of anything." Their looks went on and on, past the recent events that had put a strain between them, past the two agreements they had made, past the time she had spent with Aunt Ada, perhaps right back to the time her parents were alive and she had been confident of being cherished, valued and loved.

Liz returned, a smaller bouquet in her hands. "I rescued these. Made sure there weren't any bees." She filled a jar with water and arranged the flowers in it, then put them in the middle of the table.

Susanne looked at the bouquet. It seemed to signify something, though she wasn't prepared to say what it might be…or what she wished it might be. She looked again at Tanner and smiled.

A faint smile barely curved his mouth, but his eyes filled with a thousand stars.

Liz slipped out again.

Tanner's smile deepened and Susanne's heart opened to new possibilities.

He pushed to his feet. "I need to get the crop in."

She stood, too. "Thanks for the flowers and every-thing." The word ended breathlessly.

"I hope the sting won't bother you."

She'd already forgotten it. Though the memory of his touch was seared permanently in her brain. She brushed her hand to the back of her neck. "I barely feel it." Her nape tingled with the memory of other fingers there.

"Until later?"

She nodded, liking that his question sounded like a promise. "Until later."

Chapter Twelve

The flowers were meant to put her at ease. Tanner wasn't sure he'd accomplished that. They seemed to have cleared the air, but then, he suspected, she was uncomfortable with her reactions.

As was he.

He smiled and looked at the tips of his fingers that had examined the bee sting on her neck and applied the baking soda paste. They still tingled. He understood more fully her uneasiness with her reaction for now he felt the same.

It would prove challenging to go back to the way things had been, to be neighbors working together for mutual benefit. Though perhaps it had never been quite that simple.

His smile lingered throughout the morning as he and Pat planted the crop. A few more days and the crop would be in the ground. He'd then turn his time to working the horses.

The children played. Susanne left the house only once and wandered to the garden. He knew by the way she fell on her knees that a few early plants were already poking through the ground, though they might only be weeds.

Susanne straightened and waved at him before she returned to the house.

The morning slipped away on slow, measured steps. Uncertainty reared its head as the sun moved overhead and he took Pat to water. Would she be too busy to bring him dinner?

When the door opened and Susanne stepped out, a plate in each hand, his heart sang.

He left Pat to eat and rest a bit, and waited by the side of the barn as she crossed to him. She slowed and stared. Did his expression give something away? Their gazes caught and held as she drew steadily closer. She stopped three feet away though the space felt like nothing. He could feel her in every pore. Each breath filled with her sweet presence.

"I brought you dinner." Her voice seemed husky. Or was it only his brain that made the words deeper, more emotional?

"Thanks." He took the two plates, one loaded with egg sandwiches on thick slices of bread and the other with a large piece of chocolate cake. "Smells real good."

"Lots of plants are coming through the ground in the garden." She sat with her back against the barn and he did the same, side by side, their shoulders brushing. "Go head and eat. Don't let me stop you."

He did so and she talked as he ate.

"I helped Jim with the garden last year but this is the first year I've been in charge. It's kind of exciting to see things growing. Just think how much food I'll be able to produce to feed the children." She chattered on about peas and beans and potatoes before she suddenly ran out of words.

He studied her. A frown creased her forehead. "What's wrong?"

"I just realized how much the future depends on what grows in the garden and how many things can go wrong. So much depends on the weather."

"That's true." Too much rain, too little rain, hail, frost, insect pests, even deer could destroy a crop and a garden. "Farmers are truly dependent on things they can't control."

"That's true but—" she brightened "—I can trust God to meet our needs."

"You've seen firsthand how a family survives when the crops and garden fail?" He wanted to know what she based her faith on.

"I'm not a farm girl. I told you that. So my experience is somewhat limited." Her gaze went beyond him to the distance. "But time and again I saw God meet my needs in unexpected ways when I was living with Aunt Ada. She was miserly. She wouldn't buy me new clothes even when I was in desperate need and I told you what happened when she lent me an old dress."

His fists clenched. "She sounds very unfair." He could think of a dozen other ways to describe her but had no desire to give Susanne more reason for the troubled expression that always came to her face when she talked about her aunt.

"Well, she took the dress back even though I desperately needed something that fit. I prayed and reminded God of the fact. Not that He didn't know but I needed to let Him know I trusted Him. I might have asked the preacher's wife for help but Aunt Ada had forbidden it. Nor did she believe in accepting charity."

"Or offering it."

"That's true." Susanne's amused smile eased his thoughts. "You would never guess how I got four dresses that fit me."

"I don't suppose I would." It was enough to know she'd had her needs met and her faith honored.

"In a garbage heap. I had taken a bucket of garbage to the place and saw a bundle on top. I examined it and there were four dresses and a pair of shoes in it. All I had to do was wash and mend them and they were almost like new."

He schooled his face to reveal none of his dismay. What kind of woman would treat anyone that way, let alone her niece? And yet it had not hardened Susanne or made her equally miserly. She was a joyful, generous woman who loved her nieces and nephews and did not fail to show it in every way she could. Perhaps because of the way she'd been treated. "You have every reason in the world to be resentful."

She favored him with a smile full of sunshine, her eyes shining brightly. "Does anyone have the right to be resentful? You see, I am not responsible for how others act, only how I act. And I chose to believe God loves me even though I lost my parents and have an aunt Ada."

"I guess it applies to me, as well. I can choose to believe God made me who I am and He loves me no matter how others view me."

She pressed her hand to his. "Isn't it wonderfully freeing?"

He planted his other hand on top of hers, sandwiching it between his two. "It is. Thank you." His words did not begin to express the hope she planted in his heart.

She glanced at his empty plates. "I won't keep you." She took the dishes and headed for the house.

As he went to get Pat, he looked back and saw her doing the same. They both grinned, but neither of them moved. He would not have been the first, except Pat snorted as if to say it was time to get back to work. He waved and went to the field. Again he glanced toward the house.

Susanne stood in the same spot still watching. He bent over the hitch, pleased beyond reason that she did.

He worked all afternoon breaking only for the cold drink and more chocolate cake that Susanne and the children brought out. Then it was time to go home. Three more days and he'd be done seeding. He would miss this routine. Not likely would anyone see fit to bring him a snack when he worked with the horses.

On the way home, he did some planning. Tomorrow was Saturday. He wouldn't be planting on Sunday, but perhaps he could do something else.

He reached the ranch, took care of his horse then joined the others heading for the house. He kissed Maisie on the cheek, sat at the table and bowed his head as Big Sam asked the blessing.

Big Sam concluded his report on his day by saying, "I'll move the herd up to higher pasture next week."

Maisie turned to Tanner. "How was your day?"

"I reckon it will take three days to finish seeding. I checked on the horses. You know leaving them alone to settle in was a great idea. They're getting used to people around them." He ignored the teasing way Levi and Johnny nudged each other as he continued, speaking directly to Maisie. "I was thinking Miss Collins and the children must get lonely, so I wondered if you would mind if I invite them over for dinner on Sunday."

Levi and Johnny dropped their jaws.

"He's inviting a lady friend!" Johnny could hardly get the words out.

Tanner didn't bother acknowledging the comment.

Maisie smiled. "That would be a lovely idea. Please extend an invite from me."

He nodded and the conversation shifted to Johnny, who couldn't seem to think of anything except to repeat, "He's inviting a lady friend."

Inviting them over still seemed like a good idea in the light of day, but now as he rode toward the Collins farm, Tanner couldn't think how to extend the invite.

As always as he neared, he eyed the surrounding area. He'd seen nothing of Charlie since the man had staggered up the hill, but Tanner still knew how vulnerable Susanne was. Today he would teach her to use that gun.

He reached the barn, unsaddled Scout and put him in the nearby pasture to graze. "Good morning," he said to Frank, who was in the barn.

Then he headed for the house. Janie rushed out to greet him and he swung her in the air. He did the same to Robbie, who was on her heels. Liz came out with a bucket of scraps for the chickens and paused to say good morning.

Susanne stood in the doorway, all smiles, and offered him a sunny greeting.

He stopped six feet away and grinned at her. "Good morning to you, too."

"Isn't the sun lovely? And not a cloud in the sky."

He glanced up though the view wasn't half as nice as the one before him. Not that he was about to say it. "Maisie says you are invited to dinner at the ranch tomorrow."

Her eyes lit. The children crowded close to see what she'd say. "Would you like that?" she asked them.

"Mrs. Harding seems like a nice lady," Liz said.

"She brung me home and she wasn't mad at me," Janie added.

Frank said, "I'd like to see the ranch and the horses."

Robbie's eyes were big. "How would we get there?"

"I'll come and get you," Tanner said. "I have to check on the horses anyway."

Susanne nodded. "Then it's decided. We accept."

"Good. Now one more thing. Before I go home, I will give you lessons in handling the rifle." He deliberately made it an announcement, not a question.

Susanne shooed the children away and confronted him. "I'm not sure I want to know how. I could never bring myself to shoot a man."

"I'm not suggesting you should. But at least you can scare off any intruders, whether man or beast." He could not bear to think of her alone and defenseless. "Let's do it at noon." He narrowed his eyes and did his best to look fierce. "High noon. The traditional time for a shoot-out."

She laughed. "Guess I can't refuse now without looking yellow."

He grinned. "Sounds like you've been reading the same dime novels I have."

"Jim enjoyed them and I got a little bored over the winter."

"Noon it is, then." He returned to seeding, counting every hour until noon arrived.

The sun finally reached its zenith and he took Pat in. Susanne brought him dinner, looking at once eager and reluctant.

"You aren't going to chicken out, are you?" he asked.

"Not a chance. But I am a little nervous. Frank says I'll feel the recoil. It might hurt, he says."

"It doesn't have to." He'd make sure it didn't. "Bring the rifle and bullets out while I eat." He had the sandwiches down before she reached the house and finished the chocolate cake before she stepped out with the rifle.

The children clustered about. "Can we watch?" Robbie asked.

"You stay here and we'll go out there." He pointed to a grove of trees where they could safely shoot away from the house and not put anyone in harm's way. "Liz, Frank, you make sure Robbie and Janie stay right here."

Each of them grabbed a child's hand. They wouldn't be going anywhere.

Together he and Susanne walked the hundred yards to the trees. He stacked hunks of wood on a fallen log. Not that he cared if she hit a target or not. Step by step he showed her how to load and cock the rifle. He had her do it several times until he was confident she knew what to do.

"Now hold the rifle butt to your shoulder good and tight." He stood behind her and showed her what he meant, then reached around her and steadied the rifle.

"Ready, aim, now squeeze the trigger." She did. The recoil sent her stumbling against him. He planted his hands on her shoulders and held her safe. She lowered the gun and eased about to face him. He kept his hands on her shoulders, shifting position as she turned. Her eyes were wide, full of surprise.

Then she grinned. "I did it," she yelled, not realizing how loudly she spoke because of the sound of the blast.

He looked deep into her eyes, saw so many things. Things he wondered if she meant for him to see. Pride, contentment, gratitude and… Was it pleasure, too, he saw there? Did she welcome the excuse to be held in his arms? She smiled up at him in such a way that he allowed himself to hope it was possible.

She turned back to the targets he'd set up. "Don't suppose I hit anything."

"Listen. I suggest you either aim high or low as a warning. That should scare off anyone. Now try it again."

She nodded and reloaded with care, lifted the rifle to her shoulder and looked at him. Whether or not she meant it as invitation to stand behind her again, he willingly took it as such and again cradled her in his arms, steadying the rifle and holding her against the recoil.

His senses filled with the scent of her—the smells of baking and freshly turned soil—though that might be coming from him. Her hair was soft as newly washed cotton and smelled like sunshine. Her arms were warm and her muscles firm. The skin on her hands where he held them against the rifle was smooth, making him want to run his fingers up and down the back of her hand. He breathed deeply, branding every detail in his brain.

She squeezed. The bullet exploded from the gun and thudded into a nearby tree. The recoil pressed her into his chest. She lowered the gun, but apart from that neither of them moved.

He would freeze the moment here forever if that were possible. But the children waited nearby. Pat would be ready to get to work. The rest of the crop still had to be put in the ground.

He released her. She darted a look at him from under her dark lashes as if the moment had been as packed with awareness for her as it had been for him. A loud, insistent part of his brain said he should stay away from her.

A quieter part said he wasn't running from her or the children.

Tomorrow was Sunday and he would take them to the ranch. He could hardly wait. He'd seen her life; now it was time for her to see his.

Sunday morning came and Susanne prepared to visit Sundown Ranch. She looked at her dress. Was it suitable? Not that it mattered. It was the only good dress she had. At least it wasn't wool. She'd grown used to wearing cotton every day. This dress used to belong to Alice. Jim had given it to her, assuring her he didn't mind if she adjusted it to fit. At first, she thought she'd be uncomfortable in one of Alice's gowns, but by the time she finished with it, it felt like hers and she quite liked it.

Earlier in the day they'd had their customary church service, again outside as the weather was so nice. She'd cut the Bible lesson short as the children were restless, always jumping up to see if Tanner had arrived. Truthfully, she was almost as bad. Her nerves had been taut with wonderment and hope since the shooting lesson yesterday. Being held firmly against his chest had triggered feelings she'd long buried. A sense of having come home, belonging to someone, being cherished.

She'd tried desperately to convince herself it was only the result of many years in Aunt Ada's home. The experience had made her so needy she about melted at any sign of kindness. She'd told herself over and over that Tanner showed no special interest in her. Yes, he was kind and concerned. But she knew better than to read anything more into the situation. At least she ought to by now.

But talking to herself had accomplished nothing. Her feelings refused to be ignored. And she could not convince herself that the way Tanner pressed his hands to her shoulders had anything to do with shooting the gun—they'd lingered there far too long. And yet he'd removed them far too soon.

She turned her attention back to preparations for the day and fixed her hair with extra care, then braided the girls' hair. Thankfully she's recently cut the boys' hair. She gave a final inspection of the children and looked in the mirror for her own final assessment. "We're ready for the day." Whatever it might bring. Part of her tingled with excitement at an outing and at seeing the ranch where Tanner lived. An equal portion of her twisted with questions. Would his family approve of her? That one was uppermost in her mind.

"Here he comes," Robbie called. "He's driving his mama's buggy. He's stopping at the corrals. Going inside." He sighed. "Guess he's got to check on the horses." He alternately held his breath and then gasped in air as he watched and waited. He perked up again. "Now he's back in the buggy. He's coming this way. Yay." He was off the chair and at the door before Susanne could say to slow down.

Janie ran after him. They pulled open the door and waited as Tanner jumped from the buggy.

"Good morning," he called, his gaze coming to Susanne last. His eyes were filled with gladness. Today he wore jeans and a blue chambray shirt that emphasized his dark coloring. My, she thought, but he was handsome.

"You look very nice." The words were out before she could stop them. Her cheeks burned. How terribly bold of her to speak them. She knew he would see the warmth steal up her face, so she jerked her gaze away. "We're ready."

"You look nice, too. All of you." She wondered at the way his voice caught.

He led the way outside and hoisted the children into the back. The two older ones sat prim and proper, having been warned to be on their best behavior. The younger two bounced so excitedly the buggy jerked about.

Susanne made sure the door was firmly closed and gave a look around for Daisy. She was tethered firmly to a tree with plenty of grass nearby. Pat grazed placidly in the pasture next to the barn. What if Charlie came back? Would he enter the house and paw through their things?

"You're worried about Charlie, aren't you?"

She didn't realize Tanner had moved so close and forced herself not to reveal her surprise by jerking about to face him. He was only twelve inches behind her and turning about would put them toe-to-toe. "Do you think he might return?"

"I doubt it." He didn't sound very certain. "If he does, I'll deal with him."

It was small comfort but there was little else she

could do. She certainly had no intention of staying home and guarding the house with a loaded rifle. Not when a day at Sundown Ranch beckoned.

She eased past him and went to the buggy. He held out a hand to help her up. When she took it, her heart kicked into a gallop. He pressed a hand to her waist to steady her and her mouth dried so fast she couldn't even swallow. She settled on the bench. Tanner trotted around. The buggy tipped as he climbed aboard. Then he took the reins and guided the buggy along the trail toward the ranch.

The children asked a thousand questions about the things they saw on the trip. Why was the hawk flying over top of them? What was that mountain called? Were his brothers going to be there? Tanner answered each question, saving Susanne from having to make conversation. Sitting so close to him, she wasn't sure she could have pulled an intelligent word from her brain.

All too soon Sundown Ranch came into view and the children pressed to the back of the seat.

"It's big," Frank said. And that about said it all.

Susanne stared in awe. Somehow she had not imagined so many buildings. The place made her feel small and insignificant. A feeling she was all too familiar with, thanks to Aunt Ada. She drew in a strengthening breath. She would not let her aunt exert such influence over her.

"Tell us what all the buildings are."

Tanner slowed the buggy. "The house is to the far right."

Susanne studied the low and rambling structure. It was not what she'd expected, but then she really didn't know what she expected.

"The bunkhouse and cookhouse are next. Then the horse barn and a foaling barn. Beyond that are the breaking pens and then the pigpens."

The hot breath of the children blasted against Susanne's neck. Their tension edged knifelike up and down her arms.

"I don't see any children." Robbie sounded concerned. "Aren't there any children?"

"Not since the three of us grew up, but look." Tanner pointed. "See that tree between the house and the bunkhouse?" They all squinted, trying to pick out the tree he meant. "The big one with a rope swing on one branch."

"I see it," Janie squealed. "Can we use it?"

"I put new rope on it last night just in case you might want to."

All the children sighed as if sensing they would be welcome at the ranch. Susanne wished she was equally confident.

They continued on their way. Tanner drove past the cookhouse and stopped in front of the house.

Maisie hurried out. "I'm so glad you came to visit." Behind her came an imposing figure of a man. Susanne understood why he was called Big Sam.

Tanner helped them all to the ground, then introduced his father.

Big Sam gave a little salute. "Pleased to meet you, ma'am." He greeted each of the children by name.

Levi and Johnny stood in their father's shadow.

"You've met my brothers." Tanner didn't seem real pleased about their presence.

"Come in, come in." Maisie indicated they should step indoors.

Susanne hesitated, but Tanner took her elbow and

ushered her in. She looked about and slowly relaxed. It was a kitchen not unlike her own. Larger, of course, but with the stove and cupboards to one side and a big wooden table on the opposite side of the room. Aromas of roasting meat and applesauce and a thousand delicious things filled her nostrils. Through the open doorway she saw a large, comfortable-looking sitting room with bookcases full of books, chairs before a fireplace and a maroon couch beneath a wide window. She glimpsed two doors along the facing wall. There might have been more.

"Let's visit." Maisie led the way to the sitting room. Yes, four closed doors faced her.

She and the children sat on the maroon couch. Maisie and Big Sam pulled up chairs to face them. The three younger men lounged nearby. Susanne caught Tanner's eye as he leaned against the door frame. His smile put her at ease and she sat back.

Big Sam wanted to know how she was doing on the farm with Jim gone. "I was sorry to hear of his passing. He was a good, hardworking man."

"Thank you."

"I'm sure you're all missing him. And your mama." He addressed the children.

Janie and Robbie pressed to Susanne's side and the older two blinked back tears though Frank tried hard not to acknowledge them.

After Big Sam had finished asking his questions, the conversation lagged.

"I'd like to show them around the place," Tanner said.

Susanne gladly followed him outside. They went directly to the swing.

"Push me, push me," Robbie yelled as he perched on the wooden seat.

Tanner went behind him. "Ready? Here you go." He pushed the child gently, but Robbie prodded him to go higher.

"More. More."

"Hang on." Tanner gave a big push and Robbie sailed clear to the overhanging branches.

Robbie laughed and Susanne held her breath.

Tanner pushed him several more minutes then let him slow down. "Janie's turn."

Janie paused before she climbed to the seat. "Maybe not quite so high."

"Only as high as you want."

Janie laughed as she flew through the air.

After a few minutes, Tanner lifted her from the swing. "Liz's turn."

With a little giggle, Liz sat down and let him push her.

"Want to go higher?"

"Yes, please." So higher she went until Susanne couldn't look.

Liz got off.

"Frank's turn."

Frank hesitated. Susanne could see him struggling between wanting to be treated like a child and wanting Tanner to consider him a man. But it didn't take him long to make up his mind and he sat on the swing.

Tanner pushed him the highest of them all and Frank laughed like she hadn't heard him laugh since…well, since Jim died.

Frank got off the swing.

"Auntie Susanne's turn," Tanner said, his eyes silently challenging her.

She swallowed hard, unable to tear her gaze from his. She shook her head.

He quirked his eyebrows and pointed toward the swing.

"It's fun, Auntie Susanne," Liz said.

Janie tugged at Susanne's hand. "You'll like it. I did."

The children prodded her forward until only the wooden swing separated her from Tanner. His gaze was riveted to hers. She couldn't blink, forgot to breathe.

He caught her shoulders and turned her about. She sank to the wooden seat and took the ropes. He pressed his hands to her back and pushed. Her breath whooshed in and out as she swung out and back. Then he pushed again, his hands warm and firm on her back. She soared higher and higher, her heart rising in time to her upward arcs. Higher and higher. She closed her eyes as a rush of emotion flooded her. Freedom and laughter rang through her. She never wanted to stop.

What a foolish thought. Of course she didn't want to do this forever. She dragged her feet along the ground to slow down. "I've had my turn." She got off.

"Mr. Tanner needs a turn," Robbie said.

Susanne froze just feet from the swing.

"I'm too big," Tanner protested.

Good. Because if he got on, the children would certainly expect her to push him.

"Come on. You need to have fun, too."

The children tugged and prodded him to the swing.

"Auntie Susanne, you push him," Janie said, and four children looked at her expectantly.

Slowly she shifted her gaze to Tanner, saw challenge

in his eyes. And more. Was it a warning? Or was the warning coming from her own brain?

The children pulled her behind Tanner and stepped back. What could she do but give the man a push? She planted her hands firmly on his back, feeling his warmth clear to her heart. She pushed and he swung away. She immediately wished to touch him again. He arched back and she put her hands to his back again. Back and forth. Touch and loss. Warmth and cold. Satisfaction and aching.

Her head hurt. Her arms quivered. It was too much. She stepped away, moved about to watch him. His eyes captured hers. She couldn't say what he thought, only that his look made her want to cry out his name.

He got off the swing, letting the empty seat swing back and forth. "Who wants to see the rest of the place?"

The two younger children grabbed his hands and he took off with them.

Susanne, Frank and Liz fell in behind him. Both the children were quiet. She felt their guarded study of her. Had they seen more than she meant for them to see? Read more into the simple act of swinging on a rope swing than they should? She reached for their hands and squeezed.

Any change in their lives would be troublesome at this point. How could she assure them things weren't going to change?

Especially when everything about Tanner left her unsettled.

Chapter Thirteen

Tanner couldn't get his thoughts sorted out. What made him think swinging would be a harmless pastime? Having her hands pressed to his back was about as harmless as eating candy while it still boiled in the pot. He could feel her in every nerve and muscle of his body, in every thought in his head. But he'd seen the concern in the faces of four children and understood they saw his reaction and feared he'd take their aunt away. He had no such intention, but he knew words would not convince them. He must make his actions prove it.

He shifted his mind from Susanne to the tour of the ranch, starting with the bunkhouse. "About a dozen cowboys live here, except most of them are out herding cows at the moment." He let the children look at the long, low building with its open veranda. Ropes and harnesses hung under the protection of the veranda roof.

Susanne stood behind him. He would not allow himself to turn and speak directly to her.

"Can we see inside?" Robbie asked.

"Certainly." He opened the door and the children

crowded into the opening to look. Susanne did not move forward.

"It stinks." Janie held her nose.

"Janie, mind your manners," Susanne said.

Tanner laughed. "She's right. It gets a little ripe in here."

They moved on, Susanne trailing in his wake. His nerves twitched. He didn't care for her being behind him—unless she was pushing him on a swing, he amended. He turned and reached for her. "You'll want to see this." It was the cookhouse, where a cigarette-smoking man by the name of Soupy fixed meals for the cowboys. He opened the door so she could see the long table and the big stove and cavernous cupboards. "This is Soupy's domain. He cooks for the hands. Right now he's out with a crew."

"Soupy?" Frank asked. "Is that his name?"

"Only name he uses."

"That's funny," Frank said.

The girls giggled.

He turned to look directly at Susanne. "He takes his work very seriously. No one complains about his food. Not twice anyway." He relaxed when she grew interested.

"How's that?"

"He won't serve a man who complains."

She chuckled.

Feeling wholeheartedly better, he pulled her hand around his elbow and rested her fingers on his forearm. The touch was innocent enough, but it made his heart go crazy.

They continued past the barns. Frank quizzed him

about the horses and how the cowboys worked with them. The boy had a real interest in ranching.

They came to the end of the buildings and turned to retrace their steps. They had reached the barn when the dinner bell rang.

"Maisie's calling us for the meal."

Susanne picked up speed, but he continued to hold her hand against his arm so she couldn't fly away. Nevertheless, they rushed breathlessly into the kitchen where Maisie had the table set and bowls of food ready.

Susanne broke from him even before they crossed the threshold. She hurried to Maisie's side. "I'm so sorry. I should have helped you. What can I do now?"

"No need to apologize. I could see Tanner was showing you the place."

He glanced toward the window. What else had she seen?

She handed Susanne the platter holding a roasted chicken the size of a small turkey. "You could put this at the far end so Sam can carve it."

Susanne hurried to do so. She spoke to Liz. "See that the little ones wash up."

Tanner led the children to the washbasin and supervised them while Susanne hurried back and forth helping Maisie take the bowls of food to the table.

Maisie indicated Susanne, Liz and the little ones should sit on one side of the table while Tanner, his brothers and Frank sat on the other. Frank sat tall at being included with the men rather than the children. Tanner squeezed the boy's shoulder.

Tanner sat almost directly across from Susanne and gave her a smile of encouragement, which earned him a jab in the ribs from Levi. He nobly ignored it.

Big Sam stood. "I'll ask the blessing." He held out his hands and everyone joined hands around the table.

So many emotions roiled inside Tanner. Longing and caution, wishing and denying. He must guard his thoughts and actions more closely.

For a few minutes the conversation centered on passing and serving the food.

Levi looked at Susanne. "Is this brother of mine doing a good job of putting in your crop?"

Susanne gave Tanner one fleeting look before she shifted her gaze to Levi. He wanted to push his brother aside so she'd look at him again. So much for guarding his thoughts and actions.

"I believe he is."

Levi and Johnny studied Susanne as if hoping for more.

"Huh." Johnny filled the sound with surprise and doubt. "The last thing we expected was to see our big brother behind a plow. Why, I recall when he used to say he planned to roam the woods living like our native forefathers."

Tanner also remembered a time when they were all much younger that such a remark would have earned Johnny a challenge to wrestle. He could always best both his brothers. Still could, but he no longer used it as a way of dealing with anger.

Susanne's gaze came to him. "Is that a fact?"

He raised his eyebrows. He wasn't about to deny it nor explain that things had changed.

Maisie made a soothing sound before Tanner's brothers could say more. "God has a way of putting things in our pathway to nudge us in directions we hadn't even considered. Take me for example. I was set on being a teacher in a girls' boarding school when I saw Sam's notice seeking a governess for his sons out in Montana Territory. It sounded so romantic and adventuresome. My father—may he rest in peace—opposed the idea."

"But yet you came." Levi spoke in awe.

"My only regret was leaving my father, but if I hadn't come I would not have fallen in love with Sam and his three sons." She smiled around the table.

Tanner kept his face turned toward Maisie while still watching Susanne. She looked at Maisie with a mixture of longing and regret. No doubt she wished someone like Maisie had become her guardian rather than her aunt Ada.

Maisie continued. "What I'm saying is don't be afraid of following God's surprises."

Tanner blinked. God's surprises? Was that what Susanne and the children were?

Johnny chuckled. "I think there might have been a few times when you regretted taking us on. The three of us were as wild as the Montana wind, especially Tanner here. He wanted to sleep outdoors and wear nothing but a loincloth."

Tanner rolled his eyes. "The children do not need to hear this." The four of them looked at him wide-eyed. Amusement lingered in Frank's eyes. "Besides I thought I was honoring my ma by living wild and free."

Maisie smiled one of her rich, welcoming smiles. "I knew you all had to deal with the changes in your lives in your own particular way."

"And you prayed lots," Levi said.

"Yes, I did."

Big Sam gave her an adoring look that some might consider silly on such a tough man, but Tanner knew it was sincere and Maisie deserved his esteem. "And you loved us lots."

"I still do."

Susanne looked about the table. Tanner and his brothers had reason to regret the events of their lives that left them without a mother, yet they obviously did not resent Maisie as an intruder. They were happy and content in the certainty of Maisie's love.

She looked at her charges. She loved them lots and prayed for them. Would they turn out as happy and content as the Harding boys?

Maisie took Liz's hand. "You and your sister and brothers have had much sorrow in your young lives. I will pray that you find your way of dealing with it and allow God to lead you. You all deserve God's best." She looked about the table. "I believe you will find what you need in being strong together."

"Thank you," Liz whispered. "I try to be the sort of girl that would make my mama and papa proud."

"And you are." Tanner smiled at each of the children. "Your ma and pa would be proud of all of you."

Frank ducked his head to hide his pleased smile. Liz and the little ones favored him with adoring looks.

Susanne feared she would do the same and forced her eyes down, as if to study her plate.

Thankfully, Maisie rose at that moment to serve pie and coffee and Susanne jumped up to help.

She kept her attention on the food and the conversation that turned to other things as they finished the meal. She worked very hard to keep her gaze from roaming too frequently to Tanner and from lingering there when it did.

As soon as the meal ended, she sprang to her feet. "We will help with the cleanup."

The men wandered outside, Frank with them, while Liz and Susanne helped wash and dry dishes. "I very much enjoyed the visit," she said. "This is a nice family."

Maisie turned toward Janie and Robbie drawing on some pages she'd given them. "It is so pleasant to have young children visit. Be sure and come often."

"Thank you." But Susanne had not gained enough confidence around Pat to try to hitch him to a wagon, and she had no reason to think Tanner would be offering to take them back and forth.

Soon it was time to leave and all the children said thank-you to their hosts, as did Susanne. Tanner held her hand and assisted her into the buggy under the watchful eyes of his brothers. He did not let his touch linger one second longer than necessary and she hoped she did not show the slightest reaction to his hand on hers.

"Did you enjoy your visit?" he asked after they had left the ranch buildings behind.

The children chorused yes. They quickly settled in the back, content to watch the passing scenery.

Tanner turned to Susanne for her answer.

"I enjoyed it very much. You have a nice family."

He grinned. "I suppose I do." He paused as he seemed to consider what he meant to say. "I was every bit as wild as Levi suggested. Even more. I suppose I thought I could hold on to my ma by turning to her past ways."

"I can understand that. I suppose much of what we do is a reaction to events in our lives. I can't count the things I've done, or not done, the things I've thought—

sometimes wrongly—in accordance with what I would expect from Aunt Ada."

"Seems like a long time ago we made an agreement to forget our pasts."

"It's been a challenge for me. So often I hear Aunt Ada reminding me of the obligation I had. But I do believe it's getting easier to not listen to her voice. How about you? Are you learning that not everyone is offended by who you are?"

The reins were slack in his hands and he stared straight ahead. She was afraid she had inadvertently reminded him of the very thing he wanted to forget. She touched the back of his hand. "I hope you can at least see that the children and I aren't. We appreciate you and what you are doing for us."

He slowly brought his gaze to meet hers. "It helps to hear it from you." A smile broke forth with such power she almost shaded her eyes. "You make me believe it doesn't matter."

"Good. Because it doesn't."

"Not to you?" His voice had grown very soft.

Afraid to reveal too much of her heart and risk having it broken, she said, "Not to any of us." She nodded toward the children behind her. The little ones had fallen asleep against their older brother and sister. "It shouldn't matter to anyone."

He turned his attention back to the horses.

She should have been more honest, but he'd given her no reason to hope for the things she longed for.

"Are you anxious to get back?" he asked after several seconds of silence.

"I suppose not. What did you have in mind?"

"I'd like to show you something if you have no objections."

"None whatsoever." She'd make this afternoon last forever if she could. Besides, she heard a hint of eagerness in his voice that made her think he had something special in mind.

He turned aside, crossing rough, untrodden prairie. They climbed higher, crested a hill and followed the slope for a few miles, then he drove down into a wide, sunlit valley with several thick groves of trees. He pulled to a stop and stared straight ahead, his jaw muscles clenching and unclenching.

She touched the back of his hand. "What's wrong?"

He released a deep breath. "Remember I told you about the trees where my mother fell on her knees and worshipped?"

She followed the direction of his gaze. "This is the place?"

He nodded. "I almost went into the center of the trees the other day."

She waited as he gathered his thoughts.

"Will you come with me?" he asked her.

"I'd be honored to. Do you want the children to come, as well?"

"Of course." He jumped to the ground and hurried around to help her down. His hands lingered at her waist and he studied her face. "I'm sure it will be completely different than I remember."

"Either way, it will bring your mother's memory close."

He nodded and lifted the children down. Robbie, now awake, as was Janie, took off at once. Susanne collared him. "We'll follow Tanner."

Tanner left his hat in the buggy, then faced the trees. He wiped his hand on his trousers and sucked in a breath. "I think this is the spot where we went in." A faint trail parted the trees. "Animals must be using it." He pushed aside the overhanging branches and held them as Susanne and the children followed. The path was narrow and covered with more branches.

"Where we going?" Robbie asked.

"It's a place Tanner hasn't been to since his ma died," Susanne explained. She hoped the children would realize how important this spot was to him.

"His first ma?" Robbie asked, sounding a little worried.

"Yes."

"Oh." After that the children were silent. They understood how important memories of parents were. Each of them had something of Alice's they cherished. Susanne had never gone through Jim's things. She couldn't bring herself to. When the time came, she would see that they all got to choose something of his to keep.

Tanner broke into the open. She followed with the children right behind.

"Oh." Totally speechless, she stared about. They stood in a round clearing with the tree branches arching overhead to form a light-dappled canopy.

"It's like church," Liz whispered in wonderment.

"An outdoor cathedral," Susanne echoed her sentiments.

Tanner turned full circle. "It is exactly as I recall it." He moved to the center. "Ma knelt right here." As he looked upward, light pooled on his face. He closed his eyes as if in prayer.

Susanne drew the children back, wondering if he wanted to be alone.

He opened his eyes and held his out hands, inviting them forward.

He pulled Susanne to his side and the children clustered about them.

"This is a very special place," he said. "I have never felt closer to God than I did here when my ma prayed. And I feel it again. Do you?"

The children nodded.

"Look up."

They did so. The branches parted in the overhead breeze and light flooded them. Each of them closed their eyes as if lost in awareness of God. Susanne could not take her eyes from them.

Tanner squeezed her shoulder. "You try it."

She lifted her face, and light and warmth washed over her. She closed her eyes and let the cares and worries of her life slip away until she felt free. "God is so good. He loves each of us in a special way."

No one replied. They simply stood there so aware of God's love that there was no need for words.

Birdsong came from a nearby tree. "A robin," Tanner said.

The moment ended and the children stepped away to explore the clearing, their voices muted.

Susanne did not want to break the closeness that she shared with Tanner. His arm remained about her. Neither of them moved. The sun passed from overhead and the clearing grew chilly.

"I should get you home." But Tanner remained motionless.

"Liz and Frank, take the younger ones back to the

buggy. We'll be there in a minute or two." She sensed Tanner needed a few minutes alone, but when she made to follow the children, he held her.

"Stay here. I want to hold this moment in my memory forever."

She relaxed with his arm about her shoulders. "I'm honored that you chose to share it with me."

"There's no one I would rather share it with." His gaze claimed her. In that moment she knew she was eternally changed. Life would never be the same for her. His look went on and on, searching her very soul.

"Susanne." Her name was music on his lips.

"Tanner," she whispered. The word came from deep inside.

His gaze traveled over her face and came to rest on her mouth.

She couldn't breathe for fear of shattering the special feeling between them in this fragile moment.

He lowered his head, then seemed to think better of it.

She tipped her face up to him, inviting the kiss she knew was on his mind.

He smiled and claimed her mouth in a reverent, sweet kiss full of promise and possibility.

She clung to his shoulders, not wanting to end the moment, but he drew back.

"I shouldn't have done that, but I can't find it in my heart to say I'm sorry." He didn't sound the least bit regretful.

"I'm not sorry." She said it with utmost conviction.

He laughed with such pure delight her eyes stung.

The children's voices reached them and they shared

one more special smile, then returned to the buggy and headed home.

It wasn't until he'd said good-night and departed, and after the children were tucked in bed, that she had time to think about the afternoon.

And the kiss. Neither of them had said what it meant though she cherished the possibility that it might mean something very special.

Chapter Fourteen

Tanner returned to the Collins farm Monday morning and continued putting seed in the ground, every minute a joy as he watched Susanne and the children go about their chores. He worked very hard to appear normal as he went in for dinner and then enjoyed the afternoon break. But would anything ever feel truly normal again?

The sky was bluer, the air clearer, and the mountains more majestic. The children's laughter rang more joyously and he was certain Susanne's smile was warmer.

He tried not to linger as he said goodbye at the end of the day, but it took supreme effort to pull himself from Susanne's questioning gaze. It was as if she wanted to know if yesterday's kiss had changed him. She would never guess how much, and he feared saying anything would shatter the joy flooding every barren corner of his heart.

Partway home, he left the trail and headed toward the cathedral of trees. He dismounted and slipped into the clearing, where he sat cross-legged at the center. The sun sent rays of light through the branches.

He was flooded by memories of his ma worshipping

in this spot, intermingled with the more recent memory of Susanne and the children being mesmerized by their experience here. It seemed his life made sharp turns at this place. First, his ma died leaving him confused, then he discovered a different kind of love with Susanne and the children. He lifted his face to the sky as joy flooded his heart. He loved Susanne.

Dare he hope his feelings were more than dreams? Or that they might eventually be reciprocated?

He bowed his head to the ground. "Father God." His prayer went no further. It was enough to acknowledge God's presence.

After a bit he sat up again. In a day or two he would finish the seeding though it wouldn't put an end to going to the farm. Not so long as he needed the corrals. He would not think past the time that would come to an end. He recalled something Maisie had said. "I wonder if the poor girl ever gets to town. If not, she could be getting low on supplies."

He knew a way to solve her dilemma, but would it work?

Midafternoon Wednesday he finished seeding, put the equipment away, gave Pat an extra good rubdown with Frank helping, then he sauntered to the house. To all outward appearances he was relaxed and casual, but his insides churned.

Susanne came to the door and waited.

He almost forgot his rehearsed speech at the warmth of her smile. "I've finished seeding."

"I'm grateful. You must be anxious to start work on the horses."

He nodded. "I'll get at it, but tomorrow I am taking

you and the children to town." It was not at all what he'd planned to say and he rushed on. "We need to celebrate having the crop in."

Her expression went from surprise to caution to eagerness. "That sounds like a fine idea."

"We'll need to get an early start."

"I'll be ready. I'll pack a picnic lunch."

Her words of agreement eased some of his tension. He would have suggested they go to the small dining room in town but the last time he'd been there with his brothers, there had been a scene because some of the patrons objected to the presence of Indians.

The children gathered round, tugging at his arms and asking questions.

"Papa always bought us a candy when he went to town." Janie's bottom lip quivered. "Will you buy us a candy?"

Liz took her sister's hand. "Papa wouldn't want you asking that." Her bottom lip quivered, too.

Tanner looked at the boys. Robbie sucked his fingers. Frank gazed into the distance.

Had he made a mistake in suggesting the outing? "If you don't want to go to town we'll do something else."

Robbie and Janie looked to the older ones for direction.

Liz and Frank turned to each other, some silent message passing between them. Then Frank, as the oldest, spoke, his words soft yet firm. "We'd like to go to town. It will be fun."

The little ones relaxed.

Tanner was still uncertain. "If I do something or say something that bothers you, you tell me. I don't want to make things difficult for you."

Janie tugged at him and he squatted down to face her. She wrapped her arms about his neck and hugged him. "You don't make things hard. You make them easy."

He hugged her back, his throat too tight to speak. He hugged Robbie and squeezed both Liz's and Frank's shoulders, then pulled his gaze toward Susanne.

She wiped a tear from her eye.

He eased the children out of the way and went to her. "What's wrong?"

She ducked her head.

He caught her chin and lifted it so he could see her expression. Her eyes were awash with tears and he groaned. "I've made a mess of things, haven't I?"

She shook her head but he wasn't convinced. She pressed her palms to his chest. "Tears aren't necessarily bad. Sometimes they're healing. That's what you're seeing here. You've given the children the freedom to acknowledge their grief. Like Janie said, you make things easy."

"Me?" How was that possible? Much of his life his presence had made things difficult.

She patted her hands on his chest, sending drumbeats through his heart. "Maybe someday you will realize that lots of people appreciate you and recognize your abilities."

He wasn't sure he wanted to wait for someday. He caught her hands and clasped them close. "What are my abilities?"

Her smile teased. "You captured wild horses that many have wanted to catch. That's one ability."

Shaking her hands slightly, he silently demanded more.

"You offer help to a poor farm lady. You—"

Her words were cut off by Frank. "You made me feel important…like a man," he said.

"You hug me," Janie added.

Liz ducked her head. "You're nice to me."

Robbie wrapped his arms as far around Tanner's waist as they would go. "You throw me up in the air."

Tanner wondered how much of this his heart would take before it exploded. Yet, he wanted more. He wanted to hear from Susanne. He held her gaze, seeking words from her.

She smiled so sweetly he was sorely tempted to kiss her. "It's just the way you are…who you are."

Funny, she didn't say anything specific and yet her words were exactly what he needed to hear. She appreciated him for who he was. Something startling and cleansing rushed through him like a hot spring wind driving away the dirty remnants of winter. Something stung his eyes. He nodded in acknowledgment of her assessment, then wheeled around and rushed to the barn.

He mounted Scout and paused to wave at the family. "See you tomorrow." He galloped from the yard and didn't slow down until he was almost home.

A cool wind the next morning made Tanner study the sky. Clouds hung over the mountaintops in the west, but they were white and puffy, harmless looking. Still, it would be a good idea to keep an eye on the weather. He hitched the horses to the buggy and left for the Collins farm. The day promised enjoyment.

The children heard him coming and waited outside as he approached the house. They allowed him to set the brake before they climbed aboard.

Then Susanne came to the door looking fine in her blue dress. The first time he saw her in it he'd thought she looked like a flower. He didn't change his mind now.

"Do you need help?" he asked, and she indicated a large basket and a gallon jar of water, which he picked up. She lifted another box that held dishes.

He stowed them all in the back, then put his hands on her waist to help her aboard. Not content to let her climb up on her own, he lifted her to the seat.

She laughed as her feet left the ground.

He jumped up beside her, his heart overflowing with anticipation. A whole day to enjoy Susanne and the children. A warning bell sounded in his brain. Going to town hadn't always been enjoyable for him. There were those who still harbored resentment toward the Indians and funneled it in his direction even more so than at his brothers because he looked the most Indian of the three. But he pushed the worry aside. Today was for pleasure. Besides, hadn't Susanne said he made her life easy? He couldn't ask for more.

The children bounced up and down, constantly asking questions. "How far?"

"Are we almost there?"

"Is that an antelope?"

He welcomed their questions as it provided him something to talk about, something to occupy his thoughts apart from the awareness of Susanne at his side.

The trail followed the trickling creek that bordered the south side of the farm. Two miles later, it ran into Granite Creek, the little river that gave the town its name. They followed it several miles until they had to cross the river to head toward town. He slowed as they drove into the water and followed the rocky crossing to the other side.

"Robbie, don't lean out so far." Frank held the boy by the back of his trousers to keep him from tumbling into the river.

Susanne reached back and pulled him safely to the seat. "What were you doing?"

"Did you see those rocks? They shineded like gold."

Tanner knew the boy had not seen actual gold. "There have been lots of people looking for gold here and none have found any."

"It was gold," Robbie insisted. "Someday I'm going to find gold."

"That would be nice." Susanne sounded soothing, then to divert the boy, she pointed to a gopher watching them.

The trip took more than three hours and as they neared the town an expectant hush fell over them all. He suspected the children were both curious and excited. As for himself, he felt his muscles twitch. Could he hope to spend a few hours in town without encountering any difficulties? He had to try, for Susanne.

"Where to first?" he asked.

"The general store, please." She pulled out a piece of paper and stub of pencil and added something to her list.

He parked the wagon in front of the store and helped them down. Susanne took Robbie's hand and hurried up the steps with the other children close behind. He hesitated, not sure that following them into the store was a good idea. Maybe he'd wait out here. He lounged against the hitching post and watched the comings and goings of the little town.

A man and woman came toward him, saw him, paused, then clung to the far side of the sidewalk as they passed.

He sighed. He'd worn jeans and a plain shirt rather than leather trousers and a fringed shirt in the hopes people would ignore him. Maybe he should have taken the feather out of his hat, too, but it had been given to him by an old Indian chief who had known his ma. It stayed no matter what others might think.

Maybe he'd be less conspicuous inside. He straightened just as three ladies sidled past him and into the store.

Now what?

He stopped himself. He was a Harding and had every right to go freely in and out of any place of business. He crossed the threshold and waited for his eyes to adjust to the dim interior.

"Oh good," Susanne said. "Would you mind carrying these parcels out for me?" He noticed a sack of flour, others of beans and coffee, numerous boxes and packages. She must have been very low on supplies.

He filled his arms. "I'll be back for the rest." He took the purchases to the buggy then returned just as the three ladies clustered about Susanne. The children were on the other side of the store looking at a display of men's wear. Tanner stopped. He'd wait until the ladies moved off before he'd get the rest of Susanne's things. No one had noticed his entrance and he withdrew into the corner.

"You're Jim Collins's sister, aren't you?" The speaker fussed with her gloves as she spoke.

"Yes. Did I meet you at his funeral?"

"My husband and I were there. A fine man, your brother was."

"Thank you."

A lady with a black bonnet edged forward. "How are you managing out on that farm so far from town and with four children to take care of? Why, it's simply astonishing that you stay there."

Susanne widened her eyes, though Tanner knew it was not in surprise. She objected to the suggestion she should leave the farm. "I'm managing quite fine, thank you. The Hardings have helped put the crop in."

The three ladies tilted their noses upward. "Do you mean that half-breed I saw outside? You should not be associating with the likes of him."

Tanner clenched his fists. Bad enough he had to deal with such animosity—they had no right to involve Susanne in their dislike of him. He straightened, intending to intervene, but then waited, wanting to know how Susanne would deal with the situation.

She gave each of the ladies a look that should have curled their hair, but they remained oblivious, stuck in their own self-righteousness. "Have you ever considered that he comes from noble people on both sides of his lineage? Or have you ever taken time to notice his strengths?"

"His mother was an Indian."

"From what I've heard she was very strong. She survived being injured and lost for days. I wonder if any of you could handle such a challenge."

The lady in the black bonnet looked down her fine nose. "Why would we have to?"

"Let me make one thing clear." Susanne's voice rang out. "I judge a person not by things they have no control over but by things they do control. Like how they treat others and whether they are kind and generous." Her voice softened. "I wonder how you ladies would fare under such an evaluation."

They were undaunted. "You must think of the children and how your association with such a man will affect them," one of them said.

Susanne's determined look never faltered. "It's been very beneficial for them."

"Humph. I can see you have no sense," said the woman in the black bonnet. "There will come a day you regret your foolishness." She and the other two women stormed out of the store without looking to the right or the left.

The storekeeper clapped. "That was a mighty fine speech, miss. I agree with what you said, but I fear you have turned those ladies into enemies."

Susanne shrugged. "I don't consider it a loss."

Tanner remained in the corner, not wanting Susanne to know he'd overheard her.

The door slapped as a boy of about fourteen rushed in. Tanner followed on his heels as if he'd entered at the same time. He hoisted the bag of flour and grabbed a handful of other things and returned to the buggy. As soon as he loaded the supplies he leaned against the wheel and gathered his thoughts.

She had defended him. Stood up to three highfalutin ladies to do so. Did she really mean what she said? He knew she did and it left him struggling to think what it meant.

The door creaked open and the children rushed out. "We're going to the post office," Robbie yelled. He skidded to a stop. "What's the post office?"

Tanner laughed. It was hard to get lost in thought with the children around, and he welcomed the diversion.

Susanne stood framed by the closed door. "It's where we get letters." She seemed to be waiting for something.

He was about to ask what when she tipped her head.

"Are you coming? There might be mail for the ranch."

He sprang to her side. "I need to check." Pa had ordered him to do so. They passed the lawyer's office and the hotel and stopped in front of a small wooden structure where the Stars and Stripes billowed in the wind.

The children were ahead of them and stopped at the sign to wait.

He and Susanne led the way in. Frank and Liz waited by the wicket as Susanne requested the mail. Janie clung to Susanne's side. Robbie found a chair that swiveled and spun around in it.

Mr. Wigley, the postmaster, cleared his throat.

Tanner joined Susanne at the wicket. "Mail for the ranch, please."

Mr. Wigley didn't reach for any but scowled in Robbie's general direction.

Susanne realized what he meant and pulled Robbie from the chair.

Only then did Tanner receive the handful of letters—three addressed to hired cowboys, the rest to Pa and Maisie. Susanne received a few magazines. He couldn't tell if she got any letters.

When they left the building, Liz confronted Robbie. "That man did not like you spinning his chair. You shouldn't have done that."

"It was fun."

"Mr. Wigley objected," Tanner added.

"Mr. Wigley?" Robbie stared at Tanner in disbelief.

"That's his name."

"A wiggly man." Robbie laughed so hard he set the other children laughing.

Tanner looked at Susanne and shook his head. "What are we to do with them?"

The children tried to stop but failed.

She grinned. "Maybe if we feed them?"

"To whom shall we feed them?" he asked.

That set the children off into more helpless giggles.

Janie suddenly grew serious. "Would you feed us to someone?"

He scooped her up. "Not a chance, though you are about sweet enough to eat." He tickled her as they made their way back to the wagon.

He helped Susanne aboard though he did not swing her into the air for fear someone would see and misjudge his action. He had no wish to bring any more criticism down around her head. "Wait a minute. I've got something to do." He trotted into the store and made his purchase, then took his place beside Susanne. He glanced back to the children. "Who would like to go on a picnic?"

His question was answered with cheers.

He knew the perfect place. The creek, a river at this point, curled around and passed the town on one side. It was a pleasant spot where they'd be alone to enjoy a picnic.

Right now he glanced over his shoulder at the buildings. He couldn't help it. He was eager to get out of town, away from people who could be watching and, more importantly, judging.

Susanne tried to think when she'd ever enjoyed a day more. Not, she decided, since her parents had died and she was but an innocent child. The drive to town had been fun and relaxing—no demands, no expectations that she should be doing something else.

At the store, she'd liked having the freedom to purchase the supplies she needed without Aunt Ada pinching every penny. Seeing the children laugh so freely outside the post office was the icing on her cake of joy.

Only one thing marred the day ever so slightly. The three women's cruel comments about Tanner. It eased her mind some that he hadn't overheard them. She'd tried to respond graciously and politely when she wanted nothing more than to put them in their place. Tanner was a noble, good man.

How often had the likes of those women said things to make him think otherwise?

Well, he needn't believe them. Their opinion mattered not at all.

Tanner stopped the wagon at a place he'd declared perfect. She had to agree. The nearby river gurgled in the background, and thick trees sheltered them from the town. As the children ran off to explore and release some of their energy, she spread a quilt on the grassy spot and looked about. "It's very nice here."

She wanted to look into Tanner's eyes but feared doing so would make her forget the children, the picnic and anything else she should be thinking of.

Tanner brought the boxes from the buggy and set them by the quilt. "Did you get everything you needed at the store?"

"Yes, thank you." Her words felt stilted as she tried to keep from looking at him.

"Good." She could feel his waiting silence.

"Is something wrong?"

"Not at all." She concentrated on taking out the sandwiches and cookies.

"Are you concerned about what those ladies said?"

His question brought her to her feet to face him.

"I was there," he said. "I heard every word."

The tips of her ears burned. Not with embarrassment but with regret that he'd heard the conversation. She grabbed his arms. "Then you heard what I said."

He nodded. "Thank you for defending me."

She studied his eyes, saw the caution there just as she heard the flatness of his words. "Did you think I defended you out of duty or obligation? I thought we were past that."

"They were right about one thing. Associating with me will mark you in an unpleasant way."

"Then I guess it's a good thing I live so far from town. Even if I didn't, their opinion is of no importance to me."

He held her gaze though doubts lingered in his eyes. She had to convince him she was sincere. "My aunt Ada was a proper lady who had her rightful place in society and look how she treated me. If that is what it means to have the approval of ladies such as those, then no thanks. One thing I learned from her was that people need to be treated fairly and kindly. If you can't believe that of me, then—"

She stepped away, her heart burning that he would think her the least bit like those three women or even Aunt Ada.

He touched her arm, stopped her flight. "I don't believe you are the least bit like those women, but I'm not sure you should have defended me."

"I would be remiss not to."

She spun around and their gazes collided. She meant what she said and she could tell he believed her. For now. How many more times would this come up and make him wonder? It didn't matter. She wasn't about to change her mind; nor would she stand by while someone said cruel things about him.

The children raced back. "I'm hungry," Robbie yelled. Someday she meant to teach him to talk in a normal tone of voice but not yet. If yelling made him feel better then he could yell.

"First we pray." She looked to Tanner to say grace.

He blinked. Why would he be surprised that she asked? Because he didn't think God approved of him? Surely he was beginning to see that God had created him in love. And after visiting the trees that were like a cathedral he could not doubt God's nearness.

Then he nodded. "Father God, the great provider. Thank You for blessing us with this food. Amen."

She tucked a smile into her heart. For a man who claimed not to feel God cared, he certainly knew how to talk to Him. Perhaps she could direct his thoughts to God's love and care.

He sank to the ground at her side and she passed around the food.

The children ate hurriedly so they could return to the trees to play. Before they left, Tanner gave them each a piece of candy, which earned him four hugs.

When they were gone, she leaned back and looked at him. "I meant to tell you that I really enjoyed visiting the cathedral of the trees."

"Me, too. And now it has a name." He chuckled as if the idea pleased him.

"I can see why your mother considered it a special place. God seemed so close there. I needed the reminder that He is that close to me wherever I am."

"Is He?"

"Pardon?"

"Is He that close wherever you are? For instance, when your aunt Ada was berating you, was He close then?"

She nodded. "There were times I forgot it was so but other times, when I remembered, I was comforted, even though my aunt was so cruel and cold." She wanted to say more, to explain that God didn't change despite changing circumstances.

He looked toward the river. "I'm learning to believe God doesn't speak through the mouths of people like those women in the store."

"I'm glad to hear that finally." She touched his hand. "I know it must hurt, just like Aunt Ada's actions and words hurt me. But God's love for us never changes."

Before she could gauge his reaction to her words, he bolted to his feet.

"What is it?" she asked.

"Robbie's by the river and I don't see any of the other children." He was halfway to the water before he finished speaking and she scrambled after him, her heart thick as winter molasses. She had a healthy fear of water since her parents drowned.

"Robbie, stay away from the water," he yelled.

Robbie looked over his shoulder. "I am." But his feet told a different story. He'd been about to step on a rock sticking out of the water.

Tanner reached him first and scooped him up.

Susanne rushed to Tanner's side. "Robbie, what were you doing?" She patted him all over to be certain he was okay.

"I wasn't going to get hurt. I just want that shiny rock." He pointed to the one he meant.

She took him from Tanner, gripped his arms and gave him a little shake. "You must never go into a river, you hear?"

He nodded.

"Now go back to the buggy and wait." Her limbs shook, as did her voice, revealing just how frightened she'd been.

The other children gathered round.

"Take your brother to the buggy," Tanner said, though his eyes never wavered from Susanne.

When they were back at the picnic area and she began to put things away, he stepped in front of her and put his hands on her shoulders to still her.

"Susanne, are you okay?"

Her eyes felt too wide. She couldn't blink. Couldn't form a rational thought. "What if he drowned?"

"He didn't. He's okay."

She rocked her head back and forth. "He could have. Just like my parents." A shudder shook her from the top of her head to the soles of her feet, then settled into the pit of her stomach. "I hate water."

He rubbed his hands up and down her arms. "I can see why. But Robbie is okay and there is no water near the farm so you don't need to fret."

She hugged her arms about her. "I know but that fact doesn't make me any less fearful." She tried to laugh, the sound coming out as more of a wail.

He pulled her closer, his hands firm on her arms. If he would wrap her close, press her to his heart, her fear might subside. But they were not alone. She glanced past him to the children by the buggy and beyond them to the houses and businesses of Granite Creek. Not that she cared what the good folk of the town might think, but she did care how her actions would affect him and the children.

"I'm okay," she managed, but she could not force herself to move away from his touch.

But he'd seen her look toward town and dropped his hand. "We need to start back."

They packed up and were soon on their way back home. She breathed deeply and prayed silently for the gripping fear to end.

A flash of lightning jerked her from her thoughts. Dark clouds rolled and twisted overhead. Thunder echoed down the hills and pounded inside her heart. "We're getting a storm." Her voice squeaked from her tight throat.

"I'm hoping we beat it home." Tanner sounded calm but perhaps only because he sensed her fear.

She shivered in the wind that had turned suddenly and drastically colder.

He pulled to a stop. "Put this around you." He wrapped a woolen blanket about her shoulders, then covered the children with a fur robe.

"Are we going to drown?" Janie asked.

"Of course not," said Liz, trying to sound brave.

Tanner faced the children. "A little rain never hurt anyone. The worst that can happen is we get wet."

Susanne clamped her teeth tight and still they chattered, though not from cold. Tanner was wrong. Rain could hurt people. It could cause flash floods and people could drown.

Chapter Fifteen

Tanner darted a glance to the west where the rain came down in sheets. If only he could get them home before the storm reached them. Susanne still shuddered every few minutes from the fright Robbie had given her playing so close to the river.

He kept the horses to a steady pace knowing they could not gallop the entire distance.

Lightning slashed across the sky. He counted the seconds before the thunder clapped. Ten. The storm was still a long ways off. But every flash, every rumble caused Susanne to jolt.

They reached the ford across the creek.

Susanne stared at the dark waters. "It's higher than when we came."

It was but only marginally. It wouldn't be long, though, before the waters from up the mountain rushed down and made the creek rise. He kept his thoughts to himself as he guided the horses across the rocky ford.

Susanne sat white-knuckled.

"Robbie!" Liz's voice jerked his attention from the rocky path to the children.

Robbie had slipped from the shelter of the fur robe and leaned dangerously far out looking at the water.

He grabbed the boy and set him back in the seat.

Frank wrapped the robe around him.

Robbie jammed his arms over his chest and glowered at them all. "I only want to see the gold. It's there, you know."

The buggy tilted to one side. Tanner grabbed the reins and pulled the horses back to the rocky roadbed.

Susanne keened softly. He pulled her to his side and pressed her close. "You're okay. You're safe." He held her until the horses pulled the buggy to shore. "We're across. We'll soon be home."

They followed the trail for several miles and she kept her eyes on the creek beside them even though the sight of the water obviously frightened her.

The wind increased in velocity. Lightning flashed and the time until the thunder echoed grew shorter. Moisture filled the air. He flicked the reins to hurry the horses along. If only they could make it home before the rain came.

He cupped his hand to Susanne's head and pressed her face to the hollow of his shoulder so she couldn't look at the water. "Liz, Frank, what was that hymn you sang the Sunday I was there when you were having church? Why don't you sing it for us?"

The children sang loudly, but the wind carried their voices away.

Finally they left the creek and turned toward the farm and Susanne began to relax.

When Tanner pulled up to the house, Frank unwrapped the children and he and Liz helped the little ones down and then carried in the things Susanne had purchased. The wild horses whinnied and raced about the enclosure, frightened by the storm. He could do little about it at the moment and hoped they would not injure themselves.

Susanne clung to Tanner. He hated to let her go, but as soon as his feet hit the ground he lifted her down and carried her inside.

He barely made it through the door when the skies opened.

He set Susanne on her feet. She clung to him, her eyes much too wide.

"It's raining."

He nodded. "Yes, it is, and that's good news for your garden and crop."

She barely acknowledged his words. "What if we'd gotten caught in it and had to cross the creek?" Her thin voice quavered.

"We didn't but even if we were still out there, we'd get wet. That's all."

Her gaze clung to him, full of disbelief.

"Auntie, are you scared?" Robbie asked.

The boy's words made her draw in a shuddering breath and Tanner could see her shoulders relax. "I'm okay now. Why don't you children change?"

The sound of the frightened horses carried on the wind.

"Will you be okay if I go check on the animals?" Tanner asked.

She scrubbed her lips together. "It's just rain." As if to prove her wrong, lightning turned the world outside to silvery white. A few seconds later, thunder shook the house. She shuddered.

"I'll stay." He'd turn the whole herd loose if it would erase the fear from her face.

She closed her eyes, perhaps in prayer, then sucked in a deep breath. "We're safe and dry inside. You do what you need to do."

"I'll be back in a minute." He pulled his hat low and ran into the rain to the corrals. The horses milled about, the whites of their eyes showing large. If only he'd spent more time with them since he brought them in, perhaps they'd be comforted by his presence. Nevertheless, he swung over the top plank and sat down. Not knowing what else to do, and aware it was the method many cowboys used to calm a herd of cows, he began to sing an old trail song. "'Whoopie ti yi yo, get along little dogies.'" He raised his voice as loud as he could.

It worked. The horses slowly settled down. The lightning moved down the hills away from them and the thunder grew more distant. The rain settled into a gentle patter.

He stopped singing and waited to see if the horses would grow agitated again. They didn't. He slipped to the ground and dashed across the muddy yard to the house.

Susanne stood in the same spot where he'd left her, facing the door. She exhaled loudly when he came in. "Is everything okay?"

"Right as—" He was about to say *rain*, which would have been the normal word to use. "Sunshine."

Recognizing the change in his word choice, she smiled. "You're soaked." She handed him a towel.

"I'll dry. But I'm dripping all over the floor."

"It's just water." She tipped her head and considered him. "Did I hear someone singing?"

"I don't know. Did you?" No one had ever suggested

he had a musical voice and he was somewhat embarrassed that she'd heard him.

"Ti yi yi," Robbie shouted. "You was singing to the horses."

He turned and saw the children sitting at the table. "They seemed to like it."

"Me, too." Robbie ran around the kitchen, half singing, half shouting "Ti yi yi" over and over.

Susanne uncrossed her arms and threw back her head as she laughed at Robbie.

For the first time since the storm had approached, the tension eased from Tanner's nerves.

They watched Robbie for a few moments. But Tanner's jeans were heavy with water and every time he moved his head, water dripped from his hat. "The storm has moved off and I better move off, as well."

She met his gaze. "Thank you for everything."

His eyebrows went up. "Everything?"

A smile teased her worried eyes. "The trip to town, getting us home safely and all that."

"My pleasure." More so than she would ever guess. "Goodbye."

The children clustered about him to say goodbye. Susanne stood in the open doorway as he returned to the buggy. "Goodbye," she called as he grabbed the reins. Reluctantly, he turned the buggy toward the ranch. He paused once to turn and wave and once more just before he rode out of sight.

She remained in the doorway watching.

That simple little fact warmed him all the way home.

Finally. Tanner was heading to the farm to work with his horses. He greeted the children, who ran toward him as he approached the house, but his eyes sought Susanne. He saw no sign of her. Was she ill? Had the storm yesterday given her a chill? "Where's your aunt?"

"In the barn." Frank pointed. "Trying to put a handle on a hoe. She's been trying for a long time but the hoe keeps falling off. She told us to go away because she was getting frustrated."

Tanner chuckled. "I'll go see how she's faring."

The children began to follow.

"Maybe you should stay back just in case."

Janie's lips trembled. "Is she going to get into trouble?"

He scooped up the child. "No, you little sweetheart, she isn't in trouble. But like Frank said, she might be a little frustrated."

Liz leaned close and whispered in his ear, "She was really, really frustrated. Said she might take the sledgehammer to the whole works. Then she said she couldn't because it was the only hoe she could find."

The grin that widened Tanner's mouth came from a place deep in his heart. "I'll see what I can do." What had happened to the other hoe they'd used when planting the garden? He knew the answer. One of the children had used it for something and not returned it. He'd look for it later.

He put Janie on her feet and strode into the barn. In the tack room that Frank had organized Susanne was bent over an anvil, a hammer in her hand. Strands of hair fell over her face as she tapped the sleeve of the hoe around the wooden handle. He stood back and watched her, enjoying the scene far more than he should.

She lifted the hoe, banged it on the floor. The handle and the head parted ways. "What is wrong with you?"

she said in an exasperated tone. "Why don't you stay together?"

"Maybe I can help?"

She squeaked and turned to him. "You frightened me. I didn't know you were here." Her eyes narrowed. "How long have you been standing there?"

He stepped into the little room and took the handle from her. "Long enough to see you need a lesson in putting a handle on a hoe." He decided it best not to ask how it got loose in the first place.

"It *looks* easy enough." She scooped up the head of the hoe and scowled at the offending tool.

"It's not difficult once you know what to do." He measured the shank on the head of the hoe, cut the tip of the handle so it would fit in properly, then jammed it into the hoe. "See these two holes? They're for securing the handle." He found two nails, pounded them through the holes and shook the hoe. "There. That's good and firm. Now I'll sharpen it for you." He took it to the grinder and sharpened the edge. "There you go."

She took it, jabbed at the floor and crowed with delight when it didn't fall apart. "Thank you. And about yesterday…" She leaned on the hoe and looked at him with a regretful expression. "I'm sorry to have made such a fuss about nothing."

"It wasn't nothing. You were frightened. I understand that."

"I can't seem to get over it even though I tell myself I'm being silly."

He brushed his knuckles along her cheeks, reveling in the smoothness of them. He caught a strand of runaway hair and tucked it behind her ear. "You have every reason to be afraid of water."

Her eyes clung to his with such hungry intensity that his hands grew still and he forgot to breathe. "I don't want to pass my fear on to the children."

What could he say? It wasn't as if her fears were irrational. He spoke the only words that came to his mind. "What do you think of when you see the waters of a river?"

"I think of what the people said who came to inform me that my mama and papa had drowned. They said the dark, turbulent waters had sucked them under. And I feel myself being sucked under."

"What would happen if you looked at something besides the waters?"

"Like what?"

"Well, the sun won't be shining if it's raining out." He thought of his own life. "When I was younger I used to touch the yoke of my ma's dress and it would drive away my fears. Do you have anything like that?"

"I have my mother's brooch."

"Would it work to think of that instead of the waters?"

"I don't know. I could try. I'm willing to try anything."

That settled and the hoe repaired, they headed for the door. The children still waited outside, each wearing an anxious expression. Liz studied her aunt, and when she saw the hoe in her hands, her face broke into a grin. "I guess it's okay to talk to you now."

Susanne hugged the child. "I'm sorry if I was short with you. Fixing a hoe handle is easy if you know how."

"Are you going to work on the horses now?" Frank asked. He jiggled from one foot to the other as if he couldn't wait for Tanner to get started.

"That's my plan."

"Can we watch?"

The horses were already used to the children so he couldn't see it would be a problem. "Sure."

He expected Susanne to object or to wander off with the repaired hoe, but she leaned it against the barn and joined the children at the fence. Unlike the children she watched him, not the horses, making the muscle in his legs move with awkward stiffness as he climbed into the pen. He tried not to be aware of her attention, knowing he needed to be completely focused on his task.

He meant to gentle-break the horses, teaching them to trust him and then obey him because of that trust. He'd work with them one-on-one, which meant guiding each one in turn into the smaller pen that Jim had built for that purpose. Pretty Lady was the most likely one to cooperate so he started with her, working her around and into the pen. She already associated him with food so he used it to get the horse to come to him.

All morning he worked at gentling and teaching the horse.

At noon, Susanne brought out some dinner even though he didn't expect it now that he was not working for her. But he sure did appreciate it. Almost as much as he enjoyed her company while he ate.

He worked all afternoon, pausing only to gratefully accept a drink of cold water and a handful of cookies, then resuming work until he knew he must leave or worry Maisie about being late.

When he went to the house to say goodbye, all he could think about was saying hello in the morning.

After a restless night he returned to continue working with Pretty Lady. Already she ate from his hand and let him pet her.

At noon, when Susanne brought him food, he climbed over the fence and sat against the barn with her at his side. "I saw you out in the garden. How's it looking?" He'd watched there, knew when she stopped to go inside to make dinner and waited eagerly for her to bring something out to him. He counted the seconds, which had mysteriously grown long and plodding.

"Little seedlings are popping through everywhere. And weeds, too, of course. I'm making good use of the hoe. I think of you every time I chop out a weed." She slanted him a look so full of teasing and something more that he choked.

She patted his back. "You okay?"

He downed water and nodded. "That sounds rather ominous." He threw his arms up as if to protect himself from her hoe.

She laughed and rubbed his arm. "Not those kinds of thoughts."

The world stood still. The seconds ceased to pass. His heart slowed. "Oh? What sort of thoughts, then?"

"Very nice thoughts." Her eyes shone with what could be teasing, but he hoped there might be something else in them. Perhaps a tiny bit of sweet regard for him. "I thought how nice it was of Tanner to help me plant the garden, to plant the crop when he wanted to be working with his horses. And then to fix a hoe so I could hack at weeds."

"Oh." Had he hoped for more? Something beyond the work he did?

"Maybe I thought, too, of how nice it was of you to show me the cathedral of trees and to take me to town." Her eyes darkened as all teasing fled. Her voice dropped to a whisper. "How nice it was to be held and comforted when I was afraid." She ducked her head. "And other stuff."

He laughed, not out of amusement but out of sheer joy. He knew what she meant by "other stuff." She meant their kiss. He cupped his hand over her neck. "Other stuff was nice, wasn't it?"

She nodded. "It was nice." Her eyes said things her mouth did not.

They looked deep into each other's eyes, searching probing, asking. He'd never felt more welcomed, more at home than right here at this moment.

Robbie's laughter brought them back to the everyday things of life.

She gathered up the dishes and returned to the house and he returned to the horses. As he stepped over the corral fence, his mind was still reeling, his heart still pounding. He wondered if Susanne experienced the same powerful feelings he had.

All he knew for certain was that he would never be the same old Tanner after today.

Susanne had said more than she should have. But she didn't regret it. Her regard for Tanner had grown steadily and surely since the first day she saw him. Life would not be the same ever again.

"Auntie, what did you want me to do with these?"

She looked up toward the house and saw Liz in the yard holding two sheets, waiting for Susanne to remember that she'd asked the girl to bring them. They each had tears and she wanted to mend them. Normally she'd sit at the table to work, but not today. "It's so nice out I believe I'll sit outside."

Liz didn't appear to think the idea strange and helped Susanne carry out a chair and the mending basket. From where Susanne sat against the house, she could see the corrals and caught fleeting glimpses of Tanner as he worked with the horses. Frank, too, watched him, though his attention was dedicated and constant. She knew the boy meant to become a rancher someday and likely would capture his own wild horses. He couldn't learn from anyone better than Tanner.

She cast a glance around the farm. The little ones, who had grown bored with watching the horses, played in the trees. Liz had wandered down the trail and sat on a fallen tree, relishing her solitude.

Susanne sighed as a sense of peace settled about her.

It was, however, short-lived.

Later that afternoon, after she'd taken Tanner a plate of food and shared a few secret glances, his dark eyes clinging to hers for several seconds, she'd returned to her mending chores. She'd barely done any stitching when Liz rushed to her side.

"Auntie, someone's coming."

Susanne glanced down the trail. The rider was too far away for her to recognize, but only one man ever rode up from that direction. Alfred Morris. Perhaps he'd see she was busy and leave her alone. At least Tanner was nearby if the man should get too direct in his advances.

"Liz, stay with Janie and Robbie. Keep them away while I talk to our visitor." She gripped the needle between her fingers so tightly it would leave a mark. What would she have to do to make Mr. Morris realize she was not interested in having him calling on her?

Not that he'd ever asked her permission. He simply took it for granted she would comply with his decrees. Little did he realize she had done all the complying she meant to do while under Aunt Ada's roof.

She carefully wove the needle into the fabric of Frank's shirt where she'd been mending a tear. Perhaps for safety's sake it would be better not to have the needle in her hand.

Mr. Morris rode up slowly, inspecting every inch of the farm with his narrowed eyes. His gaze lingered at the corrals where Frank sat. No doubt the man could also see Tanner at work. Not that it was any of his concern.

He stopped ten feet from where she sat and swung off his horse. He meticulously tied the reins to the hitching post and rubbed his hands together. For what reason? she wondered, the muscles in her neck twitching. There was something about that gesture that filled her with tension.

"Good day to you." He touched the brim of his hat without removing it. Again she found it disturbing that he saw no need to show her that little courtesy.

"Good day to you, Mr. Morris. What brings you our way?" She congratulated herself on sounding neighborly.

"I've come to visit. And to again point out how foolish it is for you to stay out here alone."

"I have four children. I'd hardly say I'm alone." She stayed seated. She did not invite him inside; nor did she mean to bring a chair out and encourage him to sit for a spell.

"The children can do little to protect you."

"I don't expect them to. I mean to protect *them* if a need should arise."

He rubbed his hands up and down the sides of his legs. "Your position is so desperate you are forced to accept the help of a half-breed."

So that's what this was about. She sat up straighter and faced him squarely. "I am not 'forced,' as you seem to think. I choose to accept his help."

"At what price? Surely he expects something in return."

How dare he make such a suggestion? Anger flared deep within her and she tamped it into submission.

"I see you understand my meaning." He took her silence for something other than anger. Perhaps he thought she was sorry, regretted her decision, perhaps even that she was afraid. "No man is so noble and self-sacrificing to do the amount of work he's done in planting the crop and not expect something in return." He closed the distance between them until she felt crowded. Trapped. "Susanne, he will have certain expectations. And how will you prevent him from exacting payment?"

Expectations. The word reverberated through her heart. How often had Aunt Ada told her that every kindness had a cost? So often the words echoed inside her head, causing her to falter. But she knew better than to think they applied to Tanner.

"No." She spoke firmly. "It's not that way at all. Some men *are* noble. Some men have principles and live by them. Tanner is such a man."

"He's a half-breed!" He spoke the word with such bitterness she shivered. "Have you no idea of the cruelty of the Indians? Why look at what happened to Colonel Custer!"

Before she could bark out a retort, he leaned over her, forcing her to lean even farther back in her chair to maintain a safe distance between them.

"Susanne," he ground out, his breath hot on her skin, his eyes flashing, "hear me and hear me good. No woman I mean to marry will entertain the likes of that man. A half-breed. I order you to put an end to him coming here."

She sprang to her feet forcing him to back up, shooting him her fiercest, most defiant look.

He scowled, not liking it.

"You can't order me about. I am not your wife. Nor will I ever be." Arms akimbo, she took another step at him and knew a moment of triumph when he backed away. "I suggest you ride out. And don't bother coming here again."

He glowered at her, but she did not relent, instead challenging him with her narrowed eyes. After a few, interminable seconds his face darkened and he grabbed his horse. But rather than mount up and ride out, he crossed to the corrals.

"Get lost, kid," she heard him say to Frank.

Alfred Morris climbed over the fence and dropped out of sight into the corral where Tanner worked.

Chapter Sixteen

Tanner had watched the man ride into the yard and recognized him immediately. He'd run into Alfred Morris a few times in town. All very unpleasant encounters. With his cruel and cutting comments, Morris had made it clear he hated anyone with Indian blood.

Apparently, too, the man had a hard time getting a message through his skull. Susanne had asked him not to return to her farm, but here he was again.

Tanner ground his teeth together to think that such an odious man would think he could court Susanne. A woman like her would have nothing to do with a man like him.

Tanner's opinion of Mr. Morris didn't change when he ordered Frank to get lost.

Mr. Morris stepped over the fence and dropped into the pen, sending Pretty Lady into frightened retreat to the far corner.

Tanner positioned himself between the horse and the man, hoping the horse would realize he meant to guard her.

"You." Mr. Morris jabbed his finger toward Tanner. "Who do you think you are?"

"I *know* who I am." Tanner shrugged. "Do you need me to tell you? I'm Tanner Harding, eldest son of the Lakota woman Seena and Big Sam Harding, of the Sundown Ranch. The biggest ranch in the area. Maybe you hadn't noticed."

The man's nostrils widened and he breathed hard. "I don't care who you are."

Tanner shrugged again. Too bad it wasn't true.

"Have you any idea what you being here is doing to Miss Collins's reputation? Why, why…" He tossed his hands upward. "You might as well paint her red."

Which was the color Tanner saw. "Red?" Did he refer to him, a redskin? His fists tightened. His jaw muscles bunched into a knot.

"Yes, you fool. That's how people will view her when they learn that she's been keeping company with you. Why, you should have heard the rumble after you escorted her to town." The man's beady eyes grew even more narrow. "People even saw her in your arms down by the river." The man seemed to vibrate with rage. "Who is going to consider marrying her when they learn she's been escorted about the country by a half-breed? You dishonor the lady."

They stared at each other, Tanner's eyes, no doubt, as full of fire as the smaller man's.

He could thrash the man for the way he besmirched Susanne's name. But he knew to do so would only give Morris more reason to think poorly of both Tanner and Susanne.

"If you were half a man you'd leave this place while her reputation can perhaps be salvaged." With a muttered oath, he climbed the fence, swung to his horse and galloped away.

Tanner's insides churned. Much as he might want to deny it, there was some truth to Mr. Morris's rant. No doubt Tanner's presence on the farm tarnished Susanne's reputation. Should he, in fact, ride away? His head and his heart went to war, a battle raging between what he thought he should do and what he wanted to do. He didn't know which would win.

One thing was certain. He could not stay here right now, could not hope to gentle his horses when anger and pain filled him. He needed to calm himself.

He swung over the fence, saddled Scout and rode away without a backward look.

He would not return until he had his thoughts sorted out.

The children remained at the window long past the morning hour Tanner usually arrived, despite Susanne's urgings they come away.

She saw silent tears drip down Janie's face and off her chin. The child had cried herself to sleep last night because he hadn't said goodbye.

"He'll come back," Frank said over and over as they watched out the window.

Liz said nothing, but she held Janie and, every once in a while, wiped her eyes.

Another half hour passed before Robbie jumped from the chair and kicked one of its legs. "I'm going out to play."

Frank sighed as he turned to Susanne. "I better see that the horses have water." Nothing said they all knew he wasn't coming more than those few words.

"Come on, Janie, let's go look for flowers." Liz perched her little sister on one hip and shut the door behind them.

Finally, Susanne was alone and could give way to her fears. Whatever Mr. Morris said to Tanner it was cruel enough, vicious enough to drive him away. No doubt the man had made Tanner regret who he was.

Susanne closed her eyes and groaned. Little did he know that he was exactly what she wanted and needed. But she'd failed at convincing him. Would she get another chance?

Please, God, let me see him again.

She looked about the kitchen. She needed to keep her hands busy and her thoughts diverted from missing him. The big pantry needed a good cleaning. In a few minutes, she had everything pulled out and set about scrubbing the shelves and walls with hot water.

While the wood dried, she sorted out the items she'd pulled out. The food items she'd put back, and the odds and ends she'd put in another place. Like the handful of screws and nails. Jim had gotten careless about keeping organized in the past couple of years. She understood so well how Alice's illness and death had left him struggling. She felt much the same way now. Without Tanner, what did it matter if the cupboard was clean, the items organized?

Only her rigid training under Aunt Ada enabled her to continue while her heart hemorrhaged pain.

The door flew open and her heart jumped for joy. He'd come. She'd known he would. But when she spun around, her heart sank. It was not Tanner but her two nieces standing there holding out a bouquet of wildflowers. She forced a light to her voice that she did not feel. "I see you found lots of flowers."

"We would have found more," Liz replied as she filled a jar with water and put in the flowers, "except there's a storm coming."

Susanne rushed to look out the door. Thick black clouds rolled in waves across the sky and a cold wind battered the house. She'd been so lost in thought she hadn't noticed. "Boys," she yelled. "Come to the house."

Frank stepped from the barn and closed the door behind him. As he trotted across the yard, lightning flashed and thunder rolled. She wanted nothing more than to close the door behind her and block her ears to the sounds. But she was missing one child.

"Robbie. Robbie." She called again and again, but Robbie didn't come.

She closed the door. "Is he in the house?" He might have slipped in while her head was in the cupboard.

Frank and Liz searched the rooms. "He's not here."

The rain had begun, slashing against the house. The lightning and thunder intensified.

"I'll go look for him." Frank headed for the door.

"No. I'll go." Her teeth chattered and not because she was cold. "You stay here. Do not go out for any reason, you hear?"

"We hear," Liz replied on the children's behalf.

Susanne put on Jim's old black slicker, which covered her clear to the ground, and pulled the waterproof hood around her head. It might protect her from the rain, but what would protect her from the storm?

She thought of bits and pieces of verses she had memorized years ago. *Thou hast been a refuge from the storm... Thou wilt keep him in perfect peace whose mind is stayed on Thee: because he trusteth in Thee.* The words became a litany in her mind.

The last time she saw Robbie he was playing in his favorite spot among the trees. *Oh, God, don't let him be struck by lightning.*

She ducked her head and tried to run to the spot, but the long slicker caught about her legs and she was forced to slow down to a jog.

"Robbie, are you here?" she called out over the wind that roared through the leaves. The lightning blinded her and the thunder sent her heart into erratic beating. But still she searched. To no avail. She returned to the barn and looked in every nook and corner. No Robbie.

She searched the corrals, every bush, and still did not find him.

She returned to the house. "Did he come back?"

Three pairs of eyes filled with tears. "He's not here," Frank managed.

"What was he doing? Where was he when any of you last saw him?"

"Maybe he went to the creek," Frank replied, his voice thick with fear. "He kept talking about those gold rocks."

Susanne closed her eyes and forced herself to take slow, calming breaths though they failed entirely at their aim. The creek. It was the last place in the world she wished to go in the midst of a rain storm. Dark, turbulent waters reaching for her, pulling her under, suffocating her.

What had Tanner said? Think of something else. She shrugged out of the slicker and went to her bedroom. With trembling fingers she pinned her mother's brooch to her dress. *I will think of your smile, how much you believed in me and loved me. Most of all, I will remem-*

ber how you taught me about God. How He will never leave me or forsake me.

She returned to the kitchen, pulled on the dripping slicker once again. "Stay here until I get back."

"Are you going to the creek?" Frank asked.

"It seems the most likely place to look."

Liz sobbed and Janie clung to her sister. Susanne reached out to hug them, repeating her command. "You stay inside and keep safe."

Frank followed her to the door. "You'll be okay?" He sounded so much like Jim that her heart felt new grief at her brother's loss.

She patted his cheek. "I'll be back when I find Robbie." She stepped out into the storm. It had not lessened while she was indoors. If anything it raged even worse. She pressed her hand to the brooch on her chest and walked into the storm.

It was two miles to the creek. Two miles of slashing rain, blinding flashes of lightning and deafening thunder that rolled from one clap to the next. Two miles of canvas slicker slapping at her legs and slippery mud pulling at her feet. Two miles of fear and prayer. But she kept going. She had to find her nephew.

Tanner watched the storm approach and wished he had gone to the farm despite the continued turmoil of his thoughts. His brothers noticed his frame of mind and at first had teased him. But now they watched him out of the corner of their eyes.

Maisie had asked why he didn't go to the farm. He'd only said he had other things to do. Then he'd had to dream up something that might look important. Trimming and cleaning Scout's hooves had to do as an excuse.

Now he stood in the open barn door and watched the threatening black clouds. Susanne would be frightened by the heavy rain that was no doubt coming. Would she be okay?

His nerves twitched.

All his life he'd believed words such as Mr. Morris spoke. Believed he should stay away from nice white girls. But Susanne was different. She never made him feel anything but acceptance.

He smiled despite his concerns. She'd kissed him and almost came right out and said she'd enjoyed it. That didn't sound as if she thought he might be a danger to her reputation.

Lost in thought, he didn't hear Levi and Johnny until they joined him in the doorway.

"Lots of lightning and thunder," Levi said.

"Going to be quite a storm," Johnny added.

"Your horses going to stay put in this?" Levi gave Tanner a hard look.

"They'll be some riled, I think." He made up his mind in a flash. "I better get over there and calm them down."

"You need help?"

It was on the tip of his tongue to say no, but the horses really would need calming and so would Susanne. He couldn't be both places. "Wouldn't mind."

In a matter of minutes the three of them were mounted and racing toward the farm. They'd just made it off the ranch when the sky opened up in a deluge. Wind-driven rain slashed at them, but they pulled their hats lower and rode on.

The horses were milling about, frantic in the storm when they arrived.

"I'm going to check on the family." Tanner barely waited for his feet to hit the ground before he turned toward the house. "The horses like singing," he hollered to his brothers.

He didn't bother knocking, instead throwing open the door and stepping inside. As soon as the children saw him, they rushed to his side, hugging him despite his wet clothes and talking at once. He couldn't make out what they said except for two words—*Susanne* and *Robbie*.

"Slow down. One of you tell me what's going on."

"I will." Frank stepped back, drew in a deep breath and fired out an explanation. "We couldn't find Robbie. I think he might have gone to the creek to find those gold rocks he thought he saw. Auntie Susanne went to find him."

Completely at a loss for words, Tanner stared at the boy.

"She's been gone a long time," Frank added.

She'd gone to the creek! The creek that would now be swollen with the heavy rain from farther up the mountains.

"I'll find her." He bolted from the house. At the corrals he called to the others and explained his plan. "The children are in the house but they're okay for now."

Johnny squeezed Tanner's shoulder. "You go find her. I'll take care of the horses and Levi will keep an eye on the childr—"

Tanner was on his horse before Johnny finished and he raced toward the creek.

The dark clouds turned the day to dusk and he

strained to see through the rain, hoping, praying he would encounter Susanne and Robbie before he reached the stream.

He didn't.

At the creek he reined to a stop. The waters had risen as he expected but he didn't see Susanne or Robbie anywhere.

He bellowed their names. All that came back to him was the sound of rushing water. Upstream or down? Which way was the correct one? He had no way of knowing. All he knew for certain was that Susanne would be cold, wet and very frightened. If Robbie had gone into the water…

He couldn't finish the thought.

But if Susanne had seen him she would have gone after him despite her fear.

He'd ride downstream. "Please, God, let me find them safe and sound."

He guided Scout along the bank, peering into the turbulent waters, which had already risen at least two feet. The lazy little creek was now a raging torrent. He rode onward, leaning over the saddle horn, calling their names over and over.

Nothing. He might have swallowed a hundred knives so sharp was the pain ripping through his insides. A couple of miles downstream he encountered a tangle of bushes. To spare Scout, he dismounted and pushed his way through the branches until he reached the edge of the creek. He scanned to his right and left.

He saw nothing but water, rain and dripping leaves.

The place was nothing like the cathedral of trees but for the first time in many years he felt a desperate need to call upon God. He lifted his face into the rain, letting it pelt his skin. "God in heaven, please help me find them and keep them safe." He shuddered at the possibility of finding them otherwise. He remained with his face heavenward for several minutes until a calm peace filled him. He would find them. He had to believe that.

He pushed forward through the rest of the bushes. "Susanne. Robbie. Can you hear me?"

He strained for the possibility of a voice answering him in the storm.

At the edge of the trees he whistled for Scout and remounted. Slowly, afraid he would miss them in the poor visibility, he rode onward, his complete attention on the waters though he hoped not to see anything there unless it was Susanne and Robbie clinging to a rock or a branch.

Scout tossed his head and refused to move.

"What's wrong, old pal?" His horse must have noticed something amiss and Tanner sat up to look about. He saw nothing but a big rock a distance from the creek and a trickle of mud running from the nearby trail.

He blinked. In the rain it seemed the rock had moved. He knew it was only a distortion from the rain but, nevertheless, he was desperate enough to find hope in anything and nudged Scout in that direction.

The rock moved again and this time he knew he wasn't imagining it. Then a boy sat up. Tanner was off his horse and hit the ground running. "Robbie." He hugged the boy, then wiped his hands over Robbie's face. "You're okay."

"Auntie Susanne." Robbie pointed toward Susanne, lying in a heap on the ground. Wrapped in a black slicker, he had mistaken her for a rock.

Tanner set the boy aside and bent over her. He touched

his fingers to her neck but felt no pulse. His own stopped, too. Then he caught the faintest thread of her heartbeat. "She's alive." Her skin was like ice. Slowly, tenderly, fearfully, he rolled her over and pressed his hand to her chest hoping and praying to feel it rise and fall. When he did, he almost collapsed over her in gratitude.

"We have to get her home," he said to Robbie who hovered at his shoulder. He scooped her into his arms and struggled onto Scout's back. He reached down and took Robbie's hand and pulled him up to ride behind him. "Now hang on. We're going home."

He climbed to the trail and kept the horse to a steady canter. He dared not go any faster for fear Robbie would fall off. With his arms full of a cold, still Susanne, he rode directly to the house, not stopping until he was close enough to kick at the door.

Levi opened it. "What's wrong with you? Oh." He saw Tanner's hands were full and lifted Robbie from the horse. He handed the young boy to Frank, then steadied Tanner as he dismounted and carried Susanne inside.

Liz stared at them. "Is Auntie Susanne—" She couldn't finish.

"She's alive but cold," Tanner answered.

He issued orders. "Levi, throw more wood in the stove. Liz, get some blankets. Frank, see to your brother. Janie, find some dry clothes for Robbie."

Then he lowered himself onto a chair, his arms still cradling Susanne. He tossed back the hood and pushed away the wet strands of hair that clung to her face. Slowly he eased the big black slicker from her shoulders. She was soaked to the skin. He would have taken all her clothes off but, mindful of the children and Susanne's reputation, he hesitated.

He sent Levi a helpless look. "We need to get her wet things off. Any suggestions?"

Liz returned with a stack of blankets. "I can do it."

Tanner gently lowered Susanne to a blanket the girl placed in front of the stove, then he and Levi held up another blanket to provide a curtain. "Let me know if you need any help." He clenched his fists at feeling so helpless.

Liz bent to her task and after a bit of grunting said, "I am done. I've put her dressing gown on and a blanket over her."

Tanner bent over Susanne, Levi hovering at his side. Her skin was cold and white, her lips bluish, her breathing shallow. "What should we do? Warm her up fast or slow? Rub her to restore circulation? You know more about these things than I do." Levi often took care of Maisie when she was ill. "Shouldn't she be coming to?"

Levi rubbed the back of his neck. "I don't know for sure. I think we should warm her up slowly and wait and see."

"I don't much care for the wait and see thing."

Levi gave him a sympathetic look. "It's the best I can offer."

The children clustered around. Robbie's skin was pale though he was now in dry clothes. Still, Tanner wrapped him in blanket and held him. The boy was like a block of ice.

"I's scared," Janie said. Tanner made room for her on his lap beside Robbie. The two older ones sat on either side of him.

"Is she going to be okay?" Liz asked.

"I hope so."

"We should pray," she said. "That's what Auntie Susanne would do."

Levi raised his eyebrows, well aware that Tanner struggled with believing God heard him.

Maybe later, Tanner would explain that his faith had changed since he'd met Susanne. It had grown and flourished. "We should certainly pray." He bowed his head. "Father God in heaven, thank You for helping me find Susanne and Robbie. Thank You for bringing them home alive. Now please hear our prayers and make Susanne well and strong again. Amen."

"Amen," Levi said, and the look he gave Tanner was full of both surprise and pleasure.

It was nice to leave his little brother guessing from time to time.

They sat in silence, watching Susanne, until Levi asked, "Where did you find her?"

"About a mile downstream. I almost missed her." Tanner gave the details of his discovery.

"What happened? How did she get so far away?"

A shudder snaked across Tanner's shoulders at how easily he could have missed them. "I don't know."

"I was stuck on a rock in the water." Robbie's voice quavered. "The water was deep and scary. Auntie Susanne walked into the water to get me." He choked back a sob. "She tried to carry me to the dry ground, but she fell." He buried his face against Tanner's chest, and Tanner rubbed his back and made soothing sounds.

He wished someone would do the same for him. To think of them both struggling in the dark, turbulent waters turned his insides icy. "Then what happened?"

"We kept falling down. Auntie Susanne kept getting up. We got to the side and she pushed me out of the water." He turned wide, frightened eyes to Tanner.

Tanner's heart ached at the way the boy sought comfort and so much more from him.

"She fell back in." Robbie's whispered words were barely audible. "Then she got out. Is she going to die?"

Tanner could not say and would not offer false hope. But if she didn't, what would he do? She'd given him so much—acceptance, a sense of family and belonging, and restored faith in God's love and care. Would all that disappear if she didn't survive?

No. It would dishonor all she had done and all she stood for if he returned to the Tanner he'd been a few short weeks ago.

"She moved!"

At Liz's announcement, he jumped. He put both the younger children to the side and went up on his knees to watch Susanne. She moved again, and coughed. It was the most pleasant sound he'd ever heard. Her eyelids fluttered.

The children scooted closer to their aunt and he leaned over her. "Susanne, say something." He squeezed her hand where it lay beneath the blanket. "Say something."

Her eyes opened. "Robbie?" she croaked.

"He's here." He pulled the boy closer so she could see him. "He's fine. Just fine."

She nodded and her eyes closed again.

Liz sobbed. "She's not waking up."

Frank stood behind Levi, his expression hard, as if preparing for the worst.

Tanner had to reassure them. "She did wake up. That's a good sign. I expect she is very tired." He tucked the blanket up under her chin. "And she's still cold. It will take time."

Levi got to his feet. "Have any of you eaten?"

"No," Liz answered for all of them.

"You know what we should do," Levi said. "We should make a big pot of soup so when your aunt wakes up she can have something hot to eat. Who would like to help me?"

None of them moved, then Liz heaved herself to her feet. "I'll help. So will the others."

Between Levi and Liz they soon had each of the children doing some task. Tanner would have helped too, but he did not want to leave Susanne's side or let go of her hand.

Several times he felt Levi studying him. He ignored his brother. He cared not that his feelings were so obvious. All that mattered at the moment was praying for Susanne to waken and staying at her side until she did.

She moaned and stirred, and he leaned over her. "Susanne, wake up."

She swallowed hard. Her eyelids fluttered half-open several times before she saw him and focused on his eyes. "How did I get here?" She could barely speak.

Levi handed Tanner a cup. "It's warm, sweet tea. It will help her."

Tanner slipped an arm about her shoulders and helped her sit up. He held the cup to her lips and let her drink.

"That's better," she said. "How did I get here?" she asked again.

"I found you."

Her blue eyes clung to him, unreadable. Then she

smiled and he saw gratitude come to life in them. "I'm glad."

The children clustered around her, touching her, patting her.

"You're okay?" Frank asked as he knelt at her side, his hand on her shoulder.

"I'll be fine." She pulled her other hand from under the covers and patted the boy's cheek.

Tears dripped down Liz's cheeks. "I was so worried."

Susanne cupped her hand to Liz's face. "I'm sorry to frighten you."

Robbie rocked back and forth on his knees. "It's all my fault."

She pulled him close and kissed his cheek. "All that matters is you are safe and sound." And then she reached for Janie and kissed her. "All of you are safe and sound." Her voice shook and Tanner knew the effort of comforting the children had exhausted her.

"Levi, why don't you give these children each a bowl of soup?"

Levi nodded, his eyes saying he understood what Tanner wanted. "Come along, all of you. Let's see if our joint efforts made a good soup."

Frank didn't go directly to the table. He slipped into the other room and returned with a wooden rocking chair. He put it beside the stove. "For when Auntie Susanne wants to sit up."

"Thank you," she whispered, then turned to Tanner. "Would you help me?"

The words were no sooner out than he tucked the blanket around her and lifted her to the chair. He stood awkwardly at her side. What did he do now?

She slipped her hand into his. "Stay here with me."

Levi shoved a kitchen chair in Tanner's direction and Tanner sat beside Susanne, her small cold hand in his. Nothing had ever felt so good and right.

Johnny tapped on the door, then entered. "The storm is over. The horses are calm. How are things here?" He studied Susanne, lowered his gaze to the clasped hands and looked about the table. "Good. Everyone is safely home."

Levi filled a bowl and indicated Johnny should sit.

Even from where he sat Tanner could see Janie eyeing Johnny curiously. She shifted her attention to Levi and then to Tanner. What was going on in her little head?

She again looked at Levi. "Mr. Tanner is our friend."

Levi grinned. "Can I be, as well?"

The child nodded. "Okay." She turned her wide blue eyes on Johnny.

"I'd be honored if you'd let me be your friend, too," Johnny said.

She nodded, then ducked her head, returning to her soup.

Susanne squeezed Tanner's hand and he turned to her. She smiled. "Janie likes having friends." She lowered her voice. "So do I."

He couldn't pull his gaze from her. Didn't even try. Friends? It sounded fine. Was it all she wanted? Was it enough for him?

Several hours later, Tanner and his brothers rode toward home. He had no choice but to leave Susanne even though he wanted nothing more than to stay and make sure she was okay. They'd remained until she had eaten soup and had moved about the kitchen a time or two. She was tired, but she assured them she would be fine.

They'd had to say goodbye in a public way. Her hands had clung to his and his to hers. Their gazes had gone on and on until Johnny cleared his throat. Then Tanner had reluctantly released her and bade them all goodbye one more time.

Levi rode close to Tanner's side. "You obviously care about that gal and she for you. Have you told her of your feelings?"

"Why would I do that? The last thing she needs is to be associated with me." He told his brothers how the ladies in town had acted and about Mr. Morris visiting and his words of warning.

Johnny grunted. "How did Susanne handle it?"

He chuckled as the memory sweetened his insides. "She as much as told the ladies she didn't care what they thought. She said I was honorable and noble."

Johnny slapped his thigh and chortled. "The gal's a keeper for sure."

"Mr. Morris has a point, though," Tanner said. "I'll be branding her with the same intolerance I face if I continue to hang around her."

Levi made a scolding noise. "Tanner, there will always be people like those ladies and like Mr. Morris. You can ignore them, but why would you ignore someone who looks at you like Susanne does? What do you have to lose by telling her how you feel?"

He didn't explain that he might lose the friendship she'd freely offered. Was it worth risking that in order to tell her what filled his heart?

Chapter Seventeen

Susanne sat wearily in the rocking chair. Tanner and his brothers were gone. She'd assured them she would be fine on her own though she dreaded being alone.

But they couldn't stay all night.

She appreciated good neighbors, and still she wanted more. Not from Levi and Johnny, though they had been helpful and kind. No. She didn't mind saying goodbye to them, but saying it to Tanner about sucked the life from her.

She wanted to be able to hold his hand anytime she needed a touch, to feel his arms about her when she wanted comfort. She wanted to share a "good morning" upon waking and a secret smile over the children's antics. She wanted someone to be there to hear her deepest fears and wildest dreams.

She loved him and wanted him to love her in return. But would he ever believe love was possible between himself, a man he identified as a half-breed, and herself, a lonely, longing white woman?

Almost overcome with exhaustion, she let Frank and

Liz settle the younger two in bed, dragged her weary body to her room and crawled under the covers.

Please, God, let him see he's everything I want and need.

He's handsome, strong, noble and...

Her prayer went unfinished as sleep claimed her.

She felt sore all over and a little weak when she rose the next morning. But it was nothing that wouldn't improve with time. Unlike the emptiness inside as she wondered if Tanner would come back. Almost certainly he would, but would he pretend he didn't care? Or was it pretense? A thousand uncertainties tumbled about in her mind.

"I'll look after Daisy," Frank said, and she let him tether the milk cow for the day.

The sun had burned off the early morning mist. Puddles glistened in the yard. A pungent odor rose from the pens where Tanner's horses contentedly ate grass.

It promised to be a hot, humid day.

And a lonely one.

Tanner had not come. She'd given up looking for him to ride over the hill. Perhaps he was never coming again.

One of the horses whinnied. The animals would bring him back even if he cared not enough for her to return.

It was Sunday so she held a quiet service with the children. Afterward, to keep busy, she selected a book from the shelf in the other room and sat down to read it.

"Auntie, Auntie," Liz called as she rushed indoors. "Look. They're coming." She pointed out the window.

Susanne joined her niece. Three riders were approaching from the direction of Sundown Ranch. Even from this distance, she recognized Tanner. The other two had to be his brothers. Her heart sank. Had they come to take away the horses? If so, Tanner would not have a reason to return.

She turned away, but she couldn't remember what she had been doing. Unable to remain still, she took a mixing bowl and set it on the cupboard though she had no idea what she meant to do with it.

The hoofbeats of the animals drew closer.

Men called good-morning to the three children outside, then Liz opened the door. "Good morning."

Tanner's voice returned her greeting. It was echoed by his brothers.

Then he said, "Good morning, Susanne. How are you feeling?"

"Fine, thanks." She kept her eyes on the mixing bowl, unable to bring herself to look at him. She did not want to see the goodbye he hadn't yet voiced.

"I'll see to the horses." Johnny's boots thudded away.

"Come on, kids. Show me around." Levi left with the children talking rapid fire to him.

That left only Tanner. "Susanne, what's wrong?"

She sucked in a strengthening breath and brought her gaze to him, shooing away any emotion. "Nothing. Thank you again for rescuing us yesterday, though I can't recall any of the details." She shuddered as she remembered the dark swirling waters and how Jim's slicker had weighed her down. She'd pinned Ma's brooch to this dress and touched it now. "I remembered what you said about thinking of something else. This brooch was my ma's. I pinned it to my dress and thought how my parents would want me to be brave."

He closed the distance between them and caught her

shoulders. "You were very brave." The words caught in his throat. "And you frightened me more than I want to think about."

Their gazes filled with emotion. Her heart overran with longing.

"Are you up to a little walk?" he asked.

She nodded. She'd find the strength to follow him to the moon and back.

He took her hand and led her from the house. He kept hold of her as he led her past the corrals, past the pens, past the pasture where Daisy was tethered. They climbed a little hill, past a colorful riot of flowers scattered up and down the slope, and stopped at a copse of trees. They ducked under the shade of a big quaking aspen. With warm, claiming hands, he caught her shoulders and turned her to face him.

His look went on and on, searching the deep, most secret places of her heart.

She let him see everything, including her love for him. Would he read her emotions correctly and respond as she hoped?

He smiled. "I'm so happy you're okay."

She smiled back. "Me, too."

He trailed a finger along her cheek, his eyes following its path. He touched her bottom lip, sending shivers throughout her body.

"Susanne," he whispered, his voice husky and tentative, "I must say something even though I know it puts our friendship at risk."

Her heart stalled. She didn't have the strength to hear the words she feared he was about to utter. *No, don't tell me you want to leave.*

He caught her chin and tipped her head so she faced

him. She fought the need to look into his eyes, fearful of what she'd see there. But she could not resist. She gazed at him and his eyes overflowed with a longing that echoed in her heart.

Could it be that he returned her feelings?

"Susanne, I know you might find the idea of loving a man like me beyond your imagination, but I must say it anyway. I love you."

A thousand joys erupted in her heart. To know the love of such a man fulfilled a dream that had lingered since she was orphaned. The dream she'd only recently acknowledged was to be loved so much her heart overflowed.

But she must stop him from his disclaimer. She pressed her fingers to his mouth before he could tell her again how he was a half-breed and she couldn't possibly love him. "Tanner Harding, it is a great honor to be loved by a noble man such as yourself."

He drank up her words.

She had more to give him. Words and love that would hopefully fill his need. "I love you from the depths of my heart. I love you more than words can ever say. I love you with every breath I take. You're my first thought when I waken and my last when I fall asleep."

"You love me?"

"I love you."

He whooped so loud she was certain those back at the farm could hear him. He grabbed her around the waist and danced them in a crazy, dizzying circle as he laughed.

Then he sobered and set her down, his arms still encircling her. A look of doubt clouded his eyes. "Susanne Collins, will you marry me?"

She chuckled. "It would be my great honor to marry you. Just so long as you remember I come with four children."

He tipped his head back and laughed. "I wouldn't have it any other way. I love them like they were my own."

She knew it to be true.

He sobered and his expression grew serious. He shifted his attention from her eyes to her mouth and back again. "May I kiss you?"

She was honored that he asked. "I was beginning to think you never would." She lifted her face to him and he claimed her lips in a sweet, promising gesture. She wrapped her arms about his waist, pressed her palms to his back, thrilled at the strength she felt. He cupped the back of her head and prolonged the kiss, until she lost all sense of time and space and floated on a cloud of joy and belonging.

It was like coming home after a very long and lonely journey.

After a sweet time of enjoying their newly confessed love, Tanner and Susanne returned to the house. Several times Tanner resisted the urge to pinch himself to see if he was really awake. It seemed he'd ached for this kind of love and acceptance all his life. But there was one more hurdle to cross.

"I need to talk to the children and make sure they are okay with us."

Susanne grew serious. "I would never do anything to upset them."

He squeezed her hand. "Nor would I. I love them too much."

"I know."

They paused outside the door. He silently prayed for God to bring them all together in their love.

Janie pulled the door open to study them. "You look different."

A grin split Tanner's face. "You are very observant. Come here." He lifted her in his arms. "All of you." He sat down and waited as they clustered around him. "I love your aunt."

Janie giggled and Robbie looked embarrassed.

Tanner continued. "I want to marry her and help her raise all of you. What do you think?" He hardly dared breathe. He knew neither he nor Susanne would want to go ahead without the children's approval.

"I think, yes." Janie wrapped her arms about his neck.

"Me, too." Robbie climbed to Tanner's knee and patted his chest.

"Liz?" Tanner asked.

The girl grinned. "I'd like that very much." She reached around her younger sister and brother to hug him.

"Frank?" He needed all of them to give their approval.

Frank studied him seriously a moment. "It's okay with me so long as you always treat Aunt Susanne properly."

Tanner respected the boy's grown-up concern. "I promise I will and I trust you to tell me if I'm not." He held out a hand to Frank. "Agreed?"

Frank grinned as he took Tanner's hand. "Glad to see you two finally figured out what we could all see."

"We've been praying for this," Liz said, and the other children nodded.

His heart overflowing with love and gratitude, he met Susanne's gaze, finding in her look and in the acceptance of the children all he'd ever want for the rest of his life.

Epilogue

Three weeks later

Some might have wondered at how quickly Tanner and Susanne decided to get married, but neither of them cared what others might think. Susanne saw no need to wait and told Tanner so. "I can't bear to say goodbye to you day after day." She hadn't thought it was possible for her feelings to increase, but every day her heart expanded to hold more of their love.

He saw no need to wait, either. "I worry about you at the farm alone. Charlie is still prowling about. I know he won't bother you when he's sober, but he's not sober very often."

Charlie had thankfully not returned.

Having agreed not to wait any longer, they'd planned the perfect wedding. Susanne could hardly believe the day had finally arrived. She was fussing over the children when she heard a buggy pull up to the house.

Levi opened the door. "Are you all ready?"

"We are." The children wore their best outfits and Susanne wore her best dress.

"Did you get it?" she asked Levi. She'd enlisted his help to do something special for her wedding outfit.

"Right there." He nodded toward the bundle on the bench of the buggy as he assisted her aboard. "I have to say you chose an unusual place to get married and yet it's perfect for my brother." He slanted her an admiring look. "You really understand him."

"I see the man he is inside."

"And we are all grateful." He turned to check on the children, who had climbed into the buggy. "Everybody sitting down?" When they answered yes, he urged the horses forward. They took the path that led to the ranch—now a well-defined track. Partway there, they turned off the trail and climbed the hills until they reached the cathedral of the trees.

"Is he here yet?" Susanne didn't see Scout but nevertheless asked.

"Johnny said he'd give us time to get here first before he let Tanner go. Johnny said he would hog-tie him if necessary."

Susanne gave a delighted chuckle. Now that Tanner had confessed his love he was free and open about it. And she loved that about him. Just as she loved everything about him from his dark, shining eyes to his golden skin to his gentle humor to his—

She decided to save her thoughts until she could share them with Tanner. She smiled as she thought how he would respond.

They made their way through the trees into the clearing. The sun overhead filled the space with shimmering light. She paused in the center and looked upward, her eyes closed, a prayer in her heart that God would bless this marriage with joy and peace. Then she reached for the bundle that Levi held.

"Liz, come help me." They slipped into the trees, out of sight of those in the clearing. She opened the bundle to reveal the yoke of Tanner's mother's dress.

"It's so soft," Liz said.

"And the beadwork is exquisite." She slipped it over her head and positioned it about her shoulders so that her mother's brooch was visible at her neck. She removed the pins from her hair and let it cascade down her back.

Liz's eyes glowed. "You're beautiful."

The rattle of a wagon and clop of horses informed her the others had arrived.

Maisie's voice reached her. "What a beautiful spot. Why have I never seen it before?"

Big Sam's deep voice rumbled. "This was Seena's favorite spot. Guess none of us have been back until now."

Susanne strained to hear Tanner's voice and smiled when he said, "Where's your aunt?"

Levi parted the branches. "Everyone is ready." His eyes widened as he took in her outfit. "Tanner is going to be blinded with joy."

Susanne smiled. "I hope he will be pleased." She took Levi's arm and prepared to go to Tanner's side.

Liz went ahead of them. At the edge of the clearing she picked up a basket of wildflowers and scattered them before Susanne who walked on Levi's arm.

Tanner watched them. She knew the moment he realized she wore his mother's yoke. His eyes widened and overflowed with love.

Big Sam had arranged for the preacher from town to marry them and she joined Tanner before the man.

"Do you, Tanner Harding, take this woman—"

Tanner interrupted. "With my whole heart."

His family and the children were the only ones in attendance and they laughed at his enthusiasm.

She cherished his words in her heart, where she would keep them always.

She vowed to love him through good times and bad. Always.

As the preacher declared them man and wife, they sealed their vows with a kiss.

"God has brought us joy out of our past," she whispered to her husband.

"I could have never dreamed He would bless me with a woman like you." His gaze lingered on her, then he reached for the children. "And with a family."

Susanne joined them in a hug that included all of them, her heart too full for words.

Her life promised to be full of love, family and a man who cherished her.

* * * * *

Dear Reader,

It bothers me to see unfairness. I remember a time I witnessed an overweight child being tormented. Before I could intervene, someone else did. I know things like this happen a lot. How sad.

Life isn't always fair, is it? We, or the ones we love, have to deal with prejudice, abuse, mockery and trials that we don't feel equipped to handle. But through it all, no matter what, God is at our side to help and heal. My prayer is that this story will help someone know and experience this truth. God turns ashes into beauty if we seek Him in our situation.

I love to hear from my readers. You can contact me at www.lindaford.org, where you'll find my email address and where you can find out more about me and my books.

Blessings,

Linda Ford

THE COWBOY'S BABY BOND
Montana Cowboys
by Linda Ford

When Johnny Harding rescues Willow Reames and her sick baby from their broken-down wagon, he sets aside his own plans to help the single mother track down her missing sisters. By the journey's end, will Johnny gain the family he's always wanted?

WANT AD WEDDING
Cowboy Creek
by Cheryl St.John

Pregnant and widowed Leah Swann heads to Kansas in hopes of becoming a mail-order bride. But she isn't expecting to be reunited with her childhood friend Daniel Gardner when she arrives—or that he'll propose a marriage of convenience.

SHOTGUN MARRIAGE
by Danica Favorite

Obliged to wed to protect their reputations, Emma Jane Logan and Jasper Jackson know that it is a marriage in name only. But as they are forced to run from a gang of bandits, the feelings starting to grow between them may lead to something real.

MAIL ORDER MIX-UP
Boom Town Brides
by Christine Johnson

When Roland Decker's niece and nephew place an ad to find his brother a mail-order bride, multiple women travel to answer it and mistake *him* for the groom. But he's only interested in schoolteacher Pearl Lawson—the one woman who doesn't want the job.

―――――――――

LIHCNM0316

REQUEST YOUR FREE BOOKS!

2 FREE INSPIRATIONAL NOVELS
PLUS 2 *FREE* MYSTERY GIFTS

Love Inspired® H I S T O R I C A L

YES! Please send me 2 FREE Love Inspired® Historical novels and my 2 FREE mystery gifts (gifts are worth about $10). After receiving them, if I don't wish to receive any more books, I can return the shipping statement marked "cancel." If I don't cancel, I will receive 4 brand-new novels every month and be billed just $4.99 per book in the U.S. or $5.49 per book in Canada. That's a saving of at least 17% off the cover price. It's quite a bargain! Shipping and handling is just 50¢ per book in the U.S. and 75¢ per book in Canada.* I understand that accepting the 2 free books and gifts places me under no obligation to buy anything. I can always return a shipment and cancel at any time. Even if I never buy another book, the two free books and gifts are mine to keep forever.

102/302 IDN GH6Z

Name	(PLEASE PRINT)
Address	Apt. #
City	State/Prov.	Zip/Postal Code

Signature (if under 18, a parent or guardian must sign)

Mail to the **Reader Service**:
IN U.S.A.: P.O. Box 1867, Buffalo, NY 14240-1867
IN CANADA: P.O. Box 609, Fort Erie, Ontario L2A 5X3

Want to try two free books from another series?
Call 1-800-873-8635 or visit www.ReaderService.com.

* Terms and prices subject to change without notice. Prices do not include applicable taxes. Sales tax applicable in N.Y. Canadian residents will be charged applicable taxes. Offer not valid in Quebec. This offer is limited to one order per household. Not valid for current subscribers to Love Inspired Historical books. All orders subject to credit approval. Credit or debit balances in a customer's account(s) may be offset by any other outstanding balance owed by or to the customer. Please allow 4 to 6 weeks for delivery. Offer available while quantities last.

Your Privacy—The Reader Service is committed to protecting your privacy. Our Privacy Policy is available online at www.ReaderService.com or upon request from the Reader Service.

We make a portion of our mailing list available to reputable third parties that offer products we believe may interest you. If you prefer that we not exchange your name with third parties, or if you wish to clarify or modify your communication preferences, please visit us at www.ReaderService.com/consumerchoice or write to us at Reader Service Preference Service, P.O. Box 9062, Buffalo, NY 14240-9062. Include your complete name and address.

LIHI5

"Gentlemen, please make a path and escort our brides forward!"

A smattering of applause followed his request, and from the outer edge of the platform, the crowd parted unevenly, allowing three figures in ruffles and flower-bedecked hats to make their way through the gathering to the stack of crates. Daniel jumped down beside Will and they stood on either side of the group of ladies.

Daniel removed his hat, and every cowboy doffed his own. "Welcome to Cowboy Creek." He glanced aside. "We're still missing someone."

"Mrs. Swann was with us a moment ago," the petite young woman beside him said. "She must have become lost in the crowd somewhere."

"Let the lady through!" Daniel called, standing as tall as he could manage and peering above the crowd. He was thinking that perhaps he would need to get back on the stack of crates, when he spotted a blue feathered hat on a pale gold head of hair. "There she is. Mrs. Swann! Let her through."

The poor woman steadied her wisp of a hat atop her head with one white-gloved hand and turned this way and that, speaking to men as she choreographed her way through the crowd. Disengaging herself from the attentions of an overeager cowboy, she nearly stumbled forward. Daniel caught her elbow to steady her.

"Oh! Thank you. This is quite a reception!" She glanced up. Cornflower blue eyes rimmed with dark lashes opened wide in surprise. The world stood still for a moment. The crowd noise faded into the void. "Daniel?"

Daniel's gut felt as though he'd been standing right on the tracks and stopped the locomotive with his body. "Leah Robinson?"

She was as pretty as ever. Prettier maybe, her face having lost the roundness of girlhood and her skin and bone structure having smoothed into a gentle comeliness.

Mrs. Swann was Leah Robinson, one of his best friends before the war. Will had once shown him a wedding announcement from a Chicago newspaper, and all these years Daniel had pictured her just as she had been back then, full of youth and vitality, and married to the army officer she'd chosen. That had been a lifetime ago. So what was she doing traveling to Cowboy Creek with their mail-order brides?

Don't miss WANT AD WEDDING
by Cheryl St.John, available April 2016 wherever
Love Inspired® Historical books and ebooks are sold.

www.LoveInspired.com

LIHEXP0316